## LEABHARLANNA CHONTAE FHINE GALL
## FINGAL COUNTY LIBRARIES

Items should be returned on or before the last date shown
below. Items may be renewed by personal application,
writing, telephone or by accessing the online Catalogue
Service on Fingal Libraries' website. To renew give date
due, borrower ticket number and PIN number if using
online catalogue. Fines are charged on overdue items
and will include postage incurred in recovery. Damage to,
or loss of items will be charged to the borrower.

| Date Due | Date Due | Date Due |
|---|---|---|

09. SEP 09.

06. MAR 10.

22 APR 16.

15. MAY 10.
25. 13. 11.

The confessions of
**Edward Day**

Also by Valerie Martin

*Novels*

Set in Motion

Alexandra

A Recent Martyr

Mary Reilly

The Great Divorce

Italian Fever

Property

Trespass

*Short Fiction*

Love

The Consolation of Nature and Other Stories

The Unfinished Novel and Other Stories

*Non-Fiction*

Salvation: Scenes from the Life of St. Francis

# The confessions of
# Edward Day

a novel

Valerie Martin

Weidenfeld & Nicolson

LONDON

First published in Great Britain in 2009 by Weidenfeld & Nicolson,
An imprint of The Orion Publishing Group Ltd
Orion House, 5 Upper Saint Martin's Lane
London  WC2H 9EA

An Hachette UK Company

1 3 5 7 9 10 8 6 4 2

Originally published in the USA in 2009 by Nan A. Talese,
a division of Random House Inc

A CIP catalogue record for this book is
available from the British Library.

ISBN (Hardback) 978 0 297 84499 0
ISBN (Trade Paperback) 978 0 297 85535 4

Printed and bound in Great Britain by Clays Ltd, St Ives plc

The Orion Publishing Group's policy is to use papers that are natural,
renewable and recyclable products and made from wood grown in
sustainable forests. The logging and manufacturing processes are expected
to conform to the environmental regulations of the country of origin.

www.orionbooks.co.uk

For Nan A. Talese

*intrepid night swimmer*

'Our ordinary type of attention is not sufficiently far-reaching to carry out the process of penetrating another person's soul'

—CONSTANTIN STANISLAVSKI

*An Actor Prepares*


'False face must hide what the false heart doth know'

—WILLIAM SHAKESPEARE

*Macbeth*

# Part I

My mother liked to say Freud should have been strangled in his crib. Not that she had ever read one line of the eminent psychoanalyst's writing or knew anything about his life and times. She probably thought he was a German; she might have gotten his actual dates wrong by half a century. She didn't know about the Oedipus complex or the mechanics of repression, but she knew that when children turned out badly, when they were conflicted and miserable and did poorly in school, Freud blamed the mother. This was arrant nonsense, Mother declared. Children turned out the way they turned out and mothers were as surprised as anyone else. Her own child-rearing strategy had been to show no interest at all in how her children turned out, so how could she be held responsible for them?

Proof of Mother's assertions might be found in the relatively normal men her four sons grew to be, not a pervert or a criminal among us, though my oldest brother, Claude, a dentist, has always shown far too much interest in crime fiction of the most violent and degraded sort, and my profession, while honest, is doubtless, in some quarters, suspect. For the other

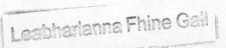

two, Mother got her doctor and lawyer, the only two professions her generation ever recommended. My brothers' specialties have the additional benefit of being banal: the doctor is a urologist and the lawyer handles real estate closings.

My mother was a tall, beautiful woman, with dark hair, fair skin, an elegant long neck, and excellent posture. She was poorly educated and, as a young mother, intensely practical. My father had various jobs in the civil service in Stamford; his moves were sometimes lateral, occasionally up. She hardly seemed to notice him when we were around, but there must have been some spark between them. She had her sons in sets, the first two a year apart, a five-year lapse, and then two more. I was the last, her last effort—this was understood by all—to have a girl.

Even if Freud hadn't encouraged me to, I think I would still have to blame Mother for my craving to be someone else, and not only because she wasn't satisfied with who I am, though she wasn't, not from the start. My middle name is Leslie and that's what I was called at home; I became Edward when I went away to boarding school in Massachusetts. Mother had "gender issues," but none of us realized how serious they were until after she died. This mournful event took place when I was nineteen, a freshman at the University of North Carolina, and it was preceded by a seismic upheaval that lasted six months, during which time Mother left my father for a woman named Helen, who was ten years her junior and bent on destruction.

Mother wasn't naturally a warm person—I know that now—and she must have been lonely and frustrated for years, surrounded from dawn to dark, as she was, by the unlovely spectacle of maleness. A frequent expression upon entering a room in which her sons were engaged in some rude or rowdy masculine behavior was "Why are boys so . . ." As the youngest, I took this to heart and tried to please her, not without some success. I kept my corner of the bedroom spotless, made my bed with the strict hospital corners she used on her own, rinsed my dishes at the sink after the pot roast, meat loaf, or fried chicken dinner, and expressed an interest in being read to. I wasn't picky about the stories, either; tales of girlish heroism were fine with me, hence my acquaintance with the adventures of such heroines as Nancy Drew, the Dana Girls, and all the travails of the shrewdly observant Laura in the Little House books. I know, as few men do, my fairy tales, from Rumpelstiltskin to the Little Goose Girl, stories certainly grisly enough to terrify even a stalwart little boy and which I take to explain the surprisingly violent images that so often surface in the consciousness exercises of young actresses. Mother was a good reader; she changed her voices for the different characters. She had a cackling crone, a booming good fellow, and a frightened little girl in her repertory, and she moved from one to the other with ease. Long after I could read myself, I approached her after dinner with a book clutched to my chest and asked if she "felt like" reading to me. Many times she didn't, and she wasn't terribly nice about refusing me. But when she agreed, I was invited to lean against her on the couch, watch the pages turning beneath her bloodred fingernails, and feel her voice through her arm. She was a smoker, so there was the cloud of smoke wafting up from her lips as

Nancy cautioned her dopey boyfriend Ned not to open the suitcase they'd found in the empty house. It was all very comforting and at the same time confusing, also mysterious and sexually disturbing. But I like to remember Mother that way, and myself, her favorite, her Leslie, the good boy who hung on her words.

When I went off to school and became Edward, I had no clear idea of myself; perhaps that was why I was drawn to acting. Inside a character I knew exactly who I was, the environment was controlled, and no one was going to do anything unexpected. It seemed a way of playing it safe. Of course, real acting is the farthest thing from safe a person can get, but I didn't know that then. Perhaps in some corner of my adolescent consciousness, I understood that my mother would eventually crack under the strain of the role she herself was playing with increasing reluctance and incredulity. On school vacations she and my father were glum and irritable. One night she put a roasted chicken on the table and announced that it was the last meal she was cooking. She joined a reading group, but this quickly bored her and she decided to become a potter. This led to sculpture and ultimately ironwork. On my next vacation there was a welding torch on the kitchen table and all food was takeout. A few days before I graduated from high school my father called me to say Mother was moving out; she would be living with a "friend" named Helen, someone she had met at the artist co-op where Mother had rented a space to do her sculpture.

I saw Mother and Helen together once. They were living in an apartment in Brooklyn, two rooms above an Italian deli, strong odor of provolone and red sauce. Helen spent my visit turning over the pages of a fashion magazine at the kitchen table, occasionally fixing me with a baleful glare. She was clearly, totally nuts. Mother served me coffee and some hard cookies from the deli; she tried to make small talk, asked about my courses, disapproved of my interest in theater, recommended medicine, law, the usual. I told her I was far too squeamish for medicine; I feel faint when I see my own blood, no, seriously faint. This made Mother laugh, which provoked Helen to push back her chair and shout, "I can't stand to see you like this. I hate this part of you," after which she stormed out of the apartment.

"She's so high-strung," Mother assured me after the door stopped reverberating in the ill-fitting frame. "She's just too sensitive to live."

When I returned from this disturbing interview, I found my father meticulously washing out a coffee cup at the kitchen sink. He was stoical—civil service does that for a man—and he was mystified by Mother's abdication of her domestic reign. "So did you see this divine Helen?" he asked.

"Briefly," I said.

He turned to me, swabbing the dishcloth inside the cup. "What did you think?"

"Scary," I said.

He nodded. "I guess your mother really wanted a girl," he said.

I went back to school and after a few months Mother's sudden and bold defection seemed almost bearable. I was absorbed in experiments of my own, concocting an identity from the flimsy material of my considerable naïveté about the world in general and sex in particular. I was smitten by a senior in my theater arts class—I've repressed her name for reasons that will shortly be obvious—but I'll call her Brünnhilde, as she was a shapely Nordic princess with eyes as ice-blue as my own. To my astonishment she indulged my fawning jokes and compliments. Our classmates referred to me as her lapdog, which amused us both, and made for crude punning about laps and lapping, etc. She lived in an apartment off campus with a roommate from New Jersey who occasionally went home on weekends. It was a dumpy two rooms above a garage, but it was the height of sophistication in our set to be invited to Brünnhilde's Friday-afternoon BYOB party. One day in class our professor, doubtless sensing sparks between us, put Brünnhilde and me together for a word exercise, the results of which were so electric the class burst into applause. To my joy, my beauty leaned across her desk, pushing back her wedge of straw-colored hair and said, "Come by on Friday, after five, if you like. It's 58 Gower, in the back."

Who knows what disgusting bottle of wine I brought to this occasion; something I got a friend to purchase as I wasn't of age. Perhaps it was the ditchwater that came in the fish-shaped bottle, or the ghastly Mateus that was the coin of the realm. Or something red, to brighten the vomit that was not an uncommon occurrence late in the evening at the Gower Street gathering. My hostess only smiled and deposited my offering on the card table with the others, introducing me to the assembled guests who were all older than me, though they appeared not to notice. Soon I was ensconced on a lumpy couch, swallowing huge draughts of cheap wine and holding forth on the existential commitment required to bring truth to a theatrical performance. To be, or not to be, it wasn't just the question, it was, in fact, the method. Drivel along those lines.

The company took me up, they praised me, and I was their breathless ingenue. At some point a marijuana pipe appeared, moving steadily from hand to hand, and I had my first taste of that. It grew late, the empty bottles outnumbered the full, and couples began to drift out into the night in search of food or more licentious entertainment. I stayed on, switching to beer which was still in good supply. At last we were alone and Brünnhilde ran her hand along my thigh. "Would you like to see my bedroom?" she asked, serious as a church.

I spent the night there and most of the next day. Late in the afternoon I stumbled back to my dorm room for a change of clothes and more money, my brain grinding with amazement and apprehension. It was paradise in Brünnhilde's bedroom, but I knew I would have to be very alert, very dutiful if I wanted a key to the gates. I scarcely glanced at the message scrawled on a scrap of paper by the phone. *Your mother called, 6 p.m. Your mother again 10:30. Mother again, MIDNIGHT.* So she knew I'd been out late, but would she care? I didn't want to waste time making excuses because I was in a hurry to get to the café near the university where my darling had agreed to meet me. It would be un-loverlike to keep her waiting on what was, after all, our first real date. I would call my mother back at the earliest opportunity.

It was Sunday evening before I got the news and by that time Mother wasn't making any calls. The new message read: *Your father called. Urgent, call at once.* Even this, in my state of elation combined with sexual exhaustion, didn't make me suspicious. "Where have you been?" my father said when he heard my voice.

"Exam tomorrow," I said. "I pulled an all-nighter at the library."

"I want you to sit down, son," he said. "Something terrible has happened."

So I sat down and he told me that my mother and her girlfriend Helen had committed suicide together in the Brooklyn apartment sometime in the early hours of Saturday morning. When Helen failed to turn up at her regular Saturday appointment, her psychiatrist made repeated attempts to reach her self-destructive patient. At last on Sunday morning she called the landlord who let himself in to find his tenants in bed, naked in each other's arms, the empty bottles of Seconal lined up next to two glasses of water on the bedside table.

I wonder now what I said. I remember a torrent of incredulity; for several moments I simply didn't believe my ears. I looked around at the suddenly unfamiliar furniture of my Spartan dorm room and spotted, of course, the scrap of paper with the message that concluded: *Mother again, MIDNIGHT.* The ensuing sob that rose from very deep within me came out as an agonized groan of pain. "Son, do you want me to drive down to get you?" my father said.

"Oh Dad," I wailed. "Oh Dad . . ." But I didn't say, *She called me,* and I never did tell him, or anyone else for that matter. My roommate knew but we were hardly more than acquaintances and he, out of courtesy perhaps, never said anything about the messages. When I got home my brothers were all there and it was clear that she had not tried to call any of them, or my father, either. Just me, the baby, Leslie, who made her laugh with my horror of blood. She'd left a note, addressed to no one, two words: *I'm sorry.*

After the funeral, I returned to school. You can imagine my confusion. I was nineteen, an innocent, and my emotions were in an uproar. I wasn't so naïve as to equate sex with death, though my experience certainly suggested the connection forcefully: have sex, your mother kills herself. Rationally I knew I had nothing to do with Mother's despair, though I couldn't resist speculating about how differently things might have gone if I'd been what Mother wanted: a girl. Would a daughter have walked into the cramped apartment, taken one look at Helen, and said, "No, Mom, you're not doing this"? Worst of all was the second-guessing about the missed calls; if I had been studying in my room like a diligent student, could I have saved her? This question kept me awake at night. For months I woke to a refrain that sent me out of the dorm and into the late-night diners near the campus—*She needed me, I wasn't there.*

Of course word had gotten around that I was a motherless boy, and sympathetic female arms stretched out to me from every direction. I said Mother had died suddenly in her sleep, which satisfied everyone and wasn't entirely a lie. Brünnhilde was suitably tentative when next we met. Though I said nothing about the manner of Mother's death Brünnhilde understood that the proximity of the event to our first coupling might be disturbing to me. I declined the halfhearted invitation to the Friday gatherings and in a few weeks she had a new lapdog, a budding playwright who wrote monologues about his miserable childhood in Trenton, New Jersey.

Gradually the shock wore off and I began to take an interest in my feelings as opposed to simply feeling them non-stop. My acting classes were particularly useful for this. As Stanislavski observed, "In the language of an actor *to know* is synonymous with *to feel.*" My studies offered access to the very knowledge I most required. Many actors are called to their profession by an insatiable craving to be seen, to be admired, and to be famous, but for me acting was an egress from unbearable sorrow and guilt. My emotions at that point were the strongest thing about me; they did battle with one another and I looked on, a helpless bystander. This, I realized, mirrored the position of the audience before the stage. I wanted to find a visceral way to give an audience everything they needed to know about suffering, which is, after all, the subject of most drama, including comedies, hence the expression "I laughed until I cried." I studied my peers and attempted to assess my position among them. Many were drawn to the theater because they possessed such physical beauty that they stood out in a crowd, they looked like actors, but what, I wondered, possessed the overweight girls, the hopelessly nerdy guys who would be doomed by their physiognomy to a lifetime of character parts? One in particular fascinated me, a short, scrawny, colorless boy named Neil Nielson, who cultivated a scanty reddish mustache beneath his pudgy inelegant nose and gazed upon the world through wire-rimmed lenses that magnified his lashless, watery eyes to twice their size. Physically there was nothing appealing about him, but he had a voice that was the envy of us all, as

rich and melodious as a cello. When he laughed, a smile flickered on every face within earshot. Naturally, he was called "the
voice." A future in radio beckoned him, which was too bad because he was a gifted actor. If you saw him sitting at a bar you
wouldn't look twice, but on a stage he had a weirdly erotic
force—he would have made a great Richard III. He was interested in me because girls were, and he hoped to pick up on that
action. I liked his company because he had serious things to say
about acting. His approach was remarkably selfless; he found
his character outside himself. We once did a Pinter scene in a
workshop; I think it was from *Betrayal*. We exchanged roles after a break and did it again. I was astounded by what his interpretation did to my own, it was as if I was being subjected to a
minute and continuous analysis by someone who could see
right into the heart of me, my motivations and anxieties laid
more bare with each exchange. Later I asked him how he did
what he did and he said something I've never forgotten: "I get
myself from what I see you getting about me." It sounds like
nonsense, but I think I understood it. Neil was doomed to
bring out the best in lesser actors and to his credit, he didn't
seem to mind. He played Rosencrantz in the production of
*Hamlet* that was the triumph of my senior year. We did eight
performances and our brief scene together was different every
night. If there was a scintilla of suspicion in my greeting—*How
dost thou Guildenstern! Ah Rosencrantz!*—he picked it up and
proceeded with utmost caution, but if my manner expressed
pleasure and relief to discover true friends in the prison that
was Denmark, his overconfidence was his death warrant. He
made keen play of his small bit, and as our Polonius was a life-

less drone, my heart lifted when I saw Neil's pointed little beard and glinting glasses enter the pool of light that it was my sovereign right to occupy in the universe of that play.

There was nothing especially intelligent or innovative about my own performance, though everyone, including the local press, praised it as if they'd never seen my equal. My teachers gushed with enthusiasm; my director, a voluptuous graduate student, fell in love with me, and we had a brief affair. I knew I was feeling my way, that my insecurity was part of what made my prince Hamlet so appealing. I was, as he was, a youth, a student, and I had lost a parent in suspicious circumstances. It was during those rehearsals that I first allowed myself the thought that my mother's death was a crime against me, me personally. I could see Helen's angry sneer as she slapped the pages of her magazine against the table while Mother encouraged me to study medicine, and her bitter denouncement of the amity between us rang in my ears. "I hate this part of you." One night I woke from panicked dreams with the idea that I must find Helen and make her pay for what she had done to me. Then, sweating and cursing in my narrow dorm bed, I remembered that she had denied me that option. My lines came to me and I whispered them into the darkness: *That I, the son of a dear father murder'd, Prompted to my revenge by heaven and hell, Must, like a whore, unpack my heart with words, And fall a-cursing, like a very drab.* I wept, not for Hamlet, who lived just long enough to avenge his father's murder, but for myself.

# Part II

I'll jump ahead to a sultry morning in July 1974. College was behind me. I was in my tiny Greenwich Village apartment packing my battered suitcase, the same suitcase I took to North Carolina when I was nineteen, the same one I carried when I arrived at Penn Station four years after that, ambitious, confident, and ignorant as a post. I experienced a pang of anxiety as I held up my swimming trunks, worn and venerable as my suitcase and woefully out of style, but there was nothing to be done about them—my ride was arriving within the hour—so I tossed them in with the rest, the T-shirts, the cut-off jeans, my Dopp kit, the gray linen jacket with the Italian label that I'd gotten secondhand, the madras shirt, the oversize belt, the black dress jeans. I snapped the top down and went into the bathroom, where I stood before the mirror, combing my hair.

Stanislavski described such a moment, a man combing his hair before a mirror, as one of perfect naturalness and ease, and therefore poetic; for him it epitomized "truth," which was the condition an actor must discover in performance. He called it "public solitude," the notion being, I supposed, that we are most "ourselves" when we don't have an audience. I smiled at my face in the mirror, recognizing that smile, the one I trusted as no other, which seems odd to me now because at the time I knew nothing about that smiling young man combing his hair; he was as opaque as a clay jug. Soon I would be on the Jersey shore in my outmoded trunks and madras shirt, and with any luck I'd have my arm around the waist of Madeleine Delavergne. Would that waist be bare? Would Madeleine sport a one-piece suit, or a bikini? Was such a thing as a bikini possible on the Jersey shore?

There would be eight of us, all acting students, though we didn't attend the same schools. Madeleine and I were students in Sanford Meisner's professional program at his studio on Fifty-sixth Street, but Teddy Winterbottom, he of the Yale degree and the large Victorian beach house, studied with the great Stella Adler. I had become acquainted with Teddy over a lot of beer at the Cedar Tavern, and though I'd never seen him act, he was a wonderful raconteur and general purveyor of bonhomie. His family was traveling abroad, and we would have the house to ourselves for the holiday weekend. There were, Teddy promised, eight beds, one for each dwarf, and one more for him.

I heard the blare of Teddy's horn from the street and crossed my narrow living room to wave out the open window. He drove an MG convertible; the top was down, so he saw me and waved back. My long legs weren't designed for a sports car; it would be a tedious, hot, uncomfortable drive, but I couldn't have cared less. I snatched my suitcase from the table and, pausing only to turn the dead bolt, rushed down the four dusty flights of stairs into the street. My poetic moment before the mirror left my mind entirely.

As it turned out, the house wasn't on the beach, but it was scarcely a block away. Like its neighbors, it was large, airy, swaddled with deep porches, shingled over, and trimmed with decorative flourishes. Red was the predominating color, the shingles a sun-faded rose, the wide-board floors gleaming cadmium, with touches of red in the furnishings, a pillow here, a slipcover there. Teddy and I spent an hour or so opening windows, plugging in appliances, distributing linens to the various bedrooms and cushions to the wicker couches on the porches. By the time he announced his intention to leave me in charge while he ran out to the grocery for provisions, I was acquainted with the house from cellar to attic. "Put Becky and James in the room with the double bed," he said. "And tell the rest it's first come, first served."

He wasn't gone long when Madeleine and her friend Mindy Banks pulled up at the curb in a rusty Dodge crammed with groceries, suitcases, and a miserable dachshund named Lawrence, who hit the ground with a grunt, trotted to a poor stripling of a tree near the curb, and peed mightily. "I'm with Lawrence," Madeleine exclaimed, bounding past me up the stairs. "Where's the john?"

We had met before, casually, in class and at Jimmy Ray's bar, always in a crowd. Aspiring actresses are often damaged, neurotic girls but Madeleine struck me as unusually stable and confident. She had masses of wavy black hair, pale skin, hazel eyes, full pouting lips, and enviable cheekbones. Her only physical flaw was her hips, which were a little wide.

"There's one just off the upstairs landing," I called after her. "On your left."

"Thanks," she said, not looking back. Lawrence left off the tree and fell to sniffing my pants leg. Mindy came up carrying a grocery bag, which she handed to me. "You're Ed, aren't you?" she said. "We met one time at Teddy's."

By dinner everyone had arrived except Peter Davis, who was bringing a friend no one knew. "Some guy who lives in a rathole in Chelsea," Teddy said. "He's only been in town a few months. He works in the bookstore with Peter, doesn't seem to have any friends or family. Peter said he felt sorry for him, so I said bring him along."

I didn't like the sound of this, especially as we had far too many males in our group already. I was making good headway in my campaign for Madeleine's attention, and I didn't want her distracted. In the afternoon, I'd persuaded her to walk with me on the beach, and I'd served as her sous-chef at dinner. The food was awful, vegetarian fare—this was before the soybean had been tamed, and good bread was only to be had in dreary co-op food stores. Salad was romaine lettuce at best, mesclun was as rare as diamonds, arugula as yet unheard of on our planet. But we had cases of beer and cheap wine, various small stashes of marijuana, and a freezer full of ice cream, so we were enjoying ourselves. As the sun went down, the breeze off the ocean cooled from torrid to sultry and we moved from the dining room to the wide screened-in porch. The talk was all of theater, who was doing what plays where, who had the best deal on head shots, the relative merits of acting teachers and schools, the catch-22 of Actors' Equity, the anxieties, perils, and hilarious adventures of those who had appeared nude on-stage. Madeleine had chosen a wicker chair near mine. On our walk she had told me of her recent breakup with a boyfriend of some duration; they had lived together in an apartment on West Forty-seventh for more than a year. She made light of the matter; the boyfriend was a slob who ate bacon-and-peanut-butter sandwiches and didn't wash the pan, left his clothes on the floor, always managed to leave a smear of toothpaste on the sink drain. The end came when she returned from a weekend visit to her parents in Cleveland to find he'd let the bathtub overflow and the downstairs neighbors had called the landlord because the water was pouring down their kitchen wall. "He was working on his play and he forgot he'd turned on the tap," she said.

"He's a playwright."

"His plays are awful," she said. "He's writing a play about Simón Bolívar, for God's sake."

Madeleine was beautiful, she made me laugh, and she was evidently available: I was rhapsodic. My quandary was how to get her away from the others. The sleeping arrangements weren't ideal, she and Mindy had chosen adjoining rooms, and I wasn't entirely clear about the etiquette of house parties. I didn't want to do anything that would offend Teddy, but fortunately he was absorbed in entertaining Mindy, who had a laugh like a braying mule. She was curvy and blowsy, crude, I thought, and given to bursts of Broadway tunes, as if she saw a producer lurking in the rhododendrons pressing against the screen. Madeleine smiled at me through the wistful refrain of "Send in the Clowns." "I want to swim," she said. "Will you come with me?"

"Of course," I said.

My feelings were mixed. It was a chance to be alone with her in a romantic setting, which was enticing to say the least. The famous still of Deborah Kerr and Burt Lancaster in a clutch on the beach in *From Here to Eternity* flashed before my eyes, but that was in Hawaii and in broad daylight (or was it what is called in film "day for night"?). The waters in Jersey were rumored to contain jellyfish—would they be worse at night? Then there was the matter of the unflattering swimming trunks, and the sad fact that my swimming skills were much inferior to Burt's. But none of this weighed more than a feather in a balance that contained Madeleine in a swimsuit at night on a beach under the moon. "I'll change," she said, leaping up from her chair. "I'll just be a minute." As she passed through the doors to the dining room I noticed a wobble in her step; she pressed her shoulder against the frame and pushed on. Was she drunk? Was I? In answer to the second question I got to my feet. No, I was exhilarated, on the up not the down side of inebriation, and a stroll in the night air might be just the thing. I hastened to my room, changed into a T-shirt and the trunks, grabbed a towel from the stack on the dresser, and went out to the hall, where I found Madeleine floating toward me in a fetching costume, a two-piece suit with a tie-dyed shawl fastened at the waist to make a loose, fluttering skirt. "This is great," she said. "I love swimming at night."

"Me too," I lied. I followed her down the stairs to the front porch where we culled our sandals from the herd along the rail and flapped out to the sidewalk. The voices of our friends drifted to us, punctuated with laughter. The house next door, blazing light from every window, gave off a mouthwatering aroma of grilling meat. Overhead the sky was clear and black; the air vibrated with the salty exhalations of the ocean. "It's nice here," Madeleine said. "I'm glad I came. The city is a furnace."

"I'm glad you came too," I said. We reached the corner, crossed the empty street, and there was the sea, black roiling under black, restless and ceaseless, combing the shore. We clattered down the wooden steps and sloughed off our sandals in the sand. Madeleine untied her skirt, dropping it over the shoes, careless in her excitement. "It's beautiful," she said. "And there's no one here." She rushed away from me to the water's edge. I tossed my towel and shirt on the pile and followed. The half-moon cast a cool light that was reflected from the sand, but the dark waves sucked it up and gave back nothing. Madeleine was already waist deep in the surf, walking steadily away from me. I pounded across the sand and into the water, which was cold against my hot skin, a startling, welcome embrace. She turned to me and, as I drew closer, batted the surface of the water gleefully. "Look," she said. "It's magic."

And it was. Strips of green light darted away from her fingertips like bright snakes, and the harder she slapped the water the more there were. "It's phosphorescence," I said.

"No, no," she protested. "It's magic." Just then the cosmic magician called up a wave, banishing the snakes and tipping Madeleine into my arms. "You're right," I said, pulling her up against my chest. We kissed.

How many kisses do you remember all your life? Four or five, I think, not many. Even at that moment I knew this was one I wouldn't forget, and I was right.

We swam and kissed and swam again, enchanted by the green light attendant on our every movement. Madeleine was at ease in the water and completely fearless, a much better swimmer than I was. She swam underneath me and came up ahead of me. We floated on our backs holding hands, letting the waves carry us to shore. We embraced in the sand, then struck back out in tandem. It was foreplay with ocean, and we extended it as long as we could bear it. We treaded water while kissing, and she wrapped her legs around my waist. At some point her suit top slipped down. To her amusement my erection strained the confines of the trunks. We spoke very little until, at last, by some visceral agreement, we scrambled onto the shore and raced back to the staircase, beneath which we laid out the towel and her skirt, stripped off our minimal coverings, and amid sighs and cries muffled by the steady rumbling of the tide, finished what we had started.

When it was over I rolled off of Madeleine, light-headed, my heart churning in my chest. She chuckled softly and rested her hand on my sandy thigh. "So, you're Edward Day," she said.

"Am I?" I replied. "Are you sure?"

"That's what I've heard," she said. She was feeling about for her suit. "I don't like to think of some of the places I've got sand in," she said. We took one last dip in the surf to rinse off. Then she shook out her wrap and tied it at her waist. I pulled on my T-shirt; we slipped on our sandals and climbed the stairs to the dimly lit street. A car passed; we could hear voices from the balconies facing the shore, but they were soft now; it was late. I took Madeleine's hand as we crossed the street, and she slipped her arm beneath mine, leaning against me. "It's as if we'd been in another world," she said.

"It is," I agreed.

"Will we go there again?"

"God, I hope so," I said.

"At any rate, we'll never forget it."

We had reached Teddy's house. Some of the lights in the upstairs bedrooms were on. A flicker of candlelight and more soft humming of voices came from the side porch, but no one was in the darkened foyer. "Should we join them?" I asked. She pressed her lips together and raised her eyebrows. We said "No" together. "I'm too tired," she added. "I know I'm going to sleep well tonight. There's no exercise like swimming, don't you agree." I laughed. She rose up on her toes to kiss me. "Good night, Edward," she said.

"You can call me Ed," I said.

"I like Edward better." With that she left me, climbing the stairs with one hand on the rail, her shoulders drooping like a weary child. I watched her go up, but, certain I wasn't going to sleep anytime soon, I didn't follow.

I know the cliché. *Post coitum omne animal triste est.* The man rolls over and falls asleep, the woman lies awake wondering why he won't marry her if he hasn't already or if he has, whether she should divorce him. Maybe it was like that for the Romans, but I've never been able to fall asleep after sex. I was elated by our adventure and restless. From the porch I could hear the idle chatter of our friends, doubtless smoking pot and gossiping about Madeleine and me. I heard Teddy's hearty guffaw, joined by a thin, mirthless laugh I didn't recognize; Peter Davis and his luckless friend must have arrived. I was in no mood to meet anyone, especially an actor with a laugh like that. I slipped back onto the front porch, careful to close the screen soundlessly, picked up my sandals and carried them with me to the sidewalk. Madeleine and I had seen a fishing pier on our walk earlier in the day, the entrance flanked by an ice-cream truck and a bike-rental concession. It had been crowded with bathers and children strolling about and shouting for the sheer joy of having escaped the city and arrived at the shore. By now, I thought, it would be quiet and empty; a good place for a late-night stroll and one last colloquy with the sea and stars before attempting sleep in the single bed down the hall from the dreaming Madeleine. Would she dream of me? How would it be in the morning when we met in the kitchen with the others; would she want too much from me by way of acknowledgment, or too little? Would our comrades have marked our absence and tease us, or would they be indifferent, distracted by their own erotic campaigns? Had I seduced Madeleine, or had she taken advantage of me because I was the most attractive, available male? Wasn't there, beneath my enthusiasm and satisfaction about what had happened on the beach, a glimmer of contempt for her? I certainly wanted to have sex with her again, but the desire I felt for her had already lost its edge. A comfortable, familiar smugness took its place. As I walked though the eerily quiet town, with its closed-up shops shedding blobs of unnatural fluorescent light onto the sidewalk, I delved into every nuance of my emotions, ambling about in search of the conjunction between the mental and the physical. An actor's emotions are his textbook. I perceived that my forehead was tight, my upper lip stretched down and pursed slightly over my lower lip. Who am I? I asked. I cast my eyes to the right and left, letting my head follow. I practiced Brando, that slow, overheated appraisal of the scene he's about to disrupt, following his prick, the wolf on the prowl for a mate.

I had reached the street ending at the pier. To my disappointment, a man and a woman lingered near the bike rental, deep in conversation. As I approached, they moved off, not touching, still talking. She walked, like royalty, ahead of him. I slowed my pace, waiting until I couldn't hear their footsteps. When I got to the corner, they were gone.

There was a lamp near the stairs to the pier, but its light didn't reach past the first few planks, and as I stepped outside its influence I had the sensation that the volume on the ocean soundtrack had been turned up. The tide was high; the water broke more forcefully against the lumber of the pier than it had against the shore, with a steady thwack and suck that sounded like slow-motion sex. I thought it might be pleasant to smoke a cigarette—get in on the sucking action. I'd left a pack on the side porch which had promptly become public property and was, by now, surely empty. I thought of my friends—I didn't know any of them well, even Teddy was something of a mystery to me, but our shared passion for the theater, for a life illuminated by floodlights, enacted for the benefit of strangers, made us not a family but a tribe. If we were successful the ordinary world would be closed to us, and if we failed, well, it would still be closed, but in a less agreeable way. So we watched one another, affably enough, to see who would make his way and who fall by the wayside. I had a good feeling about Madeleine; I thought she would succeed, and I knew it was largely this apprehension that made her attractive to me. "Madeleine," I said to the saturated air. I sniffed my fingers, but there was no trace of her; the sea had washed her scent away.

I had come to the end of the pier, high above the swirling waters. It struck me that a fisherman would need a great deal of line just to get his hook down to fish level. The sky was overcast now; the moon obscured by a moving curtain of clouds. *The inconstant moon.* Madeleine would make a stunning Juliet. *O, swear not by the moon, the inconstant moon, that monthly changes in her circled orb.* I blessed Shakespeare, ever apt to the moment, whether it be for passion or reflection, and always sensitive to the bluster the petty human summons against the capricious cruelty of nature's boundless dominion.

Dreaminess settled upon me. The muscles in my shoulders and legs were vibrating from fatigue. It had been a long and eventful day. I stretched my arms over my head—yes, I, too, would sleep well—and brought my elbows to rest on the rail before me. There was a sharp crack; for a nanosecond I believed it was a shot fired behind me and I ducked my head. My elbows were moving forward and down, following the wooden rail as it slid away beneath them. Because I am tall, the lower rail struck just below my knees, serving to shove my feet out from under me. I struggled to wrench my upper body back from the edge but it was futile; gravity had the measure of me, and the only way open was down. I knew this with the physical clarity that short-circuits reason and redirects every atom toward survival. As I fell, I arched away from the pier, seeking to enter the water as far as possible from the great mass of wood that held it aloft. It was a fall into blackness. My eyes were useless, my ears weren't even listening. The distance from the pier to the water was perhaps twenty feet, plenty of time, a lifetime, of falling. My arms stretched before me, my body straightened, approximating the proper diver's position. I tensed for the moment of entry when I would have to hold my breath. Clever calculations filled the time. I should angle in shallowly—the water might not be deep and less of it could be more dangerous than more. If it was deep I could tuck in my head and roll back up, minimizing the risk of colliding with the pier. The tide would carry me in; I need only give in to it. Was one of my sandals still dangling from my toes? At last, WHAM, there it was: an icy clutch, sudden and absolutely silent, as if a bank vault had closed over me.

The water was deep and oddly still. I executed my roll, kicked up to the surface, and took a quick swallow of air before I was clubbed back down by a crashing wave. I came up again, caught my breath, and treading furiously, tried to make out the pier or the light from shore. I couldn't see a thing. Even the green snakes had abandoned me. It was all a swirling darkness above and below. I sensed that the current was behind me and struck out before it, but I had taken only a few strokes when, abruptly, as if I had collided with a truck on some aquatic highway, I was shoved sidelong and swept in the opposite direction. I went back to treading, trying to revolve in place to get my bearings, but no sooner had my feet stretched below my knees then they were swept firmly out from under me and my body, forced to follow, slipped beneath the surface. I fought my way back up and stretched out flat, gobbling air. I was being whisked along with such dispatch I expected momentarily to be slapped into the shallows, but oddly there were no swells. Then, in the near distance, I spotted the white crest of a wave curling elegantly into its trough, a sight that filled me with such wonder and panic that a shout escaped my lips, for just as there could be no doubt that the wave was rolling into shore, it was equally irrefutable that I was being carried with overwhelming force in the opposite direction.

Out to sea. A momentary contemplation of that phrase, of what it encompassed, enormous ships afloat in it, planes flying all night and into the morning to get over it, beneath its surface whales sleeping or singing, and at the end of it, Europe. I was in a vastness in which I had no more significance than an ant, but like an ant, I was programmed to struggle against the forces arrayed against me. I knew which way I didn't want to go, and so I turned into the current and swam against it, summoning every bit of energy and skill I possessed. I didn't pause to check my progress; I just kicked and revolved my arms, turning my head from side to side to suck in air. It was like running up the down escalator, any hesitation could only set me back. The water slipped over and under me, effortlessly pushing and pushing me, but I fought against it with a dreadful, stupid persistence I hadn't known I possessed. My shoulders ached, my legs were losing propulsion, indeed I could hardly feel them. I tried to concentrate on my breathing, to keep it even—in, up, out, down—but I was missing a beat every few strokes, holding my breath in when I should have let it out, which I knew would exhaust me, but I couldn't get on top of it. Start over, I thought, as if I was on a treadmill and could step outside the belt and catch my breath. I lifted my head and my legs sank down beneath me. I could see the dark bulk of the pier jutting out into the waves. It was far away, too far, I thought, and steadily receding. I wouldn't make it, but the sight filled me with hope. Back to relentless swimming. I kicked and stroked, trying to stay as near the surface as I could because I felt less resistance there. But I was still having trouble breathing and the fatigue in my shoulders made it difficult to keep my movements organized. Grim resolve battled with increasing panic. My body was giving out on me, but my only choice was to forge on. I'd lost communication with my legs, my chest was sinking with every stroke, I was swallowing more water than air. I'm not going to make it, I thought. I'm drowning. "Help," I heard myself cry, as my head slipped under the water. I thrashed back up, cried out again, "Help!" A fierce cramp in my right calf muscle sent a shock wave to my brain. I rolled onto my back, clutching my leg with one hand, treading with the free arm and good leg, but of course I sank again. Just kick through the pain, I thought, and I got back up, took a deep breath of air and switched to frog-like pumping of arms and legs, not because I thought it might help but because that was what my body did. I had run out of thoughts; only terror and sadness inhabited me, only emotions. That's what we come down to after all.

I struggled on, but I kept going under, each time a little

longer, each breath of air more shallow than the last. It was silent below, above the only sound was my gasping and my heart pounding in my ears. "Help!" I heard myself cry as I went down and "Help!" again as I battled my way back into the air.

"Be calm," a voice commanded. Was it my own? No, it came to me from out of the air. In the next moment something big, something powerful slammed into my legs and grasped my waist. I kicked to free myself, but it held me fast, swarming up my body, pulling me down. A man's head surfaced close to mine, his arms slipped under my own, holding me close. "Don't fight me," he said.

I clutched his neck. "Save me," I pleaded, clinging to him.

"Don't push me down, you idiot," he said. "You'll drown us both." He grasped my hands and pulled them apart, pushing free of me.

"No," I cried. "Don't leave me."

He caught hold of my shoulder and pulled it, turning me away from him. "Lie on your back," he said. "Make yourself as flat as you can."

"I can't," I said, but I tried, and as my legs came up he brought his arm across my chest and pulled me in so that my head rested against his sternum.

"That's it," he said. "I'll keep your head up. Kick if you can."

"I can," I said and I tried, but my legs were numb. We were moving, however, somehow he was ferrying me through the water, not against the current but across it, so that we were still being carried away from the shore. A peculiar lassitude had taken over my senses, but I made a feeble protest. "Wrong way," I panted.

"Please shut up," he said.

I couldn't catch my breath; it was as if my lungs were frozen. Where was I? Of course, I concluded, this was a dream from which I would straightway awaken. Then I felt something swelling beneath me, lifting me so gently, and my rescuer as well, carrying us up, up, and I saw the stars, a sliver of the moon, and the twinkling of lights from the land toward which we were being forcefully conveyed on the long plume of a wave that, in the next moment, collapsed beneath us, leaving us foundering before the onslaught of the next one. I clung to my companion and held my breath.

When I opened my eyes again I was flat on my back on the sand and a man was kneeling over me, his eyes closed, his lips approaching mine like a lover. I rolled onto my side and coughed up a quantity of phlegm. He got to his feet, straddling me, without comment.

"My God," I said. "What happened?"

"You passed out," he said.

Then I remembered the rail slipping away, my plunge into the waves, the current carrying me against my will. I turned onto my back and gazed up at him. "I was drowning," I said. "You saved my life."

In the dim moonlight I could just make out his face. His dripping hair was dark and long, like mine, his eyes were deep set, heavy lidded, his jaw was strong. He was tall, like me, and handsome, like me. He considered me, still wheezing pitiably at his feet, while the waves pounded in and the moon, obscured by a passing cloud, cast us into darkness. I was conscious of how cold and wet the sand was, and how it gave beneath me, sucking at me, ready to cover me over like the rest of the debris disgorged and deposited on the shore by the ceaseless scouring of the tides. I was sick, weak, and grateful to be alive. My rescuer stepped away from me, addressing the air. "That was quite a performance, Ed," he said.

A deeper chill invaded my spine. Had I heard him correctly? "How do you know my name?" I asked.

"Why shouldn't I?"

I pried myself out of the sand; just sitting required an exertion of energy that alarmed me. Where was my strength? "Because I don't know you," I said.

He smiled at this, a mocking smile that took offense. "You know me, Ed," he said. "I'm Guy Margate."

The name meant nothing to me but there was something familiar about him. I must have met him at some party, or in a bar. "Sorry," I lied. "I didn't recognize you. I'm not myself."

"Are you ever?"

"What?"

"I came out to have a smoke on the pier," he said, "and I heard you screaming."

I staggered to my feet. "You saved my life," I said again. "How can I repay you?"

"Oh," he said. "We'll think of a way."

I dusted the sand off my legs, looking up and down the beach. We weren't far from the pier. A car, creeping along the road, turned in toward the town.

"Can you walk back to Teddy's house?" he asked. "Or should I go get a car and drive you?"

Teddy's house. Of course. "You're Peter Davis's friend," I said. "You came with him."

"That's right. We just got in. You were out with Madeleine."

Madeleine. How long ago, that torrid, sandy coupling with Madeleine beneath the stars? It was all coming back to me now, my life. "I can walk," I said.

There wasn't much in the way of conversation between us on the brief stroll back through the somnolent town. I was too exhausted to make small talk. I took Guy's silence as a form of courtesy, allowing me to recover my bearings as well as my breath. As we turned the last corner, he said, "You don't have any cigarettes, do you? I never did get my smoke."

"I had a pack on the porch, I left them there. They may be gone by now."

"I'll check that out," he said. The house was dark, and for a moment I feared we would have to rouse someone to let us in. I wasn't up to talking about my misadventure. "It's here," Guy said, lifting a potted geranium and extracting a key.

"How did you know it was there?" I asked.

"Teddy told me. How else?" He slipped the key into the lock and pushed the door open, glancing back at me with a look I couldn't read, though it wasn't in any characterization friendly. Without another word, he switched on the hall light and went out to the porch. I dropped the key back under the pot, closed the door, trudged up the stairs to my room, where I peeled off my damp clothes and left them on the floor. Scarcely a minute after I stretched out on the bed, my head cradled in the luxurious down pillow, I was asleep.

When I woke, the sun was blasting through my window and the sound of laughter floated in from the street. As there was no clock in my room, I had no idea what time it was. I indulged myself in the luxury of not having to care. The laughter drifted away; was it our group or another? At length, I sat up and looked around for my suitcase, which gaped open on an old-fashioned ribbon luggage rack near the door. My wadded swim trunks and T-shirt, still damp, gave off a faint scent of brine. The night came back to me, all of it. Madeleine and the magic green snakes, the fall from the pier and the irresistible current, the baffling appearance of Guy Margate, who seemed to know me though I felt more and more certain I'd never seen him before; who claimed he heard me screaming—was I screaming?—and plunged into the ocean to save my life.

I pulled on a clean shirt and shorts and went down the hall to brush my teeth. The house was quiet; most of the bedroom doors stood open. I peeked in at Madeleine's; the bed was neatly made, the suitcase closed, a bottle of water, half empty, and a glass occupied the bedside table. In the bathroom I confronted my reflection. I didn't look good. Nearly drowning had left me pale and drawn. I remembered swimming and then the awful, constant pull of the water, dragging me along until I was too exhausted to resist. I slapped my face with cold water, ran a comb through my hair, and went down the back staircase to the kitchen. Teddy, sitting at the long wooden table perusing the pages of a newspaper, a half-full mug of coffee near to hand, looked up. "Here he is," he said. "The drowned man."

So Guy had told the story. Well, why wouldn't he? "What time is it?" I asked.

"A little after noon."

"Is there any coffee?"

"It's in the carafe by the stove. Mugs on the hooks there. How are you feeling?"

"I've been better."

"Bread by the toaster. Help yourself."

"Thanks," I said. "Where is everyone?"

"They're all at the beach burning themselves to crisps."

"But you didn't go."

"Truth to tell, Edward, I loathe the beach. I never go out there if I can help it, even to chase women, which is the only conceivable reason a person in his right mind would go."

I pulled out a chair and sat across from him. "I think I agree with you."

He folded his paper. "You look like hell."

"Do I?"

"Guy said you were nearly done for."

"Did he tell everyone, or just you?"

"Everyone. At breakfast. The ladies were filled with admiration."

"He's a powerful swimmer," I said.

"Turns out he was a lifeguard, several summers, all through high school. Rescue is one of his fortes."

"Lucky for me."

"Well, if it had been me on the pier you wouldn't be feeling too lucky right now. You wouldn't be feeling anything."

I detected an undertone of accusation in this remark, and it stung me. "No, I know it. I'm grateful, believe me. I'll be in his debt forever."

Teddy got up to refill his cup. "When I think I might have invited you out here and on your first night you drowned. Jesus."

"I don't know what happened. I got caught in some kind of undertow."

"A rip current," Teddy corrected me. "Guy told us all about it. Some people call them riptides, but that's incorrect. They run against the tide and open out in a mushroom shape. If you don't fight them, eventually they thin out and dump you back into the tide. If you get caught in one all you have to do is swim parallel to the shore and you'll get free."

"I didn't know that. All I knew was I couldn't get back."

"The girls were much edified. They all know what to do now, thanks to you."

"Are you mad at me, Teddy?" I said.

"Good God, no." He opened the refrigerator and peered at the contents. "I'm going to scramble eggs. Do you want some eggs?"

"I do," I said. "I'm starving."

"Bless those girls; they don't eat it but they have brought home the bacon."

"I could go for bacon."

Cradling packages of eggs and bacon in one arm, he pulled

down a skillet the size of a garbage-can lid from the constellation of cookware dangling over the stove.

"So what do you think of this—"

"Guy," he said. "It's a problem, the name."

"This guy, Guy," I said.

"I think he bears watching."

"Doesn't immediately bowl you over with confidence?"

"Yet, evidently, he's a lifesaver."

"A lifeguard, at least."

"He looks a lot like you."

"Does he? I thought he did."

"He says he knows you."

"Maybe he does. I mean, obviously he does. But just between you and me, Teddy, I don't remember the guy."

"Guy."

"Right."

Teddy had the burner up and was marshaling his forces in the skillet. "Peter likes him, at least he's sympathetic to him, but not simpatico sympathetic; the other kind."

"What did the girls think of him?"

"That's one of the things that bear watching." We heard voices from the porch, female laughter, high and bright and the screen door creaking on its hinges. "As you're about to find out," Teddy concluded.

Peter Davis came in first, resplendent in paisley swimming trunks, a bright-yellow towel draped around his neck. He greeted me, holding out his hand for a manly shake. "Ed," he said, "really glad you're still with us." Becky and Mindy followed, interrupting their conversation to gush over me. They amused themselves with an exaggerated display of hugs and kisses. "I'm fine," I assured them. "I'm fine." Over their sunburnished, brine-scented shoulders I saw Madeleine and Guy pause in the doorway to take in the spectacle. Their bodies inclined toward each other. Madeleine's droll expression suggested that Guy had just said something entertaining and he had the smug look of a man relishing his own wit. Was there a joke between them? Was it at my expense? My tongue probed my teeth in a hopeless quest for words. The dithering girls released me and alighted on Teddy, who announced that he was taking orders at the stove. Madeleine approached without speaking. Tenderly, she laid her palm along my check and dropped a chaste kiss on my forehead. "You should have gone to bed when I did," she said softly.

I turned my face into her hand, closing my eyes against the humid web of her fingers and kissing the soft pad at the base of her thumb. It came over me that, along with everything else, I had come close to losing her, and losing her before I could say with any confidence that I had found her. We'd had an intimate yet brief encounter, but now the benignity of her touch, the gentleness of her reproach called up in me an emotion so pure and deep it shook me to my core. As an actor, it is my vocation to reproduce such feelings at will, and in fact that moment has stayed with me all these years, and when I am called upon to find, for the benefit of an audience, the outward expression of inconsolable sadness and loss, I feel my eyes closing and my face turning into the warmth of Madeleine's hand.

It was a public caress, noted without comment by a lively

group intent on pleasure. My desolation was off-key, out of tune, too intense for the company, and I let it go as quickly as it had come. So did Madeleine. Briefly she pressed her palm against my lips, a subtle pressure no one else could see, and then she withdrew her hand and offered her services to the chef, who, having insufficiently separated the bacon strips, was dodging and cursing over a viciously sputtering lump of fat. Wistfully I regarded her back; when would we be alone again, how would we manage it? I sensed a movement behind me, a shadow flickered across Teddy's folded newspaper, the chair across from me gave a muffled shriek as it was dragged back from the table, and Guy Margate dropped into place before me.

I don't deny that, superficially at least, Guy looked a lot like me. We were both tall and lean, our eyes deep set, and our beakish noses jutted from the eyebrow line. We were a type; in a casting call, we were the handsome white guys. But Guy was darker than I, his hair black and straight, his eyes a deep chocolate brown. He could do an Italian, or a Latino, even an Indian at a stretch. My looks are more startling because my hair is wavy and I have light eyes. I can turn the atmosphere on a stage to ice with a sudden glance.

Guy must have envied me my eyes. He had to withhold something to cool things down, something overheated and demonic. Personally I think it's difficult for anyone with brown eyes to do a real chill. Brando could scare the life out of you, but if he turned a cold shoulder it wasn't distance, it was a death warrant, it was violence. His cold shoulder was hot. Pacino does restraint well—same effect—he's just decided not to tear your head off right this second. Jeremy Irons is an exception;

he has brown eyes, but he can do a prodigious chill. That's because he's got Britishness, which is the definition of cool on a stage; also he's slight of build, and he has a quality of longing combined with deep boredom—that's the Britishness again. You know he'd give anything to be human, to have a real feeling, but he's just not going to get there because he's dead, actually, and you forgive him for that. For me, Irons epitomizes what I call "the remove."

So, although Guy was giving me what anybody else would have characterized as a cold look over the kitchen table, my perception was that he didn't do it very well. I could do it better and for a moment I did. I smiled slightly, I allowed my eyes to rest on his face, not meeting his eyes, and I waited for him to speak.

I know what you're thinking—what kind of ingrate is this? Here he's reencountering the man who saved his life not ten hours earlier and all he's thinking about is who's the better actor. Well, perhaps you're right, but remember, Guy Margate had seen me at my most desperate. I had clung to him in panic, lost consciousness from exhaustion and fear; on the shore I had retched into the sand at his feet. Thanks to him it was understood by my friends, and especially by the woman I most desired, that my plight had been largely the result of my ignorance. Any competent swimmer could have saved himself. As every actor knows, emotions succeed each other in sequences that are often inappropriate and counterintuitive—this is what polite society was created to conceal—but one sequence that rarely, if ever, obtains is for humiliation to be followed by gratitude. If politicians could only grasp this simple precept, the world would be a much more peaceful place. I knew by all rights that I should feel grateful to Guy Margate for saving my life, but what I felt was not gratitude. I felt wary of him, but I was prepared to present him with a reasonable facsimile of the proper emotion.

"How are you?" he said at last.

Now how did he say it? That's important. Did warmth and solicitude pour from his eye, did his tone betray more than ordinary interest in the answer to his question? No and no. His interest was distant, his voice flat.

"I'm fine," I said.

"You don't look fine," he observed.

Oh, all right, I thought, all right. "I'm glad to be alive," I said. "Thanks to you."

He smiled. He had long canines and a wolfish grin, very sudden and over before you knew it. "My pleasure," he said.

Then an unpleasant thing happened. Madeleine approached with a mug. As she leaned over his back, the top of her chest pressed into his shoulder. "Here's your coffee," she said, setting the mug before him. He brought his hand up and touched the inside of her elbow. "Thanks, dear," he said.

"You're welcome," Madeleine sweetly replied, turning back to the stove. Guy lifted his eyes to mine, as my heart sank. "She's lovely, isn't she?" he said.


The rest of the weekend was torture to me, though it ended well enough. After lunch everyone but Teddy went back to the beach and I tagged along. It was agreed that I must get back in the water, just as a fallen rider is advised to get back on a horse, no matter how damaged or reluctant he feels or how blatantly vicious and unruly the animal might actually be. I wasn't unwilling; I even felt some crude masculine urge to prove myself, especially to Madeleine, but when I stood on the sand looking out at the fathomless depths, I felt my throat closing around a solid lump of panic. The beach was crowded; all manner of people were thrashing about in the water: oldsters, pubescent girls, pregnant women, children were in it, babies were being dunked in it or toddling about in the shallows. I wanted to cry out, Run for your lives! Swimming struck me as a species of madness; one might as well try to ride a tiger or leap into a vat of poisonous snakes. My friends, unaware of my stark terror, encouraged me, all but Guy Margate, who strode out into the shallows, dived into an incoming wave, and beelined at motorboat speed out past the breakers, where he bobbed like a cork gazing back at the shore. Madeleine and Mindy chortled over his prowess, reminding me, as if I needed reminding, what a bit of luck it was for me that I had managed to nearly drown within range of such a man. Drowning began to look good. I swallowed my fear and walked into the swirling waters, noting that even close to shore you can feel the pull of the tide, its willingness to take you down. Peter Davis caught up with me and we chatted as the sand declined beneath my feet and the water gripped my waist. "How long have you known Guy?" I asked him.

"A few months. He's only been in town since February."

"Where's he from?"

"I don't know. One of those states in the middle. Iowa, Ohio, something like that. Kansas, maybe."

"He didn't learn to swim in Kansas," I said.

"No? Don't they have lakes?"

I shoved off into a wave and Peter followed. It was OK, I could stand it. I wasn't going to drown with this many people around and the ocean was doing a gently pulsing, I'm-not-scary routine, which I now understood to be the equivalent of entrapment. We swam along, parallel to the shore, stopping to tread a bit and look for our crowd. I saw Madeleine swimming out strongly, rising upon a billow and disappearing briefly behind it. She was heading for Guy, who watched her approach, treading so effortlessly that he appeared to be sitting on a chair just beneath the surface of the water. In another moment Madeleine was next to him. They looked like two seals in their element, barking cheerfully at each other.

What if Madeleine had saved me, I thought. She was certainly a strong enough swimmer. Then I would owe my life to her: Would that really be desirable? I could deny her nothing and she might look upon me with pity. At best her feelings would be maternal. No, I wouldn't like that at all. "I'm going in," Peter said.

"I'm with you," I said. It was an easy return; we hadn't gone out very far. My feet found the bottom and I stood up feeling I'd vindicated myself somewhat, at least in my own estimation. Mindy was on a blanket rubbing lotion into her thighs, squinting at the sea. She spotted Peter and me and waved encouragingly.

"Teddy's sick for her," Peter observed. "I don't see it myself."

"She's sweet," I said. We arrived at the blanket and threw

ourselves down on the sand. When we were dry and broiling in the sun, Guy and Madeleine emerged from the sea and ran up the beach to accost us, shaking off water and wringing their hair over us, playful as puppies. Pretending to be excited by the madcap jollity of it all, I caught Madeleine's ankle and pulled her down on the sand. She shouted as I play-bit her calf, but she wouldn't tussle; she was on her feet in an instant, kicking sand in my face. Mindy caught some of it and complained. "It's too hot for that," she said. "Let's get ice cream." Madeleine, playing the petulant child, whined, "Yes, yes, I want ice cream," so there was nothing for it but to pull up the blanket and set off for the ice-cream emporium. Madeleine and Mindy led the way, chattering nonstop while Peter, Guy, and I crowded along behind on the sidewalk. The rest of the day went like that, Mindy and Madeleine were inseparable, as if they'd made a pact, and I wondered if, in fact, they had. At the house Teddy was loading a cooler with beer. We started drinking by four. Becky and James, our resident lovers, smooched in the shadows on a big chaise lounge while the rest of us milled about aimlessly, smoking, drinking, doing shower rotations to cool down. Even on the porch with the ceiling fan running, it was hot. I switched from beer to vodka and cranberry which only made me more irritable. Mindy put on some mix tapes she'd brought with her, one dreadful Broadway show tune after another. No one seemed to mind, even when she joined in on the chorus. Teddy, desperate to separate her from Madeleine, engaged her in a teasing version of "Cabaret," followed by a faux-tango to "Hernando's Hideaway." I took the opportunity to steal Mindy's seat next to Madeleine. Teddy whirled Mindy this way and that, a suave and confident dancer. "Teddy's a revelation," I said to Madeleine. She gave me the blandest of smiles. Guy, watching the show from the dining-room doorway called out "Olé!," his eyebrows lifted and his lips pursed, thwacking his palms together in the approved flamenco style, a parody of the excitable Latino male. Madeleine laughed. Their eyes met across the room; something sly and charged in the exchange put me over the top. "Come dance with me," I commanded Madeleine, grasping her wrist. I lurched to my feet but she resisted, throwing me off balance. I still had my drink in hand and I stumbled a few steps, trying to keep it from spilling over. I heard Guy say, "Oh, señor, be careful." Teddy was twirling Mindy in my direction as she sang the required knock code and password to give at the door of the hideaway. We collided. I poured my drink neatly down the front of her blouse. "Joe!" Mindy exclaimed. The music stopped.

"Well done, Ed," Guy said.

I looked back to see Madeleine frowning at me in a way I didn't like. Mindy, ever good-natured, only laughed. She plucked an ice cube from her bodice. "Very cooling," she observed.

"I'm so sorry, Mindy," I said. "Please forgive me."

"Don't be silly," she said.

I put my arm around her waist and led her toward the kitchen. "Let's clean you up," I said. "Let me help you out of that top."

"Teddy," she cried joyfully. "Ed wants to take off my top."

"That's a job for two men," Teddy said, enfolding her from the other side and we propelled her to the kitchen where we did get her blouse off and made a show of washing it in the sink while she poured herself a glass of wine and stood watching us in her black lace bra. Cleverly Teddy sent me to the basement for some detergent. When I came back, he and Mindy were in a clutch against the refrigerator. I ducked back onto the porch to find only the lovers and Peter Davis, who was playing solitaire at a low table he'd pulled up between his knees.

"Where'd they go?" I asked.

"They went for a walk."

"Damn," I said and Peter chuckled over his cards.

"I'm losing too," he said, "against myself."

I sat on the porch steps looking up and down the sidewalk but there was no one in sight. I was thinking about Guy's Latino impression, which had been so successful with Madeleine, and of how disarming is the ability to make people laugh. It's a gift, mimicry, but it's not acting; in a way it's the opposite of acting, which is why comedians are seldom good actors. There's an element of exaggeration in the imposture; the copy is the original painted with a broad brush and it can be grotesque, even cruel. But no one is offended. People are drawn to the funnyman who can imitate a politician or a famous actor or an ethnic type, especially his own ethnic type.

Guy was an excellent mimic. He could pick up the voice, accent, posture, inflection, facial tics, laugh, walk, and conversational manner of anyone he studied for a few minutes. He had the requisite deadpan, the refusal to enter the joke, but it wasn't willful. He was not one of the clowns derided by Hamlet *that will themselves laugh, to set on some quantity of barren spectators to laugh too.* Though he could mock those who did, Guy simply had no sense of humor. "Barren spectators," I thought. That was good.

So by disdaining a skill I don't possess, I got my mind off my present predicament and made myself feel superior to the competition, a serviceable gambit rendered worthless when at last Guy and Madeleine came into view. They didn't see me and I was free to study their approach. They weren't touching, which was a relief, but they were talking, or rather Madeleine was talking and Guy was listening closely, nodding his head as if he was taking instruction. At last he spoke and Madeleine, glancing ahead, noticed me on the steps. I raised my hand in humble, hopeful greeting. To my relief, she smiled. As they turned up the walk, they fell silent. When she was very close, Madeleine said, "Did you get Mindy's blouse off, Ed?"

"That was just a joke," I said.

"Was it?" she replied. "I wonder why it wasn't funny." She passed me, her flip-flops snapping out a brisk staccato of dismissal, concluding in a sharp rap from the closing screen door. Guy came up the steps and sat down beside me.

"Things aren't going very well for you, are they?" he observed.

"I wouldn't say that," I said. "She's obviously jealous; how bad could that be."

"That's a very positive way of looking at it," he said.

"You'll find I'm a very positive sort of guy, Guy."

"Unfortunately that's not always enough."

I took this cryptic observation as my exit cue and got to my feet, looking down at Guy's bowed head. As if addressing his knees he said, "I find myself in financial straits."

The sagacity of hindsight makes me think I apprehended something ominous in this remark, that it contained an element of moral challenge, one I sensed I might fail to meet. Perhaps I had no such trepidations, but I didn't move away and the air was oddly still, as if listening for my response.

"It's the actor's chronic condition," I offered.

"I thought you might want to help me out." He didn't say the rest of it, but I heard it loud and clear—*because I saved your life.* I heard it and I knew it was true. My life, the air moving in and out of my lungs, the blood coursing through my veins, the thoughts hurtling like traffic in the precincts of my skull, the emotions which at that moment were a rush of contradictory impulses, one of which was resentment, another, the consciousness of boundless obligation, everything I knew and cherished about myself was standing on that porch looking down on the person who, by a selfless effort, had made my standing there, breathing, feeling trapped and resentful, possible. If he had not jumped in to save me, I would have drowned. I couldn't deny it; I owed him my life and my obligation was a bond that must endure between us forever.

But it didn't make me like him. "How much do you need?" I said.

"Fifty bucks would do it for now."

Fifty dollars, at that time, was a fair amount of money. It was half my rent. I had that much in my bank account, but not a lot more.

"I didn't bring my checkbook," I said. "Can you wait until we get back to town?"

"Sure," he said. "Monday?"

"After work. I could meet you at Phebe's. Bowery and Third, you know it?"

"I can find it. What time?"

"Make it seven."

"I'll be there," he said.

Immediately I was annoyed with myself for inviting him to my favorite dive instead of choosing some impersonal, public place like Washington Square. If I just handed him the money and walked away, there could be no assumption of friendly feeling, which it seemed important to keep at a minimum. The hostility between us was not, I was convinced, all coming from me; Guy had been contemptuous of me even when I was drowning. He had called my struggle with death a "performance." Obviously shame was a large component of my feeling about the entire episode; if I could have arranged never to see his face again—with no harm to either of us—I would have done it. At the moment, all I could do was continue on my course back into Teddy's house. I went up the stairs, closed the door of my bedroom, and stretched out on the bed. I didn't want to talk to anyone.

However, as there's no such thing as a reclusive actor, after a brief nap, I rejoined the party on the porch. The men were playing cards and the women were in the kitchen torturing vegetables and the dreaded tofu into a casserole. There was no pairing off and no music, just general bonhomie until after dinner when we heard the band strike up "The Star-Spangled Banner" in the bandstand at the nearby park where, Teddy told us, there would soon be an impressive fireworks display, well worth "toddling over" to see. Off we went.

It was too American for words, this Jersey shore. The grilling hot dogs, the ice-cream cart, the stand purveying that strangest of all confections, cotton candy; gossiping oldsters, darting children, a bevy of sweating young parents dancing under the cover of an open tent near the bandstand—the scene was so innocent and good-natured it warmed my anxious heart. I sidled up to Madeleine, who, with Peter Davis, was admiring the singer, a middle-aged Mafioso with a voice as smooth as olive oil. With mock politesse, I asked if she would give me the honor of a dance.

It worked; she smiled, held out her hand, and in a few moments she was in my arms under the tent. I swelled with confidence. I'm an excellent dancer and, it turned out, so was she. We whipped through a brisk number and then I held her close as the band segued into a surprisingly soulful, languid arrangement of "Blue Moon." She rested her cheek against my chest, her hips brushed my own, but I was careful not to introduce into this public embrace anything resembling erotic play. She'd surprised me with her reaction to the admittedly poor joke I'd made at Mindy's expense, showing me a prudishness and respect for the proprieties that was unusual in young women of my acquaintance and completely at odds with her frankly provocative behavior on the beach the night before. She was complicated, and I liked her better for that. When the crooner hit the line "Please adore me," I whispered the words into her ear. She chuckled, looking up at me. "This is nice," she said.

"It is," I agreed. "Let's dance all night."

And we did. When the music stopped and the dancers abandoned the tent for the lawn where the fireworks were about to begin, we ambled over to our group arm in arm. Teddy and Mindy, kneeling on a blanket, handed out beers from the cooler. It was a clear, hot night, the sky a perfect blue-black canvas for a pyrotechnic display. Without warning the first volley sent a white streak heavenward and all were riveted by a fountain of sparkling diamonds raining harmlessly down upon us. Madeleine stood in front of me, her head resting against my chest. "Oh look," she said as a diaphanous red flower blossomed overhead. The booms of the rockets crackled in the air and the displays grew more complex. I slipped my arms around her waist and joined in the soft exclamations of the crowd. A collective "Aaaah!" greeted a spectacular burst made of bright ribbons, red, white, and blue, of course, which exploded into half a dozen concentric rings inside of which more ribbons shot up to another level of shimmering rings. Everyone knew the end was near. The pauses between explosions extended, giving the designers time to coordinate their missiles. It's like sex, I thought, glancing about me at the raised faces, all bright with expectancy. The air over the firing station was flushed with hellish red smoke. I could hear the ratcheting of the machinery and the boom and hiss of multiple shots as a dozen streamers rippled past. Not far off, literally by the light of the rocket's red glare, I spotted the only spectator besides myself who wasn't closely attending the grand finale. He was standing apart from the crowd, his gaze fixed purposefully on me, and I had the sense that he had been watching me for some time. Our eyes met and I lifted my hand in a diffident salute, but Guy made no gesture in response. Then, just to unsettle him, I nuzzled Madeleine's neck with my lips, tightening my grip on her waist. "Oh, look," she said again, softly. The sky seemed to be raining stars into a tide of blood steadily rising to meet it. I looked back at Guy, who hadn't moved a muscle. There's something wrong with him, I thought, but I got no further than that, for the show was over, and Madeleine, who had turned in my arms, brought her lips to mine.

Phebe's is spiffed up these days, and surrounded by other build-ings, but in the '70s it was a glittering oasis in the desert of the Bowery, the haunt of panhandlers, drug dealers, and actors. At Phebe's the beer was cheap, the food wouldn't kill you, and the proprietor was actor-friendly. I went there two or three nights a week. Sometimes Teddy came with me, but he preferred the more literary scene at the Cedar which was closer to Fifth Avenue and the world of his heritage.

I'd never seen Madeleine at Phebe's, but that Monday night when I went to meet Guy and give him the fifty dollars in ex-change for my life, there she was at a corner table, dragging fried potatoes through a pool of ketchup and biting off the bloody-looking ends, while Mindy rattled on across from her. They spotted me and beckoned me to join them, but their table was a two-top and pulling up a chair would have put me in the aisle to the peril of the waitress. "Thanks," I said. "Thanks, but I'm meeting someone." Madeleine swallowed more potato, somehow managing to smile around it.

We had returned to the city separately with no particular understanding, but I had her phone number and had promised to call, which I had every intention of doing. I wanted to get the Guy matter over with first. I could tell by her smile that she assumed the someone I was meeting was another woman and that, should this prove the case, she would affect indifference. Mindy had some gossip about an actor who'd been sacked at the behest of the leading lady, who said she couldn't stand kissing him, and we laughed over that, though actually it wasn't funny. The power struggles that go on backstage can be brutal and destructive, and I couldn't help imagining how I would feel if something like this happened to me, which naturally led to some thoughts about the quality of my kissing. "Couldn't they just get the poor guy a kissing coach?" I suggested and got not only the laugh I was after but an unexpected and deeply reassuring compliment from Madeleine, who said, "You could hire yourself out for that."

"Do you think so?" I said lightly, disguising the deep seriousness I felt about her answer. Mindy was silent, looking from one of us to the other, her eyes dancing with amusement.

"Oh yes," Madeleine said. "And I'm a good judge of that. I've had a wide experience."

"I'll bet you have," I said.

She took up another potato and wagged it at me. "On the stage of course," she said.

"That's the only place it really matters," Mindy added.

We all laughed at this and then Madeleine announced much too cheerfully, "Look, it's Guy Margate."

"He's coming to meet me," I said.

He passed inside and stood near the door, surveying the room critically.

"Excuse me," I said to the girls, leaving them to cut him off at the bar. The last thing I wanted was witnesses to the money exchange. When he saw me, his expression changed only slightly. Fortunately the room was crowded and we were forced to take a seat at the bar.

"So how are you?" I said after we'd ordered our beers.

"Pretty good," he said. "I have a callback. I just found out."

"That's fantastic," I said. "That's something to celebrate. Where is it?"

"Playwrights Horizons."

Playwrights Horizons was an impressive venue for a callback. It was an Equity house, they did new edgy plays, the directors were generally up and coming, and they got reviews. But, I reminded myself, a callback wasn't a part. "That's great," I said. "Good luck."

"I think I've got the job," he said. "The director really liked me."

This was an incredibly foolhardy and naïve thing for an actor to say, a certain jinx on his chances, and I marveled that he didn't seem to know it. But I wasn't going to set him straight. "That's great," I said again. He was looking around, ready to change the subject. "This is a nice place," he said.

"It is. I come here a lot."

He studied the brick wall behind the bar. "Do you have the money?" he asked.

I dug the carefully folded bills from my back pocket.

"Sure," I said, handing them over. He took the money, counted the bills, and stuffed them into his jeans pocket. "This is an actors' hangout," he observed.

No word of thanks, no acknowledgment of any kind, surely the proper reception of repayment by the debtor. Why would you thank someone for that which is owed? It wouldn't make sense. Do bankers thank you when you pay exorbitant interest on a loan? Does city hall send a thank-you note when you pay a parking fine? "Where do you live, Guy?" I said, hunkering down over my beer.

"Chelsea," he said. "Great, Madeleine and Mindy are here." I looked up and there they were, moving through the tables to the bar.

"What a surprise," I said.

"Hey, Guy," Madeleine said as she sidled between us. "I've never seen you here before."

"That's because I didn't know you came here," he said.

Not bad. Not exactly wit, but quick. Madeleine's eyes softened as they do when she receives compliments. It's hard to tell if she's taken in or just letting the moment pass. "Have a drink with us," I said. Guy was already pulling up a stray barstool and in a moment the girls were perched between us. Madeleine chose the seat next to Guy, which I took to be bad news. The bartender plunked down the glasses of red wine they requested. Guy announced that he had a callback, which focused the attention of the women nicely. They wanted to know all about it. This time, playing to his audience, he was self-deprecating—it was a small part, he probably wouldn't get it. The women affirmed that auditions were hell, rejection was more likely than not, and a callback meant you were doing something right. Mindy had heard of the playwright, an Italian from Brooklyn, he'd had a play at Yale Rep a year ago that did pretty well; she couldn't remember the title. The talk turned to other plays; who was casting what and where. We were all non-Equity at that point, so we had the option to work for little or no money. If Guy got this job he would be able to join the union and be guaranteed a minimum wage. The old chestnut "Get your Equity card and never work again" was passed around, though we all knew it was just a variety of sour grapes. Madeleine had already applied for the group auditions in April, a cattle call for summer stock companies. It was a good way to get into the union as well as spend the hot months out of town. Guy hadn't heard of this and vowed to do the same. I had a vision of Guy and Madeleine sporting on a green lawn in Vermont or the Berkshires next summer, which sickened me. "You're quiet, Ed," Madeleine said. "Are you OK?"

"I'm depressed," I said. "I'm working double shifts three days this week." This was true. I'd agreed to work overtime because I needed money to pay Guy and my rent. The worst part was, by Friday I would be exhausted and broke, so I couldn't invite Madeleine to dinner or a movie. Guy shot me a chilly look and said something to her I couldn't hear. She turned away to answer him, effectively closing me out. Mindy finished her wine and set the glass on the bar, slipping two one-dollar bills under the base. "I've got to meet Teddy at La MaMa," she said. "He's got tickets for a new show." As she kissed my cheek and slid from her barstool, a flush of fragrance rose from her bosom, baby powder mixed with sweat, not unpleasant but not enticing, either. I pictured Mindy après shower, dowsing her breasts with baby powder while she sang "Don't Rain on My Parade" at full blast. "Take it easy," she said kindly. "Don't work so hard."

"Right," I said. "Tell Teddy I'll call him." I watched as Madeleine and Mindy hugged and cooed. Guy accepted the same cheek busses I'd received. As Mindy flounced out the door, Madeleine and Guy went back to their conversation. For what seemed like a long time I sat drinking my beer and admiring Madeleine's back. What were they talking about? I found Guy's conversational mode peculiarly deadening, but Madeleine seemed both engaged and amused; her soft laughter rustled her shoulders and she nodded her head now and then in agreement or approval. I could see Guy's lips moving, his dark eyes fixed on her face with a sinister, distant interest. Now and then his sudden grin flashed; something unnerving about it, I thought, something menacing. Christopher Walken had a similar death's-head grin. I'd seen him in *Caligula* at Yale. It was amusement provoked by the apprehension of weakness, and I didn't like to see it leveled at the unsuspecting Madeleine. I shifted to Mindy's stool and leaned into the bar. "That's hysterical," Madeleine was saying.

"What is?" I asked.

She turned her bright eyes upon me. "Have you heard this? They're rehearsing a musical of *Gone With the Wind* in Los Angeles. Guess who's playing Scarlett?"

"Julie Andrews," I suggested.

"Lesley Ann Warren!" she exclaimed.

"Not far off," I said.

"And guess who's playing Rhett?"

Because I had been thinking of him, I said, "Christopher Walken."

"No, he would be good, actually. It's Pernell Roberts."

"Who's he?"

*"Bonanza,"* Guy said. "Adam."

"The strong, silent one," Madeleine added.

"Good God," I said.

"Tell him about the songs," Madeleine insisted.

Guy nodded. "There's one called 'Tomorrow's Another Day,' and 'Why Did They Die,' and 'Atlanta Burning.' " This really did make me laugh.

"It's a huge cast," Madeleine said. "More than fifty parts."

"How do you know about this?" I asked Guy.

"I have a cousin who's in it. He plays one of the Tarleton twins."

"Is that where you're from?" I asked, though I knew he wasn't.

"No," Guy said. "I've never been to L.A. Have you?"

"No," I said.

"Do you want to go?"

"No," I said. And then we talked about L.A. and how different film acting was from stage acting and how little work there was in New York, unless you happened to be British or Italian. It was banal conversation and Guy held up his end well enough, though, as we were both entirely focused on Madeleine, there was a competitive edge to it. Then, abruptly, Guy stretched his wrist out to check his watch and pretended surprise. "Gotta run," he said, kissing Madeleine on the cheek. "Friday, six thirty."

"See you there," she replied.

He turned to me extending his hand for a gentleman's parting. "Ed," he said. "Good seeing you. Get my beer for me, would you?"

"Sure," I said. "Why not?" Madeleine smiled upon us, pleased to see this amiable exchange between friends. When he was gone I pulled my stool closer to Madeleine and said, "Friday? Six thirty?"

"He's got tickets to *Jacques Brel.*"

I snorted. "That old rag?"

She regarded me coldly. "Don't be ridiculous. Jacques Brel is great. I've been wanting to see it." She finished her wine while I pictured the inside of my wallet. What a jerk Guy was to take my hard-earned money and then stick me for the price of a beer, especially since he was flush enough to buy tickets to a popular musical revue. My chance with Madeleine was at hand and I determined to take it. I signaled the bartender to refill her glass and when she demurred I insisted. "On me, please. I haven't had a minute alone with you since—"

"We went night swimming," she finished.

"Yes," I said. "You were right. That night was definitely magic."

"It was," she agreed. The bartender set a full glass before her.

Two hours later we were hand in hand, climbing the narrow stairs to my apartment, pausing on each landing for long embraces. The next morning when I opened my eyes to find her arm draped around my waist, her soft breath oscillating against the nape of my neck, I sighed with satisfaction. Guy could have the money. I'd beat him to Madeleine a second time.


Like most actors I worked for tips in restaurants that I couldn't afford to eat in. Three days a week I did the lunch shift at Bloomingdale's, where stylish ladies who had just maxed out their husbands' credit cards picked at cold chicken salad and vowed to economize, beginning with the tip. On Thursday and Friday nights I served dinners to artists and gallery owners at a trendy bar and restaurant in SoHo, which was a good gig because artists have often worked as waiters themselves, so they're sympathetic; also, not being good at math, they tend to round up the percentage. This gave me Monday and Wednesday nights free for my classes with Sandy, Thursday and Friday all day to pursue auditions. Doubling up meant losing audition time as well as Saturday night. So I spent the week resenting Guy Margate, though I was perfectly conscious that if not for him I wouldn't be working at all, I would be a waterlogged corpse tossed up after a thorough pounding on some rocky beach in New Jersey. Friday night I had the additional pleasure of imagining Guy and Madeleine out on the town on the money I was working my ass off to replace. It was midnight on Saturday when I hung up my apron and counted my take, which was unusually good. I decided a nightcap at Phebe's was in order and set out across the cultural divide of Houston Street with a firm resolution: no beer, straight whiskey.

The traffic was light, only the occasional yellow flurry of cabs and a few delivery trucks. The streetlamps hissed and buzzed overhead, shedding a blue metallic light. Phebe's glowed like a golden spaceship dropped down in a grim future world; the sound of voices and music ebbing and flowing as the doors opened to exiting aliens. As I crossed Third Avenue, a panhandler appeared from the shadows and planted himself on the sidewalk so that I couldn't pass without getting his pitch. He was a gray, wizened fellow, with hair like a mudpack, wrapped in a combination of blanket and plastic sheeting that served as both his attire and his lodging. "Jesus," I said, as he stuck out his grimy hand. "Aren't you hot?"

"Any spare change?" he said. His voice was lifeless, but his eyes were black and keen. I dug into my pants pocket; I actually had a lot of change, and extracted a couple of quarters and a dime. "You need to work on your patter," I advised him.

"Fuck you," he said. I dropped the coins into his palm and pressed past him. Actors are superstitious about beggars, perhaps because we're largely in the same line. They know this and make a point of hanging around stage doors, particularly on Broadway. Long-running shows have regulars, who call the stars by their first names. "Dick, the reviewers are in tonight." "Shirley, look at you, you're drop-dead gorgeous as always." So I didn't relish being cursed by a panhandler. He stepped back into the darkness from whence he came and I pushed on to Phebe's, feeling tentative and anxious. The bar was packed, with some overflow to the tables, and the two bartenders were constantly moving with the speed and agility of jugglers. I spotted Teddy at the far end, looking glum, his chin resting in his hand, his eyes fixed on the glass in front of him as if he saw something alive inside it. I squeezed in beside him and said, "What's wrong with that drink?"

He looked up, smiling wistfully. "I fear it is empty."

"We'll take care of that," I said. "Let's go sit at a table." I signaled the bartender, pointing at Teddy's glass, raised two fingers, and received a terse nod; he was on the case.

"Are you drunk, Teddy?" I asked.

"I have no way of knowing."

"Well, how many drinks have you had?"

He glanced at the wall clock. "About two hours' worth."

Two full glasses appeared and I lifted them carefully. Teddy got down from the stool and followed me to the table. "Well done," he said. "I'm glad to see you. Where have you been all week?"

"Working," I said. "I've been killing myself working."

"Why would you do that?"

"I need the money."

"Oh yes, they pay you." Teddy sipped his drink, opening his eyes wide. He had an actor's face, full of expression, long, pale, freckled, a weary drooping mouth, an aristocratic nose, pinched at the nostrils, hazel eyes rather round and flat, and a nimbus of curly red hair. He was slender, lithe, and quick on his feet, not handsome but appealing and wry. I knew a bit about his family—his banker father who wasn't pleased about the acting ambition; his dramatic alcoholic mother (at the beach house there was a painting of her, an English beauty with skin like a blushing rose); his ne'er-do-well older brother, Robert, who befriended thugs and gambled on anything that moved; and his talented younger sister, Moira, who was studying painting in London. He'd been to prep schools and then Yale Drama, his path strewn with privilege at every turning, but he was no dilettante. Money got him to the stage door, but only talent and dedication could get him onstage and he knew it. I sipped my whiskey, which was both smooth and potent, some brand known to the Ivy League and doubtless twice the price of the bar brand, but I didn't care. I was in a funk about the whole business with Guy and I weighed the option of consulting with Teddy. As if he read my mind he announced, "Guy Margate got a job."

This news hit me like a blow and I dropped back in my chair, struggling to accommodate it and to take account of my emotions. There was a strong element of surprise—I hadn't thought he would get the part—and a fair component of jealousy, mixed with deep resentment. Teddy watched me attentively, his chin resting in his hand, his eyebrows lifted. "How do you know this?" I said.

"Mindy had it from Madeleine. Big celebration last night."

"Mindy was there?"

"No, Madeleine called her and she called me. The celebration was just Madeleine and Guy; they had a date."

"Right," I said.

"It's Playwrights Horizons."

"Right," I said again. "Equity. What's the play?"

"*Sunburn* I think it's called. Or maybe *Sunstroke. Sunburst.*

It takes place on a beach. It's written by an Italian I never heard of."

"Guy plays an Italian."

"Presumably."

I reached for the whiskey and swallowed a big gulp.

"It will keep him busy," Teddy observed.

"That's true. And I won't have to give him more money."

"You gave him money?"

"Fifty bucks. He pretty much demanded it. That's why I had to work so much this week, but I've made it up and first thing tomorrow I'm calling Madeleine."

"That's the spirit," Teddy said. We drank in silence for a few moments. The bar was emptying out. "It'll probably flop," Teddy added.

"That's true. And it will keep him off the streets for a couple of weeks at least."

"Also true." We snickered companionably, but the likelihood that the play would fail was cold comfort against the dismal fact that stood before us: Guy Margate had a part and we did not.


When an actor has a part, he has a life, and a full one. When he doesn't have a part, his life is looking for one. Parts are few, the competition is stiff, and even if one succeeds in being hired there are still a variety of avenues that lead directly to failure. The backers can go broke before a play goes into rehearsal; the play can close after a tryout; the director may be incompetent, lack nerve, or just lose control (as evidently happened in

the profitable but unnerving production of *Hamlet* in which
Richard Burton, directed by John Gielgud, delivered a mind-
numbing impersonation of Burton saying Shakespeare's lines
very fast); the play can be difficult, unwieldy, or just banal; the
actors may be miscast; illness, divorce, or lawsuits may ham-
string the production; critics may hate the play and say so; audiences may fail to show up.

Or the leading lady may go mad onstage.

But without a part, an actor can't even fail, so when a play
is cast the thespian community recoils and regroups, simultaneously discouraged and reinvigorated, for if that miserable actor
Joe Blow can land a juicy part, anything is possible.

I'd been in the city a year and had appeared in two productions, one an Equity-waiver workshop at the Wooster Open
Space and one a two-week run of one acts at a tiny theater in
the West Village. The plays were new and forgettable and my
parts were negligible, though I did have a nice bit of comic
business in the one act, in which I got tangled up in my
trousers while trying to seduce my female employer. I went to
my classes, gossiped at the right bars, circled the roles I thought
might be suitable in the casting-call pages of *Back Stage* and
*Show Business,* and lined up at the doors with the rest of the cattle, but I wasn't getting anywhere and I knew it. The news that
Guy, an obscure bookstore clerk, new to the scene and not
connected to any school that I knew of, had a part in an Equity
production was like an injection of iron into my resolve.

On Monday, I went to class with an edge of self-loathing
that felt new and dangerous to me. Madeleine was eager to tell
me about Guy's success, but I shut her down with a grimace.

"Teddy told me," I said. She studied me a moment, her head cocked to one side, thoughtful, interested, the way adults look at a child who has revealed in some completely transparent and inappropriate fashion that he is in pain.

"Look," I said, "I'm wondering if I'm just lazy, if I'm not hungry enough, if I'm just kidding myself."

"This amazes me," she said.

"I don't lack confidence; I know I'm good, but maybe I'm too comfortable hanging out at Phebe's pretending to be an actor."

She nodded. "I've been having the same thoughts all day. It's eerie." Our eyes met and held. I think some elemental bond was struck in that look, a passion to further each other's interests.

"What should we do?" I asked.

"After class, we'll talk," she said, for the inimitable Sandy Meisner had arrived, his ogling eyes behind the thick spectacles that allowed him to see, to which was attached the microphone that allowed him to speak, sweeping the room for the girl with the most revealing top.

We went to the Cedar because it was quiet, and over beers and fries worked out our plan. We would take time off work as much as possible for three weeks and concentrate on nothing but the pursuit of parts. We would try out for everything, suitable or not, wild stretches and stuff we thought beneath us, even musical revues. We would drop our head shots off at agencies, take our meals at diners, prepare our pieces at night in my apartment. We would be relentless, we would urge each other to the limit, we would succeed.

And we did. In two weeks I had two callbacks and Madeleine had three. We stayed up late refining our readings, drinking coffee until we were revved past endurance. Then we got into my bed and blasted ourselves into oblivion with athletic sex. It was great. I felt sleek, powerful, cagey; in the mirror I detected yon Cassius's lean and hungry look. Madeleine was glowing from all the sex and edgy from lack of sleep. She was living on fruit and coffee. One of her callbacks, an enormous long shot we'd chosen because she was so definitely right for it, was for the role of Maggie in a revival of *Cat on a Hot Tin Roof.* She wanted it almost beyond endurance. The call had sent her dancing around the apartment, over the couch, knocking down chairs. "I'm Maggie," she crooned. "They know it, they know it, I'm Maggie." But they didn't know it and she didn't get the part. When the call came, she broke down and wept. She was hysterical actually; I couldn't get near her. She lay on the bathroom floor kicking her feet and pounding her fists against the tiles. Then she got up and vomited into the toilet. It was pure nerves and rage. I got her cleaned up and tucked into bed where she cried herself to sleep. In the morning she was pale and haggard, but she took a shower, disguised the dark circles under her eyes with makeup, drank two cups of black coffee, and set out for another day of rejection. She came back with a callback for a new play at the Bijou and a week later she got the part.

I'd been striking out all over town and my last shot was a new play about criminal activity in a bakery. I had a scene for the callback and Madeleine and I worked it over so scrupulously that I didn't need the book. When the audition was over the stage manager reading with me looked like he'd run into a train. The director stood up and shouted, "That does it." I had the part.

Naturally Madeleine and I wanted to celebrate. I called Teddy, got his machine, and we shouted "WE HAVE JOBS!" into the receiver. Within the hour Teddy called back, as excited as we were. "No burgers tonight," he said. "Meet me at Broome Street. Dinner's on the pater."

Teddy had an evolving theory about the importance of actors in the survival of the human species. At Yale he'd been in a play about Charles Darwin, with the result that he had actually read *Origin of the Species,* which inspired in him an informed but idiosyncratic respect for the theory of evolution. Actors, he maintained, are imposters and imposture is an evolutionary strategy for survival. He described the butterfly whose wings so resemble a leaf that even water spots and fungal dots are mimicked, a perfect imitation of random imperfection. All manner of camouflage delighted him, the lizard who turns from bright green to dull brown as he wanders his varied terrain, the deer on his father's land in Connecticut, coppery red in the coppery fall and drab gray in the winter, when the world is monotone and dull. The actor, Teddy concluded, is selected for survival, like the white moths in a British mining town which, as the coal dust blackened the local birches, mutated to black. Predatory birds couldn't see the black mutants so only blackened moths survived to reproduce themselves.

Because humans have only other humans as natural predators, and are, by nature, tribal and territorial, what could be more essential to the flourishing of one's genetic material than the ability to pass for the prevailing type, to play before the fascist, another fascist; to offer the drug-crazed, gun-wielding holdup artist a fellow in addiction. In their predilection for imposture, their insistence upon the necessity of a counterworld in which they play all parts, banker and pauper, murderer and victim, man and beast, actors are equipped for survival. They are human chameleons, born with a natural ability to take on the coloration of the psychological and physical environment. And, according to Teddy, it is this evolutionary edge that accounts for the paradox of the actor's social condition. He is both lavishly admired and eternally suspect. Actors make ordinary people uncomfortable, yet they inspire reverence and awe.

It was nonsense, but entertaining, and Madeleine hadn't heard it before, so we encouraged Teddy, over glasses of white wine and plates of grilled fish, to expand upon the struggle for existence and our part in it.

"So according to your theory," Madeleine observed, "actors are born not made."

"Exactly," Teddy agreed. "There's got to be something genetic going on. I mean, what is the attraction of a life in the theater? It's certainly not the money. Yet look how many there are in every generation who are drawn to it."

"I thought it was something to do with exhibitionism," I put in.

"The common error," Teddy said.

"But I don't want to blend in," Madeleine protested. "I want to stand out."

"Of course," Teddy said. "You want to be recognized as Madeleine Delavergne, the actress who can play all parts, from ten to ninety, male or female, aristocrat, cutthroat or tramp."

As Teddy ticked off this list, Madeleine made small adjustments in her expression and posture, her spine straightening at "aristocrat," her eyes and lips narrow at "cutthroat," her mouth ajar and eyes sultry at "tramp."

"She's good," I said and we laughed.

"Now if you want to see an actor who only wants to be seen," Teddy said, "check out Guy Margate in that Italian thing. I saw it last night."

I hadn't thought of Guy in weeks and I found I didn't want to think about him. "Has that opened already?" I said. "I've lost track of time."

"Is it any good?" Madeleine asked.

"It opened last night and no, the play's not good, though I've seen worse. Guy has a lot of lines and he's in the altogether for the whole last scene, so it feels like there's more of him than anyone else."

"He's naked?" Madeleine's eyes were wide.

"Starkers," Teddy said. "He has a towel around his neck and I kept thinking he was going to wrap it around, you know, but he never did."

"This I've got to see," Madeleine was giggling like a teenager.

"Haven't you already seen it?" I snapped.

"Darling, you don't have to answer that question," Teddy said, and Madeleine, frowning, replied, "Believe me, I'm not going to touch it."

"See that you don't," I said.

"Children, children," Teddy chuckled. "Play nicely."

I had no intention of going to see Guy's play, but the next day he called Madeleine's machine to tell us he had left two comp tickets in her name at the box office and Madeleine insisted it would be rude not to go. "Why us," I complained. "Are we the closest thing he has to friends?" To which she replied, "I don't understand this antipathy you have for Guy. After all—"

"He saved my life," I finished for her.

"Well, yes, Edward," she said. "He did."

I can hardly remember what the play was about. An Italian family, all staying at a beach house. Two brothers, one girl. Something like that. Or maybe it was a brother and sister, and the brother's friend. The older generation included a doddering grandfather. Generational conflict, the changing world, expectations too high or not high enough.

As Teddy promised, Guy had a lot of lines and in the last scene he appeared naked, save a thin towel across his shoulders which he used to pop someone, his brother or his friend, or maybe it was his father, someone who was shocked to find his friend/brother/son naked in the kitchen at nine o'clock on a Sunday morning. Guy had a nice monologue near the end, to the effect that his family was smothering him and he didn't know what to do with his life, which he delivered while holding a glass of milk.

I watched halfheartedly, one eye on the stage, the other on Madeleine, who appeared to be enjoying it much more than I was. She laughed at all the lame jokes and she followed the actors closely as they moved about. Her eyes never left the stage. When the lights came up on Guy's bare back at the open refrigerator pouring out milk, I gave her a close look, noting something, amusement, admiration, maybe just intense interest, that irritated me. Guy turned around and the audience gave the requisite inhale attendant upon full frontal nudity. There was a lot of it on the stage in the '70s, more than there is now. *Let My People Come* was just around the corner, a cast of fifteen without a stitch on for two hours, they even had an orgy onstage, so people were getting jaded about all that, still, a naked man or woman in a social setting where everyone else is clothed always creates a frisson. I looked at Guy, who was drinking his milk, staring out over the footlights, a self-satisfied smirk on his face. He was loving it; he was in heaven. His sister or girlfriend, or his brother's girlfriend, whoever she was, sitting at the kitchen table, spoke to him. He turned to her, jutting his hips forward, and praised the virtues of milk. The audience, save one, laughed. Madeleine's mouth was open, the corners lifted, her expression engaged and titillated. I studied my knees. Disgruntlement and disgust were churning into something solid in my gut. I wanted to get up and walk out, but I knew Madeleine wouldn't forgive me and I didn't want to risk that. Also, if I left, I was in effect leaving her alone with Guy, who was strutting about the stage, spewing his lines like a sick baby, while his fellow actors stood by attending their cues. What else could they do? He was a hog of an actor, over the top and out of control; he even managed to upstage the girlfriend/sister's weepy confession of her long-repressed, undying love. I recall one line—"You were a fling for me"—at the conclusion of a longish tirade about his inability to love. He tossed it at her like a brick, blindsiding her, so that she appeared to be struck dumb. It was one of those perfectly dead moments when everything comes together, the banality of the script, the ineptitude of the direction, the stereotyped superficial performances of the actors, the moment when the complete falsity of the enterprise is manifest and you know a play really stinks. If, instead of yelling the idiotic line, Guy had whispered it, there might have been hope; the actress would have had something to do, she wasn't bad, she might have made something out of it. But Guy made the scene all about his character, a big, stupid, naked, self-absorbed, unfeeling ape.

"He's got no subtlety," I said to Madeleine after the show. We were drinking beer at Jimmy Ray's on Eighth Street. "There's nothing going on underneath. If the guy's a dick, that's fine, but there's got to be something behind that, I mean, there's a reason he's a dick. It didn't just happen; he wasn't fucking born a dick."

"What did you think of his dick?" Madeleine asked.

"That's an incredibly crude thing to say," I snapped.

She laughed. "It just seems to be on your mind."

"Frankly, I was too aggravated by his acting to notice, but I'm sure you have an informed opinion."

"I didn't think his acting was that bad. It's not a great part, but he made the best of it."

"Oh please," I begged.

The play got two reviews and the critics agreed with Madeleine. One called Guy's performance "stalwart," the other said he'd attacked a difficult role with "brio."

"If the audience is conscious that the actor is attacking his character," I told Madeleine, "it's all over, it's a failed performance."

"You need to get over your envy of Guy," she replied. "It's not very attractive."

Of course everyone was talking about Guy's success; you couldn't go out for a burger without hearing about his latest coup. The reviews resulted in the acquisition of an enthusiastic agent and a callback for a play at the Public and another at St. Mark's Theater. Christopher Walken beat him out for the part at the Public, but who could complain about being bested by Christopher Walken, etc. The Italian thing ran for its allotted stretch during which time Madeleine and I began our own rehearsals, so I didn't actually see Guy for several weeks. Then, one night, Teddy invited a few friends to his apartment for drinks and there he was, the new, improved, Equityed and agented Guy Margate, lounging in an armchair before a non-functional fireplace with a glass of Teddy's good Scotch and a pretty, rabbity blonde leaning over him to give him the benefit of her cleavage. Madeleine and Mindy went into a giggling clutch at the door. "Who's the blonde?" I asked Teddy.

"She was in the play, the sister. Or was it the girlfriend?" Teddy said. "Her name is Sandy. Sandy something."

Sandy was laughing and Guy watched her with that peculiar avidity he had, the dead gazing upon the living. His shoulders were bigger than I recalled; he must have been lifting weights. He was unshaven, his hair unkempt. Was he going for an Italian-stallion look? He lifted the Scotch to his lips and his gaze, surveying the room, settled on me. I nodded—yes, I recognize you—nothing more personal than that. Then he spotted Madeleine behind me, she was still buzzing with Mindy, and his focus narrowed to a fine point. If he had used his eyes that well onstage he might have made something of that character.

Which was Guy's problem in a nutshell. He could never see himself from himself. He created character from the outside looking in, he constructed a persona. Basically anyone can do it, politicians do it nonstop. It's not, perhaps, a bad way to start. But Guy could never inhabit a character because he was himself so uninhabited. Nobody home, yet he wasn't without strong emotions. I didn't know that last part then.

Madeleine released Mindy and threaded her arm through mine, rubbing my shoulder with her chin. Guy took this in with only a compression of his lips, but I knew he wasn't pleased. I bent my neck to brush Madeleine's hair with my lips, my eyes on Guy, and I smiled at him pleasantly, complacently, as a poker player smiles when he lays a straight flush upon the table.

This brought him to his feet, narrowly missing the cleavage with his nose as he stood up. Madeleine noticed him and released my arm. "Guy's here," she said and in the next moment she was stretching up to plant a kiss on his rough cheek. His hand rested on her waist, his eyes closed as he bent down to receive her greeting, then he straightened up and held his hand out to me. "Teddy tells me you two are working," he said. "That's great."

"It is," Madeleine agreed.

I offered my hand and he grasped it heartily, tightly, and for just that moment too long that bespeaks the will to domination. "Give me the details," he said. "I'll make sure my agent shows up. She should see you two."

"That would be fantastic," Madeleine gushed.

"She's terrific," Guy assured us. "She's opening doors all over town for me. I'm up for the new McNally next week."

While Madeleine expressed her delight at this prospect, I eased past Guy and made an excuse about my urgent need for a drink. Peter Davis was talking up the now neglected Sandy near the bar, so I pressed myself on them, keeping my back to the room. My emotions were in such a tangle I felt it would take a soliloquy of some duration to sort them out, but this wasn't the time or place. Peter's gossip was about Stella Adler, who had stripped down to some disheartening underwear in her effort to break an obdurate student's performance. "No," she shouted, lurching about the stage in her high heels, bra, and girdle. "This is boring, you've got to open up, you can't be afraid, you can't be timid and afraid, you must be naked in the theater, take your clothes off, you must be absolutely fearless and naked in the theater."

"She's a genius," Sandy said.

I could hear Guy talking behind me; his voice had grown since he'd been absolutely naked on the stage and after every fifth word he said, "my agent." At some point he exclaimed, "Oh, who reads reviews!"

Teddy came up, rolling his eyes in disbelief at this remark and I put my arm around him, desperate for an ally. "Success spoils Rock Hunter," he chortled and I said, "What was there to spoil?"

Sandy, offended for her hero, said, "You two are like catty teenagers." Then the room exploded with the primate roar of Guy Margate's laughter.

Later, as we undressed in my bedroom, I remarked to Madeleine that Guy was an intolerable blowhard.

"You won't think so if his agent takes you on," she said.

"His agent isn't going to take me on," I replied. "His agent thinks Guy is a good actor."

"So if she's interested in you, you'll turn her down."

"She isn't going to be interested in me," I said.

And I was right, she wasn't. She was interested in Madeleine.


The criminal-bakery play received the mildest notices. Everything was "adequate" and "not without interest," a few of us were "promising" and the playwright bore "watching." Only "newcomer Edward Day" was signaled out for abuse. One reviewer described his performance as "erratic," the other called him "a mincing, predatory fop." Madeleine maintained that the latter designation might be a compliment but I knew better. The play was a flop but it ran its scheduled six weeks, each night to a smaller audience.

One Saturday night as I was cleaning my face in the dressing room, Guy appeared at the doorway. The dressing room was a converted storage closet, scarcely wide enough for two to pass abreast, with a long counter, wooden stools, and a hazy mirror lit by a row of bare lightbulbs. As they finished their ablutions, laying aside their characters for another night, my fellow actors filed out in a gloomy procession. We had less than a week to go and we were all bracing for the plunge back into merciless reality where none of us had jobs. Guy spotted me and stepped inside. He looked big in that room and the garish light gave his skin a greenish cast. I was in no mood to accept the obligatory compliments he had doubtless come to offer, nor did I imagine he had any sympathy with my performance. He pressed against the wall, allowing one of my departing colleagues to pass, then claimed the vacated stool next to mine. "I've been arguing with my agent all evening," he confided loudly. "She came to the matinee and she just didn't get the play. I said, 'Forget the play, what about the Day,' but she said she thought you were muddled. What a stupid thing to say."

"Good night, Ed," another colleague called to me as he went out.

Before I could answer, Guy butted in. "Hey, good night. You were terrific."

The poor fellow perked up at this praise. "Thanks," he said, "thanks a lot."

I watched Guy in the mirror, wearily noting the resemblance between us, especially marked in profile. He was wearing a black turtleneck sweater which might have been chic were it not for the specks of dandruff scattered across the shoulders. As the voices of the actors in the hall were silenced by the slam of the heavy backstage door, Guy ran his fingers through the lank hair straying over one ear, tossing his head as he raked it back like an anxious ingenue. Was Guy anxious?

I found I didn't care. Lethargy settled over me, not unexpected, as I'd done the damned play twice in a day on very little sleep. I resented Guy shouting out his agent's appraisal of me for all to hear. Surely my fellow actors were talking about it now as they rambled through the chilly night in search of a drink, agreeing with the criticism—Day is muddled; he's dragging down the whole show—each inwardly wondering if the agent might have been impressed by his own performance. Better check the phone service before bed.

I recalled, with grim specificity, the matinee. Matinees were never strong, everyone knows this. Old people with hearing aids come to matinees. Even if there was something to *get* in a play, which, sadly, in the thing about the bakery there was not, they wouldn't get it, so why waste the energy. I routinely saved what I could for the evening performance. Why in hell had Guy's vaunted agent chosen a matinee to check out my potential? I dabbed a tissue at the last of the cold cream near my mouth. Guy turned back to me. "I tried, Ed," he said. "But she wouldn't listen to me."

"Why did she come to a matinee?" I asked testily.

He was distracted by his own reflection in the mirror. He frowned, first at himself, then at me. "She's a busy woman," he said. "She had to fit you into her schedule. I didn't know when she would come. She only did it as a favor to me."

I chucked the tissue into the trash can. "Do me a favor, Guy," I said. "Don't do me any more favors." Our eyes met in the mirror, mine a glaring hound, his a wounded doe. The favor he had already done me wafted between us like stage fog and I was back in the ponderous deep, gasping and thrashing for life. I seldom thought of that night, though occasionally it recurred in a dream from which I woke with a shout. In an uninteresting twist sometimes it was my mother who was drowning and I who was trying to save her. Guy's gaze shifted back to his own reflection, which clearly soothed and pleased him, leaving me to glower at the unedifying spectacle of an actor admiring himself. He turned his cheek, raising his chin to take in the strong line of his jaw, giving himself a sly smile.

"Who are you?" I asked. "Narcissus?"

"The sad part," he said, "is that my agent is right, your performance really is a muddle. You just don't have a grip on that character, Ed, you're all over the place with him and it's not such a bad part. You throw that whole scene with the Mafia don away and he's an excellent actor. He must want to murder you."

I snorted. "You're killing me," I said. Guy assessed the other side of his face. The stillness of the theater weighed down on me. All those seats, all those empty seats.

"I was surprised, frankly," he continued. "Madeleine has a high opinion of your work. I expected something better."

"God, I hate to disappoint you," I said.

"Has Maddie seen this show?"

"She hates being called Maddie."

"Thanks for the tip. What does she think?"

"You tell me."

"Would you like me to sound her out for you?"

"Not much."

"I just don't think this teacher you've got, what's his name?"

"Meisner. Sandy Meisner."

"Right. I don't think he's doing you any good. He's got you all tied up in knots. I mean, you don't look comfortable on that stage, Ed."

"You mean I'm not upstaging everybody with my cheap theatrics. I'm not waving my arms and bobbing my head around like a puppet; I'm not wagging my limp dick at the audience?"

Guy thrust his face closer to the mirror and commenced probing the skin over his cheekbone. "Damn," he said. "There's a zit starting."

I stood up and pulled my jacket from the hook on the wall. I was uneasy about the next part. I couldn't very well leave him in the theater—he had no business there—but I didn't relish walking out with him. I had to turn off the dressing-room lights and walk about twenty feet in total darkness to get to the door. I paused with my hand on the light switch, looking back at him. "Go ahead," he said. "I'll follow you." I flipped the switch and stepped into the black hole of the hall, expecting to hear his footsteps behind me but there was nothing. Instead his voice rang out, low and serious: "We've got to stop meeting like this, Ed." It was ridiculous, it was actually funny, but there was something eerie and threatening about it that made me scoot for the door and fling it open with more than necessary force. Outside a lamp illuminated the shabby entryway. I leaned against the bar that opened the lock from the inside, gazing back into the gloom from which, all at once, Guy appeared, striding confidently toward me.

"Let's go to Phebe's," he said. "I'll buy you a beer."


Madeleine's play ran six weeks and got extended for an extra two. One reviewer found her "fresh" and "appealing," another described her as "a young actress with talent to burn." Guy's agent, Bev Arbuckle, a deeply frightening redhead from Long Island, went to the show one night, liked what she saw, called Madeleine to her office, and took her on. Bev was certain Madeleine would do well in commercials and we had a long, difficult weekend of tears and protests before she agreed to try out for a few, which she didn't get. We were back to the audition trials and it was clear that Madeleine was getting more try-outs and more callbacks than I was, but she was not gratified by this. If anything she was more apprehensive and desperate. This surprised me and it irked me: I was spending far too much energy trying to keep Madeleine's ego properly inflated when my own was sagging well below the recommended pressure level. I listened to Madeleine's side of panicked consultations with Bev on the phone and chewed my casserole to a monologue on the subject of Bev's failure to understand the full dramatic range of her new client. Sex was still good and we resorted to it for distraction, which certainly beat television, but I found myself forestalling the orgasm because it meant we would have to go back to talking about Madeleine's career. If I turned the subject to my own daily confrontation with oblivion, she reminded me that the theater was a notoriously hard taskmistress and that success was the exception to a whole universe of rules.

We didn't actually live together. Madeleine still paid rent on a two-room apartment she shared with a college friend where she dropped in once or twice a week, mostly to do laundry for us both, as I didn't have a washer. She was reluctant to give the place up because the friend needed the rent and would be forced to find someone to replace her. So though she spent most of her nights with me, she wasn't helping with my rent and it didn't occur to her that she should. She bought and cooked most of the food we ate. Her repertoire was limited, pasta with sauce, vegetable soup, and macaroni and cheese. She was no longer a vegetarian, so once in a while she roasted a whole chicken and we ate that for a few days.

Gradually we began to have arguments about small matters: the tea bags she left in saucers all over the place, the way I broke the spines of books by laying them open to mark my place. Sometimes when we went out for a beer, we sat at a table without speaking. Teddy came across us like this one evening at Phebe's. He pulled up a chair and sat in the empty, silent space between us. "Trouble in Paradise," he said.

"What do you mean?" Madeleine asked.

"Our lovebirds are not cooing," he said.

She looked at me quizzically; I raised my eyebrows and shrugged. "I'm just anxious about an audition I have tomorrow," she said. "It's a small part, but Bev thinks it could be important."

Teddy patted her hand, all fake sympathy. "That is nervous-making," he said.

"Bev is nervous-making," I said.

Madeleine gave me a sharp look. "And what am I supposed to do about that according to you?"

I let it pass and Teddy changed the subject. He'd just seen an amusing farce by Alan Ayckbourn in which a British actress spent the second act quietly attempting suicide while her friends, bent on kitchen repair, worked around her. Teddy described Stella Adler's hostility toward British actors; in her view they were inferior and she mocked students she suspected of succumbing to their influence. When someone pleased her she said, "Yes, we will have great *American* actors." Teddy did an impression of his teacher's un-American pronunciation of the word "American."

"How old is she?" Madeleine asked.

"Who knows?" Teddy said. "As old as God."

"No," I said. "She's older than Sandy and he's as old as God."

"I hope I don't wind up like that," Madeleine said.

"Like what?" I asked. "Old? It may be hard to avoid."

"No," she said. "Old and teaching."

We nodded over our beers. Madeleine had summoned a specter no actor contemplates tranquilly. The personal lives of our teachers didn't interest us; they existed, as far as we were concerned, only for what they had to give us. We treated them with respect. They could reduce us to quivering jelly with a harsh word. They had power; some were rumored to use it maliciously to elicit unhealthy dependency, as Strasberg was said to have done with the phenomenally talented Marilyn

Monroe, but ultimately we believed our fate must be to leave them behind.

"Somebody's got to teach," Teddy said ruefully. "Acting is an art, after all."

Madeleine's eyes drifted toward the windows. Outside a couple clutching their coats against a gust of wind struggled by. The temperature was dropping steadily; the first hard freeze was predicted. "I really want that part," Madeleine said.


What strikes me when I look back over these pages is not only my ignorance, which was prodigious, but my myopia. This is always the case with hindsight, when the inevitability of choices that seemed difficult and complex is revealed to have been obvious. I wanted to be an actor; I needed to act, to play a part; and I was driven by an ambition I scarcely understood. I knew that great acting is an art, one which requires dedication, study, and patience. I was open to learning everything I could in any way possible, that was my strength and this openness drew the best teachers to me. It was this and not my talent that excited them. At that time I had not found the teacher who, as the Buddhists remind us, appears only when the student is ready. She was waiting for me.

I was frustrated by auditions and my classes bored me; the relentless exercises that led to small moments when, egged on by the relentlessly nagging Meisner, I had a momentary revelation of the depths I would have to mine in myself if I was ever to act fully. I wasn't afraid; it was just such hard work and I was often physically tired from my jobs, and from keeping Madeleine on an even keel. Sandy said things like "Edward, I don't know why you can't just look at that table. Is there something that's keeping you from looking at the table?" or "Mary, that was good, you were urgent, it was good. Ed, try joining her there."

"I don't think Sandy's the right teacher for me," I told Teddy, but he only smiled and said, "He's as good as any."

Meisner was well loved by his students and occasionally successful actors returned for a tune-up with him, especially those who had been working in television and wanted to recover their energy because the daily grind of TV was so deadening. One chilly December morning the news was that Marlene Webern, a fine stage actress who had been appearing in a popular television drama about a hospital, was among us. She enjoyed directing improvisation exercises and, after consultation with Sandy, posted a list of students invited to participate. To my surprise, my name was on it.

Marlene was in her early forties then, though of course she didn't look it, and she had a long career both behind and before her. The first time I saw her she was seated at a table in the wings of a makeshift stage, turning over the pages of a script. Her heavy red hair was pulled back in a ponytail; she wore a white men's-style shirt, jeans, and a pair of short red boots, the exact shade of which was matched by the polish on her fingernails. There was a pitiful low-wattage lamp to read by so she was hunched over the page, her brow furrowed above a pair of bifocal glasses. As I approached, she whisked off the glasses and her face came to life, though her eyes were still unfocused. Her smile had about it, always, I was to learn, a trace of sadness. "Who are you?" she asked.

"I'm Edward Day," I said. "Is this where the improv session will be?"

"Is that your real name?" she asked.

"It is," I said. This meant Marlene Webern was not her real name but I didn't pursue it. Later I learned her name was Cindy Webewitz and that she came from the Bronx. Another student arrived and another until we had a troupe of eleven. Marlene herded us onto the stage, announcing that we would do a warm-up called "catch." This was a silly business in which the actors stand in a circle while one among them assumes a peculiar posture and movement. "Mark," Marlene instructed, "start with a chicken." Mark stretched his neck up, thrust out his butt, flapped his arms, and turned his legs into strutting sticks. He bobbed his head, making chicken clucks, and bopped into the center of the circle. After a bit of preening he approached a pretty young woman named Becka, who responded with a quick peck and screech, took on the chicken, entered the circle, and modified the movement into something slithery and reptilian, which she then passed on to me. I turned the snake into something, I don't remember what, passed it on, and so on. Actors love this sort of thing; it limbers the instrument and allows for fierce grimacing and eye flashing. Marlene got something piggish, transformed it into an insect walking on water, then snapped abruptly back into Marlene and said, "That's good." She went to a table and took up a folder of pages which she handed out to each of us. "These are the improvs," she said. "There are six of them. They're all two-person scenes, so pair up. I'll have to do one too; Ed you be with me. We'll do number four."

All eyes shifted to me momentarily, and then there was a brief hum as we read over the pages and couples gravitated together. Marlene assigned random numbers and sent all but the students assigned to the first exercise into the audience.

They were clever scenes. I don't remember much about the others, one was an argument in a bar, and in another a man didn't want his wife to know what (or who) was behind a curtain. But I recall every detail of my own. It was the improv that changed my life.

The scenario was elaborate. I was a young man named David who wanted to go to Japan and become a monk, but I didn't have the money for a plane ticket. I sneaked into the kitchen of my mother's house and there on the table was her purse. I decided to steal her credit card; she came in and surprised me in the act. Marlene would be my mother.

As the others created conflict and comedy and pathos from thin air on the stage, I tried to work my way into a condition of such desperate urgency that I would steal from my mother. I kept my real mother in a safe place; I seldom took her out to look at her and this bit of fluff with Marlene Webern was clearly not an appropriate venue for delving into that dark and painful cache of emotion memory. I understood that I would never have stolen a dime from my mother, no matter what my condition, so there was, in addition, no point in dredging about in my own past. I queried my character, who was my own age and determined to make a complete break from the world as he knew it. He wanted to be in Japan, and he wanted to be there right now. Why? Because he had failed somehow, because he regretted actions he couldn't repair. What sort of actions? What would make me desperate to enter a monastery in Japan? I must have betrayed someone, or someone had cruelly betrayed me, but who and how?

I was getting nowhere and the scenes were ticking by. There was a round of bright applause. "All right, Ed," Marlene called to me as she dashed up the steps lugging a large red purse. "You've got to get to Japan. Chop, chop."

Everyone laughed. I followed, stumbling behind her. I'd done this sort of thing before, we all had; exercises of this kind were our daily bread, but I felt unprepared and anxious. I've got to get to Japan, I told myself. I must get to Japan, today. If I can get the money now, I'll make the plane. I have a reservation; my bag is packed.

Marlene put her purse on the table and pulled it open, producing a leather wallet from inside. "This is my wallet," she said. "The credit card is inside." She dropped the wallet into the capacious purse. It had a satchel-style opening which she snapped closed. "You'll have to open the wallet to get the card," she added needlessly. "You come from there"—she pointed to the wings offstage right—"and I'll come from this side."

I went into the wings where I stood for a moment pulling my cheeks down with the palms of my hands. I'm desperate, I thought. I've got to get to Japan. I know Mother won't want me to go, she won't help me, but if I could get her credit card somehow without her knowing, I could pay for the ticket. I'll pay her back later, once I'm settled in Japan. I stepped onto the stage and there was the table with the purse. All I had to do was open the wallet and get the card. I paused, listening—was she nearby? Was she even in the house? But there was nothing. Now's your chance, I advised myself. Do it quickly. I rushed to the table and snapped open the purse. It was crammed with stuff, makeup, a checkbook, pens, wadded tissues, a tin of mints, but the wallet was riding on top of it all and I snatched it, glancing behind me, though I knew very well that Mother wouldn't surprise me from that direction. That backward glance stymied me—it was forced, something from vaudeville, the anxious thief fearing apprehension. I imagined Meisner chortling at my ineptitude, my loss of focus. The wallet, I thought, just get the card before she comes in. I lifted the snap and the wallet flopped open like a book. There were three credit cards on one side, the shiny edges visible above the thin leather sheaths, like toast in a toaster. On the other side was a plasticized pocket designed for a driver's license. My eye was drawn to this because it displayed not a license but a photo-graph of a naked woman. She reclined upon a couch, oda-lisquely, her red hair loose and waving along her shoulders, her chin lifted and her eyes gazing into the camera. Lovely full breasts with unusually pale nipples. My God, I thought, this is Marlene.

Should I be seeing this? What was I to do? Get the credit card, I reminded myself. This is a trick; she's playing with you. Get to Japan, that's all that matters. Take a card, any card; take the green one, that's American Express, good round the world. I extracted the card and dropped the wallet back into the purse as if it was burning my fingers, which it was. A titter of laughter from the audience exasperated me. What were they laughing at?

Though I didn't register the roar from the wings as human, much less female, I heard Marlene before I saw her. She burst upon the stage brandishing a board as long as she was tall and she came straight at me in a fury that no one would mistake for an act. My brain, confused beyond endurance, concluded that she was angry about the photo. But how could that be, she'd put it there, she knew I would find it. "Get out of my house," she bellowed. I backed away as she lowered the board, leveling it at my head for what promised to be a mighty blow. "Mother," I cried, staggering, but she kept coming. My knees buckled and I sprawled to the floor, covering my eyes with my hands. "Don't hit me," I whimpered.

"David?" she asked incredulously. The board, inches from my face, shifted to the right and came down with a crash on the chalky stage planks. "Oh my God, David," she said. "It's you. What are you doing here?"

Tears burst from my eyes; my heart hammered in my ears. I tried to sit up but an emotion of such helplessness and guilt overcame me that I rolled onto my side, clutching my knees to my chest, my head to my knees. The sharp edge of the credit card—I was still clutching the credit card—pressed into my cheek. "I've got to get to Japan," I wailed.

"What are you doing?" she cried. "Are you stealing from me? David, are you stealing from me?"

Then it was over. I got to my feet and tried to defend myself for my action. Marlene demanded the card; I refused to give it to her. We had a brief tussle over it, but it was all acting.

I was even conscious of the audience, my fellow students, and I knew they knew we were just winding down, cleverly, skillfully, but that for that one moment when I fell to the floor in terror and shame, I'd found that for which we all strove, a pure emotion expressed in my own person. There had been no space between my character and myself. I hadn't considered what David might do, or what I might do in David's place, I had simply cried out in David's voice, David's desperation, which was my own. Anyone watching understood that something real had happened in the last place one might expect to find it, inside an actor, on a stage.

Marlene stopped the scene with a raised hand and a sharp "That's it." My fellow actors burst into wild applause. I realized that I was sweating, that my knees were still weak, my heart racing. The whole business had taken about four minutes. I bowed stiffly and Marlene said, "Well done, Ed." I took her hand and kissed it, gratitude flooding up from the bottom of my soul. "Thank you," I said.

"My pleasure," she replied. I raised my eyes to her bemused, almost tender smile. She was pleased with herself and with me. It had been no accident. She had taken my measure and contrived how best to get me to the place I needed to be. The photo, so startling and confusing, the furious board-wielding territorial mother, it was all of a piece. And of course, because of what she had put me through and because of what I now knew about myself as well as about her, I was in love with her.

———

Winter dragged on. I had a small part in a play about García Lorca which got no reviews. In the spring, desperate for an Equity card, I did the group auditions for summer stock. To my surprise I secured a place at a playhouse in Connecticut.

In my first summer at college I had worked as a technical intern at a summer theater in upstate New York, so I had some notion of what to expect. We interns were the equivalent of a Suzuki orchestra of ten-year-olds, grinding out Bach on tiny violins with no idea of theory or art, running on the enthusiasm of being young and attached to a real stage. We were turned loose in an old, run-down hotel a long walk from the theater. The walls were peeling, the water was rusty, and the kitchen was inside a cage constructed of chicken wire to keep out the raccoons which patrolled the place so stealthily and determinedly that if one of us failed to secure the latch at night, in the morning it looked like a band of crazed drug addicts had staged a break-in. The clever creatures opened every door, including the refrigerator, as well as every box, jar, and carton. What they didn't eat, they scattered, and what they scattered, they pissed and shat upon. Hostilities broke out between those of us who carefully secured the latch, hoping to preserve our little stashes of comestibles—a process that required threading a length of wire through two holes—and those who couldn't be bothered. Signs were posted—FASTEN THIS GATE YOU JERK—and scrawled over with tart graffiti. Those determined to prepare decent meals (coffee and sandwiches was the platonic ideal, though one sad, anorexic girl, the child of divorcing parents who didn't care to know exactly where she was, lived on nothing but cereal for two months), tried securing cabinets with metal ties and clamps. One boy bought a steel box with a padlock in which he successfully stored a loaf of bread, but it was a pitched battle and for the most part the raccoons were the victors. My roommate opened the refrigerator one morning to find a raccoon inside, leisurely finishing up a package of sliced ham before making an escape. A sweet high-school student from Ohio was reduced to tears when she found the contents of a tea tin scattered across the linoleum in partially masticated clumps. "My aunt brought me that tea from England," she whimpered. "I only got to have one cup."

The actors were lodged in small apartments in town or in cabins in the woods. Being New Yorkers they were made anxious by the proximity of so many trees, terrified of the deer and the occasional bear, and paralyzed by the swift descent of the deep, black, unilluminated nights. Our leading lady had to be escorted, shrieking at every rustling bird or cavorting rabbit, by a phalange of techies from stage door to cabin.

Three days after we arrived it started to rain and it didn't let up for the rest of the summer. The theater was a well-designed, decently equipped proscenium that seated upward of three hundred, and our actors, if they found their way to rehearsals, were serious professionals. But the weather took a toll and when we were finally up and running we played, night after night, to audiences of forty or fifty who looked on like lost children in the wilderness of empty seats. Their applause sounded like dried peas rattling in a tin can.

This time it would be different. The playhouse in Connecticut was an old and respectable one, and I wouldn't be there to carry coffee, drive nails into frames, or escort nervous drama queens. I would be one of a company of actors. We would do four plays in three months and I would have a part in every one of them.

It meant being apart from Madeleine, a prospect I viewed with equanimity. We were having constant squabbles, some of which escalated into storms so furious even sex couldn't calm the water. In April she got a small part in a comedy she and Bev thought was poor, but it paid union wages so she couldn't turn it down. She spent hours waiting around for the five minutes a night (ten on Saturday) when she was onstage. I was looking for someone to sublet my apartment and she didn't like that. She felt our space would be invaded and violated by a stranger and would thereby be unrecoverable, but she didn't want to give up her shared place and couldn't afford to pay two rents. I put the word out at school and of course a beautiful neophyte actress from Georgia snapped it up, which put Madeleine in a state. "What am I supposed to do?" I reasoned. "Pay rent on an empty apartment in New York? No one does that, Madeleine. I can't afford it even if I wanted to do it, which I don't. Be reasonable."

"It's not about reason, Edward," she snapped. "It's about feeling."

"Feelings don't pay rent," I replied.

One evening, just a few days before I was to leave for Connecticut, I went out with Teddy for Chinese food. He was on the outs with Mindy and his father was bearing down on him to give up acting and pursue a "real" career. "Mindy takes his side," he explained over his mo shu pork. "She thinks I should go to law school. Then we could get married and she could be an actress and I could sue the producers who try to screw her."

"She wants to get married?"

"To Teddy the lawyer, not to Teddy the actor."

"Is she that blunt about it?"

"Pretty much. Yes. You know Mindy, she doesn't mince words."

"Are you seriously considering this?"

The waitress, an adorable Chinese with a long braid and quick, furtive eyes, brought another round of Tsingtao. "I'm seriously considering asking this lovely young lady what time she gets off," he said.

"You are an actor," she said in unaccented English.

"How can you tell?" Teddy asked.

"I saw you at an audition. Last month. It was at La MaMa."

Her name was Jasmine and she got off at ten. We drank beer and ate almond cookies until she was free and then headed over to Phebe's, where I was to meet Madeleine after her show. Before we left Jasmine introduced us to her aunt, Mrs. Lee, who owned the place and insisted on mixing up a round of Chinese cocktails for us in the kitchen. "Lychinis" Jasmine explained. "A lychee martini."

"Jasmine is great actress," Mrs. Lee informed us as we sipped the strange concoction. "But theater very hard for Chinese. No parts."

It was a gorgeous night; the trees, such as they were, had unfurled their delicate sap-green leaves and exhaled chlorophyll-scented oxygen into the atmosphere. We agreed to walk uptown rather than descend into the underground where breathing was a necessarily shallow affair. I expanded my chest, opened my arms to the invigorating air, and declared the lychini the liquor of the gods. Teddy observed that on this fair night in this part of town one could actually see the stars, and we paused on the curb to gape at the heavens. " 'Twere all one," Jasmine recited, "that I should love a bright particular star and think to wed it, he is so far above me."

"Are you in love?" Teddy asked.

She smiled. "On a night like this I could be. Don't you think I could be?"

We marched on, combing our brains for tributes to the stars. Teddy, overexposed to show tunes by his connection to Mindy, crooned, "Today, all day I had the feeling, a miracle would happen," which put us on the track of the most mawkish song we could find. By the time we got to Phebe's we were on "Some Enchanted Evening," and we burst into the nearly empty bar proclaiming, "Fools give you reasons, wise men never try." A few diehards nodding over their drinks ignored us, the bartender rolled his eyes. Madeleine, alone at a table with an empty glass before her, regarded us so sourly that Teddy muttered "Good luck" and steered Jasmine to the far end of the bar, leaving me to my fate. I leaned over the table, my eyes moistened by the smoky pall that hung upon the air. "Hey lady," I said, in a low-life pitch somewhere between Brando and De Niro, "can a fella buy you a drink?"

My queen was not amused. "Where have you been?" she asked. "I've been waiting for over an hour."

"We walked from Chinatown," I said. "It's a beautiful night, didn't you notice?"

"I'm tired," she said. "My stomach hurts."

"Well, have a drink with me and we'll walk home and you can go straight to bed."

She glanced at Teddy and Jasmine, who were perched on stools, chatting up the bartender. "Does Mindy know about that?"

"That's Jasmine," I said. "We just met her at the Chinese restaurant. She's an actress. What do you want, sweetheart? Have a liqueur; it will settle your stomach. Have a Sambuca."

"OK," she said. I went to the bar and answered Teddy's inquiring look with a thumbs-up all clear. When my drinks came, he and Jasmine followed me to the table where the introductions quickly yielded to the important info that Madeleine was tired because she had a job and had come straight from the theater.

"I've heard about that play," Jasmine exclaimed. "You're in that play? That's so cool. I really want to see it."

"It's a small part," Madeleine demurred.

"I really want to see it," Jasmine repeated.

"Our Madeleine plays a maid of easy virtue," Teddy said, keeping the subject where we both understood it needed to be.

"Typecasting," I joked.

Madeleine flashed me a look that made my stomach tighten. "What are you talking about?" she said.

"Mitt Borden is the lead, isn't he?" Jasmine said. "He's fantastic."

"What are you talking about?" Madeleine persisted, glaring at me.

"Just teasing, love," I said.

"What's he like?" Jasmine asked, but Madeleine ignored her. "Did you see him in that Wilson play? I thought he was hot."

"He's a good actor," Teddy agreed. "He's got a lot of presence."

"He stinks," Madeleine said, releasing me from her cold inspection.

"You don't think he's good?" Jasmine asked.

"He's an OK actor," she said. "I mean he smells bad. He doesn't wash enough."

"Oh. He stinks stinks!" Jasmine cried, collapsing into charming, girlish giggles.

When was the last time I'd seen Madeleine laugh with such simple openhearted glee, I thought. She watched Jasmine's amusement with a chilly, distant smile. She was angry at me for my remark; she had passed over it for now but I knew I'd hear about it later and I was right. On the walk home she was silent, loading up her argument, and when she got to the apartment she opened fire. I had as good as called her a slut in front of someone she had just met. It was clear I would only make such a remark to let Jasmine know that I was not in any way attached to Madeleine, that everyone knew she was sluttish, which simply wasn't true. I had no reason to make such a charge, it was outrageous and uncalled for and she wasn't going to forgive me for it. I defended myself indifferently, apologized insincerely in the hopes of toning down the scene, but she was having none of it. It was clear to her that I wanted to go to Connecticut just to get away from her and prove to myself that I didn't need her. Well good, that was good. I should go ahead.

That was fine with her. She was too busy anyway; her career was the most important thing and it was obvious that I was jealous of her because she was talented and ambitious. By this time she was weeping and trembling, genuinely exhausted, so I got her to bed, protesting my affection for her, cradling her in my arms until, in the midst of snuffling tears, she fell asleep.

I got up and fixed myself a drink. She was right, of course. I was tired of the relationship. I had been for some time, and all I really wanted to do was get through the next few days without more hysterics, get on the bus, and head for Connecticut.

On the morning I left, Madeleine was subdued and remained so until I packed my old suitcase, kissed her goodbye, and hopped on the bus. I was in a cheerful frame of mind. I didn't know who the other actors would be, but there was always a star or two, older stage actors or television actors desperate to play a scene without someone yelling cut and eager to be nearer the city where real theater still more or less thrived. Agents routinely toured the summer productions and there was occasionally a new play, which meant spending time with an ambitious playwright, always an interesting opportunity for an actor.

A theater functionary met me at the station and drove me to a rambling Victorian rooming house with a long porch across the front straight out of Thomas Wolfe. "Here we are," the driver informed me.

"Very Thomas Wolfe," I remarked.

"The actors all seem to like it," he assured me. "Most of

them are here." The porch screen drifted open revealing a
stunning young woman, all golden curls, honey skin, and startling green eyes, dressed in a white halter-top dress that reminded me of the bubbling skirt Marilyn Monroe famously
battled down against the subway draft in *The Seven Year Itch*.
She flashed me a camera-ready smile and stepped out into the
light. "I'm Eve," she said.

"I think I'll like it just fine," I told the driver.

From there things got better. Eve escorted me to my narrow room just three doors from hers, and left me to "get settled in." On the pine desk I found a folder packed with useful
information, including a list of all the actors in our company.
Here I learned that Eve's full name was Eve Vendler and that
she had studied at Yale. I didn't recognize any of the other
names, save two. One was Gary Santos, an actor I'd seen in a
good production of Joe Orton's play *Loot* in some miserable little theater downtown. The other was our star, the talented
stage, film, and television actress who, it turned out, had a long
association with this festival playhouse and was returning for
her sixth season, the immensely talented and widely acclaimed
Marlene Webern.

The first cast meeting was the following morning. As the
dress code was casual, I pulled on a T-shirt, my most faded
madras shorts, sandals, and in case of overactive air-conditioning,
the linen jacket, and went forth confidently to join my company.
The rehearsal shed was a short walk from the boardinghouse and
we actors went over in a troop, chattering away with introductions and gossip. Gary Santos, who was there for a second season,
enthused about the venue and praised the talent and tempera-

ment of our star. "Marlene is great," he declared. "Nothing pretentious about her and she's brilliant."

I said nothing, as I doubted that Marlene would remember me—though she had, in the brief encounter we had shared, changed my life—and I didn't want to embarrass myself by suggesting a connection where there was none. But when the time came and I stood diffidently before her, protesting that it would be unlikely if she recalled our little scene together, to my delight, she claimed me. "Of course I remember you, Ed," she said. "That's why you're here."

That's why you're here.

Close your eyes and imagine you are standing before a strange door in a whirling snowstorm. Your fingers are numb; you're frozen to your bones and hungry as well. The door swings open upon a sunny, tropical isle, birds are singing, exotic flowers nod in the soft breeze beckoning you, a table is spread with a magnificent feast. Bathing beauties, if you like bathing beauties, emerge from the calm waters calling your name. Ed, you're here, at last, you're here, we've been waiting for you, that's why you're here. In just that way Marlene's greeting caught me by surprise and I blurted out, "That's great," much to the amusement of my fellow actors who took me for an innocent. And so I was, so I was. But not for long.


We did four plays that summer; one was a musical, *Dames at Sea;* two were insipid pieces in which I had negligible parts; and the fourth was Tennessee Williams's *Sweet Bird of Youth.* I was cast as Chance Wayne, chauffeur and paid gigolo of the drug-addicted, over-the-hill screen star Alexandra del Lago, also known as Princess Kosmonopolis, played by Marlene Webern. Eve, the delicious Eve, was my long-lost sweetheart Heavenly Finley. Mine was a plum part albeit one in which I was castrated onstage every night. The play felt seriously dated even then; now it seems like some embarrassing relic. The shock value of drugs and venereal disease had faded through the '60s, but Connecticut audiences were perfectly content to have their prejudices about the Deep South confirmed and chalked the strangeness of the play up to its author, that gay blade who doubtless knew everything there was to know about VD and drug addiction.

Marlene was perfect for her part and she knew it, but I was miscast in every way, including the color of my hair. Chance Wayne is so golden the ladies talk about it; it's one of his great charms. I assumed I'd wear a wig, which worried me. A wig is a big deal, a serious distraction. I'd need to wear a wig night and day for a week at least just to get past it, or get even with it. So I was relieved, early in the rehearsal period, when the director took me aside and said, "I've made an appointment for you at the salon in town. It's the Wee-Hair-Nook on Main Street. Just show up at two o'clock and ask for Beatrice. She knows what to do."

One really must admire the persistence and imagination of women when it comes to approximating their ideal self-image. Beatrice was an artist and the challenge I presented excited her. She laid swatch after swatch of fake hair against my cheek, from champagne blond through honey to strawberry, with variations in between so numerous and slight I couldn't detect a difference. "This one's a little cooler," she said, or "This is pushing toward red." She kept returning to a panel of haystack yellow. "With your eyes and skin, I'm thinking we can go Scandinavian and get a real natural look."

The process was horrific, toxic, vile smelling, with a long stint under a dryer so hot I thought my scalp would fry. But when it was over and Beatrice pulled the towel away with a flourish, I gasped at the rakish fellow in the mirror. "I'll be damned," I said. "It's fantastic."

Beatrice beamed at me, drawing a few damp curls over my forehead. "There's a blond in all of us," she said. "We just let him out."

Back at the theater my colleagues were agog. "I didn't recognize you," Eve exclaimed. "It makes your face look bigger."

"You're standing different," Gary Santos observed. "Are you conscious of that?"

Then a rich, theatrical voice called from the stage. "Is that Chance? Is that my driver, Chance Wayne?"

"At your service, Princess," I said, turning to Marlene who looked me up and down so ravenously I felt a blush rising to my cheeks. "I have such a weakness for blonds," she said. "I fear it will be the death of me."

I pressed my fingertips to my lips, regarding her coolly. "You could be right about that, Princess." She shook her hair over her shoulders, reminding me of the photo she'd tantalized me with at our first meeting. It was then I decided I would have sex with her and soon. Chance Wayne wasn't a guy who would wait around for the prize to fall from the tree and I was, at that moment, feeling just as useless, hungry, stupid, hot, and blond as Chance Wayne.

As everyone knows, in my profession we go around screwing each other as much as possible, mostly to see ourselves do it. Narcissists are always making love to number one. Eve was a perfect example. I asked her to my room to share a bottle of wine and she was in the bed and down to her lacy underwear before she finished the first glass. She disported herself charmingly, wiggling around to present her various assets as if there was a paying audience seated on the dresser. She made interesting noises and urged me on with cries of "Oh my God" and "Do it." Afterward she wanted a cigarette, but I didn't have one. She pouted her pouty lips. "Eddie, I really need a cigarette," she said. So I got up, put my clothes on, and walked down to the general store to buy a pack. On the walk back, I found myself thinking of sex in general and Madeleine in particular, definitely a different ball game from Eve. More inhibited but, oddly, more intense. Eve had no shame, which wasn't as much fun as it should have been. It struck me that she might wind up in porno films, and in fact, this turned out to be an accurate prediction.

Eve was entertaining, but my real goal in the sexual stakes game was Marlene Webern. Marlene wasn't just a different ball game, she was a different planet, and one not easy of access. In public she flirted and teased, it was part of her role as Alexandra del Lago, and we enjoyed bantering in a familiar way, as if we had actually driven into town from the Gulf Coast, stopping over at chic hotels where we took drugs and she was serviced by me at considerable expense to her pocketbook and my self-esteem. It was tantalizing, but we were never alone. After a week of rehearsals I noticed that she contrived to keep it that way and I resolved to break her will.

This wasn't easy. As the star she received special perks and was much in demand. She was lodged in a private guesthouse tucked into a garden behind a mansion on the green in town. The owner, a patron of our theater, occasionally sent a chauffeured car to pick her up after rehearsal and whisk her off to private dinner parties with the local elite. When she was reduced to dining with the rest of us, she was seated next to the producer or the director, both of whom were clearly in love with her. I couldn't get next to her, except onstage, where we were very close indeed. We spent the whole first scene sparring in a hotel room. I held her in my arms, she examined my bare torso, I picked her up when she fell on the floor, and at the end, after we agreed that we were both ashamed of our degraded connection, I got in the bed with her and tried to make her believe, as she put it, "that we're a pair of young lovers without any shame."

In the Broadway production Chance closes the hotel shutter on this line and the stage goes dark, but that was in the '50s and this was the '70s. Audiences wanted to see actors making out. It was fine with me. All I had to do was call up the photo I'd seen in her wallet and I was eager to clamber on top of her and try to remove her blouse. The look she gave me as she held her arms out to me was such a combination of fragility and appetite that it touched my heart and my groin at the same time; who wouldn't want to make love to such a look as that.

We weren't exactly the people we were playing, a washed-up star and a boastful neophyte, but we could certainly imagine the desperation that would drive these two together. Marlene opened her lips beneath mine and arched her spine as I slipped one hand around her back and pressed her thighs apart with the other. She was wearing a cotton T-shirt and jeans, so it wasn't as if I could really get anywhere, and the director always interrupted too soon with his "Good, that's it, that's hot." We sat up on the bed, side by side, disheveled and overstimulated. Marlene came back to herself in an instant, patting down her hair, blowing out a puff of air as she lifted and lowered her shoulders. It wasn't so easy for me. I tried not to listen to the riot in my senses as the director droned his notes for the scene.

Scene 1 was fine, it's well written, lots for the actors to do, but after that the play is pretty much downhill. Nothing fazed Marlene; her character was entirely in place and she was convincing no matter how bizarre or nonsensical the requirements of the role. She made it easy for me; she let me act around her solid interpretation and if I came up with anything new, some little insight into my character, she followed me like a willing dance partner. We searched for Chance Wayne together. I couldn't decide how dishonest he actually was. When he said he'd slept "in the social register" in New York, was that true? Was he in the chorus of *Oklahoma!* as he bragged he had been, or was even that small distinction beyond him? Did he have an Equity card? One day when the director told me my "YIPEEEE" sounded like a death knell I spoke up. "I don't get it," I said. "Why would I brag to this famous film star that I was in the chorus of *Oklahoma!?* Am I so stupid I think that's a big deal? Did I actually do it, or did I just try out for the chorus and didn't even do that? I know I'm a loser, I've got that, but just how big a loser am I?"

Marlene, lounging on the divan, her arms stretched out over her head, flipped one of her red sandals to the floor. "Big," she said.

I turned on her. "That's what you think, Miss Has-been," I said.

She narrowed her eyes at me as if she was looking into my brain. "It's what I know, Chance darling," she said.

That's it, I thought. It's all a lie. From start to finish. I'm a complete fraud. I was never on the stage in New York. I never made it out of Florida. *I sang in the chorus of the biggest show in New York,* I proclaimed to her and to the world. *In* Oklahoma!, *and had pictures in* Life *in a cowboy outfit, tossin' a ten-gallon hat in the air! YIPEEEE.*

"That's more like it," the director said.

The rest of the rehearsal went well. I hardly thought about who I was, I just concentrated on being a liar. Everything I said could be proved false; therefore I was always in danger of being unmasked. This gave me an edge I hadn't been able to find. I appreciated the peril of my situation. At the end of the day the director's notes were distinctly upbeat. "Ed," he said, "you're getting there." I glanced at Marlene for confirmation, but she was fully concentrated on every word issuing from the lips of our director.

That night we had a cookout on the plush green lawn behind the boardinghouse. Tubs of ice sprouting beer and wine bottlenecks dotted a multicolored carpet of blankets and towels upon which we actors preened ourselves in mocking rivalry. Near the house a smoldering charcoal grill, lovingly tended by our prop man turned grill master, pumped into the warm night air the tantalizing fragrance of burning flesh. I was poking a wiener mischievously at the appreciative Eve when I spotted Marlene strolling across the lawn. She was relaxed and oblivious to the palpable alteration in the atmosphere occasioned by her presence among us. She's like the queen stopping in at the local pub, I thought. She will never know what it's like when she's not there.

"It's Marlene," Eve sighed beside me. "She's so fantastic." I got to my feet and weaved my way among the blankets. Gary Santos was pouring wine into a plastic cup while the prop man pointed out to our unexpected guest the choicest bits sizzling above the coals. I popped into the space beside her. "Princess," I said. "What are you doing out among the hoi polloi?"

She was wearing dark sunglasses, her hair was loose, and her smile was at its most enigmatic. "Oh Ed," she said, dismissing the charade of our characters. "Here you are. Advise me. What is a tofu pup?"

"It's a perfectly tasteless wad of soy cheese."

"Oh," she said. "That sounds appetizing. I'll have one of those."

"Are you a vegetarian?"

"No. I don't think so. Are you?"

"No," I said. "At least put some mustard on it." I led her away to the condiments table, snatching a beer from a tub as I passed, acutely conscious of all eyes upon us. I had her, I had her, and I didn't want to share her. I particularly didn't want to share her with Eve, who looked on with slack-jawed amazement, but no sooner had Marlene buried her pup beneath a blanket of relish and mustard than she looked out over the field of players and said, "Let's sit with Eve."

"Sure," I said. "Of course." As we settled on the blanket, Eve gushed like an overflowing bathtub. "Miss Webern," she said. "I can't tell you what an honor it is to be on the stage with you. I've admired your work for so long. I saw you in *Tiny Alice* when I was in high school and that's when I decided I wanted to be an actress."

"Was that a long time ago?" Marlene said, fiddling with her tofu pup, which had slipped out of its bun.

"Well, I was fifteen."

"Best not to tell me how old you are now. Ed, darling, how am I to eat this?"

Eve closed her mouth and sent me a troubled look.

"It's a disgusting thing," I said.

"No, no," she laughed, pressing it back into the limp folder of bread with her bloodred fingernail. "I'm sure it's delicious." As she lifted one end, mustard and relish poured out the other.

"Let me have it," I said, taking the plate from her. "It's going to squirt all over you."

"That would be discouraging," she said.

"Hold a napkin under your chin."

"I had no idea you would take such command," she said, unfolding a napkin and cupping it beneath her chin. I grasped the sandwich gingerly and brought it to her lips. "Just bite it," I said.

She obeyed, baring her teeth and taking a sharp bite, neatly catching the dripping condiments in her napkin.

"Ed," Eve whispered anxiously.

"Be quiet," I snapped. "Let this woman eat her pup."

Marlene was convulsed with laughter, but she managed to swallow what she'd taken and opened her mouth for another go.

"It's awful, isn't it?" I said.

"Completely," she agreed, chewing thoughtfully.

"Let me throw it away."

"Definitely," she said.

I got to my feet folding the plate over the soggy mess. "Do you want some corn? Or a burger?" I asked.

"No, thank you."

"More wine?"

"Yes," she said. "That would be nice. Tell me, Eve, are you a vegetarian."

"No ma'am," Eve replied as I ambled off to the nearest trash can. I was working out a plan. If Marlene wouldn't eat what we ate, I might persuade her to go somewhere alone with me. I had very little money; I certainly couldn't afford any of the chic restaurants in the town center. The only place I'd been inside was the pub and I couldn't picture Marlene tucked into a leather booth with a plate of fries and a beer in front of her. I filled a plastic cup with wine and turned back to our blanket. Eve was blathering about something while Marlene bent upon her a look of fascinated concentration, such as you might give an overturned beetle struggling to right itself next to your bare foot on the bathroom floor.

"Yale is an excellent program," Marlene was saying as I rejoined the conversation.

"Yes," Eve said. "I'm so lucky to be there."

"I'm sure luck had nothing to do with it."

I agreed. I thought Eve had probably gotten into Yale by fucking someone on the admissions committee. Perhaps the whole committee. She was a wretched actress, empty as a kettledrum.

"Now what will you do?" I said to Marlene. "You've had no dinner."

"I have plenty of food in my little cottage," she said. "It's a lovely evening. I'll just sit here a bit and then go back and fix myself something. Frankly it will be nice to be on my own."

"I can understand that," I sympathized, my spirits rebuffed. She was slumming, we were a distraction, but what she really wanted to be was alone. After a few more exchanges she got up and wandered over to the grill where she chatted with the prop man and the lighting designer. I looked on woefully, sucking at my beer while Eve told me Marlene had pronounced her horrible fake Southern accent "charming."

"You know," I said, "I think I'll get a burger while they still

have some left." I got back to my feet and slunk along the edge
of the blanket patch until I came up behind Marlene.

"I'm using a blue filter for that whole scene," the lighting
designer was saying. "It makes the palm trees black, very
spooky." Marlene drained her cup and turned to me as if I'd arrived on cue. "Perfect," she said. "Here's my driver. I think I'm
ready to leave now. Ed, will you walk with me?"

"At your service," I said, spirits surging back up like champagne behind the cork. Her cottage was a good ten-minute
walk. How much could be accomplished by a youthful suitor
in a ten-minute stroll through a sleepy summer evening? Marlene had a way of opening and closing the distance between
herself and an admirer that was something to see, like watching
a skilled angler with a bright fish on the line. She always knew
exactly where you were because she controlled the line and
understood the play of the currents. This analogy presumes the
fish, once hooked, longs to be hauled in, which is the opposite
of the truth, but I was eager to leap from the shallows into her
lap, and she knew it. I calmed myself as we left the party
grounds and set off along the sidewalk. Several conversational
openers flitted across my imagination: *Say, I love kissing you in
that opening scene* or *You know that photo you have in your wallet,
could I see it again* or *I'm in awe of you, you are my ideal* or *When
we get to the cottage, what say we hit the sack.* Playing them out
while I waited for her to speak—for I was determined that
she must set the tone, even if we had to walk the whole way
in silence—entertained me. I allowed expressions of pleasure,
wonder, yearning, bold aggression to flit across my features. A

block went by and another. The front lawns deepened and the houses accumulated grandeur.

"Ed," she said at last. "What are you doing with your face?"

I laughed. "I'm going over the things I'd like to say to you."

"Why not just say them?"

"That's a good question."

"Do you feel intimidated by me?"

"No. But I wouldn't want to bore you."

"I'm not easily bored," she assured me.

"You weren't bored by Eve?"

"Not at all," she said. "But you are."

"I wasn't thinking of talking about Eve."

"No? You'd rather not?"

"Definitely not."

"But you brought her up. You see, I find that interesting."

I chuckled. "You're good," I said.

We paused at a corner to allow a Mercedes convertible to roll by; the town was full of them. I watched Marlene watch the Mercedes, or so I thought, because her sunglasses made it impossible to tell what she was doing with her eyes; they could have been closed. She wasn't old enough to be my mother, but she was older than any woman I'd kissed before, and she had the aura of confidence and ease only actors who work a lot possess that flooded my veins with envy and desire. Her mouth was set in the cheerful lines that seemed to be their natural inclination and it occurred to me that she seldom actually frowned. She had a great line in the play—*When monster meets monster, one monster has got to give way and IT WILL NEVER BE*

*ME!*—which she delivered with verve and conviction, her eyes flashing at full star power, but there was still this quality of mild self-mocking about the mouth, this detachment behind which, I surmised, the real Marlene, the Marlene who could suffer, resided.

"It's getting dark," I said. "Don't you think you should take off the shades?"

As we stepped into the street she whisked off the sunglasses. "Shades?" she said.

"I want to see your eyes."

"You're a very bossy young man," she observed.

"Bossy?" I said.

She laughed and to my delight took my arm. "We turn here," she said. We went along another block at the end of which was a wide drive leading to a mansion. "I want to show you my cottage," she said. "It's like something from a storybook." The drive forked and we took the narrow path that curved around the house and through a garden riotous with flowers. An arbor laden with deep purple blossoms framed the doorway of a pink stucco cottage. "These are clematis," Marlene said as we passed beneath the arbor. "And here it is. Isn't it charming?"

It was certainly charming and I was on tenterhooks to know whether "showing" it to me meant I would be invited inside. Marlene released me and opened the door which wasn't locked, glancing back as she entered. "Come in and have a glass of wine," she said, "and let's see if I have something we can eat."

I stepped cautiously inside; carefully I closed the door behind me, resting my hand against the panel, advising myself with a maturity beyond my years, *This is your chance. Don't blow it.* The furnishings were summery, rattan and floral cushions, lacy curtains at the windows. There was one big room with chairs, couches, a table, a desk, and beyond that a wide arch through which Marlene passed. A painted screen partially obscured another arch which led, I presumed, to the bedroom. I followed Marlene and found her standing before a wooden tray in the gleaming kitchen, twisting a corkscrew into a bottle of white wine. "May I do that for you," I offered.

"No, you may not," she replied. "Look in the fridge and take out some cheese and there's a bit of a sausage I think."

"You're right," I said, choosing among the colorful packages of cheese with French names on their wrappers, "this is quite a fine place."

"Beats that boardinghouse?" she said. "Put that on the tray."

"Oh yes. By a lot."

"Well, they couldn't expect me to stay in a boardinghouse." Expertly she pulled the cork free and poured out two glasses. I spotted a plate for the cheese in the dish rack.

"No," I agreed.

"So you think it's fair. The whole star-system thing?"

"No question about it," I said.

She slapped a baguette across the tray and held it out to me. "Take this to the table," she said. I went out, perplexed by her line of inquiry. She was the star, why would she be lodged with the underlings?

I set the tray on the table and looked about me. There were

signs of her, a paisley shawl thrown across the back of a chair, a few magazines on the coffee table, *Vogue* and *Ms.,* papers, a book, and what looked like an oversize deck of cards on the desk. I leaned over the desk to check out the book title. It was *World of Wonders.* I'll say, I thought. I turned up the top card on the deck: a happy baby riding a horse, a smiling sun beaming down upon him. Marlene came in carrying plates, an apple, and the bottle of wine. "Do you read tarot cards?" I asked.

"I do. Does that surprise you?"

"Not really," I said, which was true. Actors are a superstitious tribe, always looking for luck and a glimpse of the future. They read their horoscopes, practice strange ritual behaviors before performances, carry totem objects with them for special occasions. Madeleine had a silver bracelet she'd worn when she won a state competition in high school that she kept in a velvet bag and wore only to auditions. Teddy had a lucky belt.

"Let's sit down," Marlene suggested. "We'll eat and talk, and then I'll read your cards."

"Great," I said.

We talked. What did we talk about? I believe we talked about me. Marlene asked me questions about what I'd read, my training, what plays I'd seen, what I thought of them, what I thought of the actors in them. She made me feel more interesting than I knew I was.

At one point she asked me what I knew about her. The photo in the wallet sprang into my brain, but even after a few glasses of wine I was cautious with her. "They say you are married and have a son tucked away in California and that you don't answer personal questions in interviews."

"Is that all they say?"

"And that you are a great actress."

"Oh, well, of course," she said. "They would say that."

"I believe it."

"You flatter me," she said, creating the sudden distance that kept me so off balance. "Now bring me my cards and let's see what they have to say about you."

When I stood up I found myself sure on my feet but light-headed from the wine. Outside it was dark and humid; a sultry breeze lifted the curtains, rustling the papers on the desk. Marlene switched on a lamp. I handed her the cards and took my seat, oddly excited by the prospect of mumbo-jumbo in a summer cottage with Marlene Webern. One could make a play of it, I thought. The ingenue and the actress. "This is fun," I said.

"No," she said. "It's serious." She fanned the deck open and extracted a card. "First we choose your signifier," she said, laying down a picture of a dark youth on a horse. "You're a blond now, so ordinarily I would choose a cup or wand, but I know your true color is dark. And this boy suits you. He stands for vigilance."

"I'm sure you can't fool the cards with a dye job," I said.

"No," she said. "You can't." She shuffled the cards and laid the pack facedown in front of me. "Now we're going to get to the bottom of Edward Day."

"I don't like the sound of that," I said.

"Cut to the left three times, three times."

"Three times, three times," I said, breaking the deck into stacks and reassembling them.

"And ask a question in your mind."

"What sort of question?"

"It should be a general question."

So I couldn't ask if Marlene would go to bed with me, though that was uppermost in my thoughts. I settled on "What will become of me?" One couldn't get more general than that.

"I hope I get the baby on the horse," I said.

She smiled. "That's a very good card," she agreed. She turned the top card up and laid it across my signifier. "Oh dear," she said.

It was the horned devil, all goat legs and bat wings perched on a block; at his clawed feet a naked man and woman, sporting horns and flaming tails, were chained by their necks to a ring on the block.

"That doesn't look promising," I observed.

"It's not so bad. It covers the general atmosphere of the question. It suggests you're in bondage to the material world."

"Oh, is that all," I said.

"Well, it could be something more extreme. It could be black magic."

"Heaven forbid," I said, refilling my wineglass.

"You're not interested in spiritual matters then."

"No. That's right. I'm not."

"Well, you should be."

"Do you think so?"

"The cards think so." She turned up the next one and placed it crosswise on the other two. "This crosses you," she said. It was a man standing before a series of silver chalices from which snakes, castles, laurel wreaths, and precious jewels overflowed. It was a dreamy picture; the cups floated on clouds.

"Scattered forces," Marlene said. "You waste your energy on fantasies."

"That can't be denied," I said.

"Well, you're young. It's natural. How old are you?"

"Twenty-five."

Turning up the next card she said, "This card refers to something that has happened in the past." She placed it carefully below the first three. For a moment we sat staring silently at my past.

The image was brutal. A man lay facedown on the ground with ten swords thrust into his back. The background was black. A liquid that was probably blood pooled near his head. "I'm really not enjoying this very much," I said.

"It's not death," she reassured me again. "Obviously in this position it can't be. It's a card of sudden loss, of betrayal."

Something about the card made me queasy, yet I couldn't look away. *I want you to sit down, son*, I heard my father say. And then, very clearly, a voice I'd heard only once in my life: *I hate this part of you.* Tears sprang to my eyes. "I'd like to stop here, if you don't mind," I said.

"Ed?" Marlene looked into my eyes with an expression of sympathy I found too bold, too easy. "Are you all right?" she asked.

I cleared my throat, clearing out my mother and her cracked girlfriend and the notes fluttering on the desk in my dormitory room: *Your mother called. Your mother again.* "Do your son a favor," I said coldly to Marlene. "Don't kill yourself."

She drew in a breath, leaning away from me. "I'm so sorry," she said.

"There's no reason you should be sorry."

"I mean, I'm sorry for you. I'm sorry for your loss. When did it happen?"

"When I was a freshman in college."

She was quiet for a moment. "It does explain something about you, as an actor."

"I don't much care what it explains," I said.

She picked up the card and examined it closely. "I don't believe in fate," she said. "And I don't think cards can predict the future. Only stupid people believe that. But the symbols on these cards are very old and they speak in a language we apprehend without having to think about it, without words. They speak to the unconscious, in effect, they speak to our emotions. That's why I like them."

"Good for you," I said.

Oblivious to the wave of ice I was sending her way, she went on. "What a strange set of circumstances," she said. "That you should come here to do this particular play with me at this point in your career. It's truly fortuitous."

"But you don't believe in fate," I said. "And you wanted me to come here, you said so yourself."

"Who are you angry with? Is it me?"

"I'm just saying it isn't fortuitous."

"You're a talented actor, Ed. You have a gift, and you have ambition. And you're not envious and competitive, that's something, that's good. Envy can be killing to an actor. Well, it's ruinous in all the arts."

"Are you getting at something, Marlene?"

"I am. Be patient. You're a good actor and you could be a

great actor, but only if you understand that your life must be given up to your art. You can have no other life. There can't be Ed having an emotion on the stage and Ed having an emotion, a strong, pure, deep emotion here in this room and a curtain drawn between. You mustn't sit here and try to push away a powerful emotion because it's painful. As an actor you have no right to do that."

"I'm not going to bawl about my dead mother, if that's what you want."

"I don't want anything. It's what you want. And what you need, from yourself, as an actor. Let go of your response to the emotion and study it. Study what it did to you, how it evolved in you, how it came about, Ed, dear, that *I* could see it and know it was real. Not faked. That it was real. You have to make use of yourself, of who you are."

"Sandy is always on about that in class," I said.

"Yes, well, he's right. Listen, you know that moment in the first scene when Scudder tells Chance Wayne his mother is dead and Chance says, 'Why wasn't I notified?' "

I'd been listening to her halfheartedly but now she had my complete attention. Incredible as it may seem, I had not until that moment connected the death of my character's mother with my feelings about the death of my own. His mother had been sick, she sounded old and petulant. That's why he'd come back to town. He hadn't been notified of her death because he'd left no reliable address. He was out starfucking, trying to get into the right crowd, sleeping "in the social registry," when his mother needed him. She had died a few weeks before he got around to caring about her.

"You always make yourself go cold when you deliver that line," Marlene continued. "You clench your jaw as if someone had just trod on your foot and you didn't want to let on. It's a dead line when you deliver it, nothing is revealed. Now I know why."

"I never feel comfortable with that line."

She handed the card to me. "Take it, look at it. Memorize it, not in words, don't say, 'It's a man with swords in his back,' just visualize it."

I took the card and did as she instructed, but words rose up in spite of me, and those words were, *It was my fault.*

"Now say the line."

I studied the card. It was myself I recognized, slain there.

Marlene gave me my cue. "Your mother died a couple of weeks ago."

I looked just past her at the curtain rustling in the breeze. A shiver, like spidery pinpricks ran up my spine. "Why wasn't I notified," I asked her. It wasn't a question, I wasn't seeking information. It was an admission of guilt.

"There you are," Marlene said. "There you are."

I held the card out to her. "Thank you," I said.

"Keep it," she said. "It's yours now."


I did keep it; I still have it somewhere, I'm not sure where, but I know I never threw it away. I didn't keep it for luck or out of superstition, but as a souvenir of that strange night when I was in love with Marlene Webern and she was generous to a young actor who had no idea what he was doing. I wanted to have sex with her, she wanted me to commit to my art. She sent me back to the boardinghouse that night with a kiss as chaste as Thisbe gave Pyramus through the chink in the wall and the next morning at rehearsal, she held her arms out to me again and I snuggled down into her warm, fragrant bosom and kissed her parted lips, sick with desire. What an actress that woman was! I never did get her into bed, but perhaps that was just as well. Best not to sully the ideal: I think she knew that.

Our play opened a week later and was, in the insular, hot-house world of summer stock, reckoned a success. The local press gushed over Marlene's performance as well they might, and I was singled out for hyperbolic praise: "A young actor of startling prowess." "Newcomer Edward Day commands the stage." Stuff like that. I was fucking the luscious Eve at night and worshipping at the altar of my goddess by day; my fellow thespians were a spirited, pleasure-loving lot; I was working hard and playing hard; and I had, at long last, an Equity card. The future was dazzling, and I gazed upon it from the evanescent interior of a bubble.

We had only one phone in the front hall of the boarding-house, so making and receiving calls wasn't easy. At the end of the first week I had left a message at Madeleine's service, giving her the number, with the frustrating addendum that there was rarely anyone in the house to answer it. A few days later I found a written message under my door: *Madeleine called; please call her at eight a.m. on Friday.* Dutifully I made the call but got the service again. "She had an appointment," the sleepy employee explained. "She said to tell you she's fine, very busy. She'll try to give you a call on Sunday."

"That's not good," I said. "We're in rehearsal all day."

"I'll tell her," he said. "How is it up there?"

"It's great," I said. "Are you an actor?"

"Why else would I be doing this job?"

"Right," I said. "Tell her I'll send her a card."

And that was the end of that. These days everyone has a cell phone stuck to his head and the idea of being out of touch is unthinkable, but at that time an exchange passed through a stranger was sometimes the best you could do. The next day I sent Madeleine a postcard with a photo of the picturesque town green.

*Dear Madeleine,* I wrote. *I'm working hard and loving it. I have the lead in Williams's* Sweet Bird. *It's a good group. The director's no genius, but he's not vicious and the theater is charming. Sorry about the phone situation. It's basically impossible. Glad to hear you're busy too. Love, Edward*

I didn't want to lose her, I thought, as I dropped the card into the postbox. I just didn't want to deal with her until we were face-to-face again.

A week later I got a card from her; the Statue of Liberty, which I took to be a good sign. *Dear Edward, Your card sounds like you're writing to someone you've recently met—or to your maiden aunt. Everything dead and hot here. I've got an audition at the Circle—wish me luck. I miss you. (You forgot to say that.) Love, Madeleine*

That last bit made me smile. Sufficiently tart, put me right in my place; that was Madeleine. I missed her too.


One evening toward the end of July, Gary Santos stopped in at the dressing room—he played the thuggish Tom Junior and took his part in my onstage castration with what I considered excessive glee—to say a friend had stopped by the boarding-house asking for me.

"What's his name?"

"He didn't say. Tall guy, long hair, beard, looks like a hip-pie. Said he'd see you after the play."

I could think of no friend who matched this description and straightway forgot about it, being absorbed by the cruel fate of Chance Wayne. The performance went well; the audience chuckled at all the jokes and took in breath during the brutal bits, applauded strongly for the full duration of our bows at the end. Marlene squeezed my hand as she smiled into the lights and I lifted her fingers to my lips, gazing longingly into her eyes. I was still in hot pursuit which amused her, but I hadn't been in-vited back into the sanctity of the cottage. In the dressing room I cleaned off my makeup, pulled on a T-shirt, and went out with a group who were heading for the local pub. We arrived in high spirits and occupied our customary booth near the back. The waitress, who knew our preferred brews, at once began ferrying icy mugs from the bar. Eve was next to me bending Gary's ear about the high professional standards at Yale, but her eyes kept drifting to the mirror behind him. "Stop admiring yourself," Gary demanded. "It's disgusting."

"I'm not," she protested.

"Right," Gary and I said in unison.

Eve giggled theatrically. "No, you sillies, I'm not. There's a cool-looking guy at the bar watching us. He looks like Warren Beatty in that movie, you know, with Julie Christie. I think I've seen him in something."

Gary and I both craned our necks for a celeb sighting. He was standing with his back to the bar, propped on one elbow, drinking beer from a bottle in a studly pose and, Eve was right, he was watching us. His black hair was long, past his chin, and he had a short, neatly trimmed beard. He raised his bottle to us in a friendly salute and flashed a disturbing smile like a coconut cracking open. With his free hand he pulled up a leather satchel resting on the barstool. "That's the guy who was looking for you," Gary said and Eve whispered, "Look, he's coming over."

"God, Ed," Guy announced as he arrived at our table. "When you came out on that stage, I didn't recognize you. I thought I was in the wrong theater. You make a fantastic blond. I think you should stick with it."

"I didn't recognize you, either," I said, which was true.

He patted the beard tentatively with his fingertips. "Oh, yes," he said. "I've changed too." His quick eyes raked the company and settled on Eve. "You were just great," he said.

"Thanks," Eve said.

"This is Guy Margate," I said. "This is Eve."

"Guy," Eve said, rising up in her place to shake hands. "Nice to meet you."

Guy fumbled in the bag and pulled out a Polaroid camera. "Can I get a picture of you guys?" he said, popping off the cap and stepping back to frame his shot. Eve grinned and leaned across the table, resting her hand on my arm. Gary and I laughed at her eagerness. "She's always ready for her close-up," Gary said. There was a flash and the zip of the magical square sliding out like a white tongue. Guy pulled it free and fanned it languidly, smiling at us.

"What brings you to Connecticut?" I asked.

"Well, I wanted to see your show."

"That's really nice," Eve said.

I didn't think it was nice; in fact I was sure it wasn't. He was up to something; he wanted something. Fortunately there was no room in our booth so I had a good excuse to separate from the group and join my old friend Guy at the bar. He passed the photo around, discharging a few fulsome compliments upon the players until the picture came back and he followed me.

"Jack Daniels," I said to the bartender. "Straight up, water back."

Guy drained his beer. "I'll have the same."

I watched the bartender pouring the drinks, unable to think of anything I wanted to say to Guy. "Man," he said at last. "I can't get over you as a blond. It almost looks natural." He pulled thoughtfully at a thick strand grazing his cheek. "Maybe I should try it."

"It wouldn't look natural," I said.

"I don't see why not."

"You're actually darker than I am," I said. "Your coloring is all wrong."

"There are lots of blond Italians."

"Is that what you are?"

"It probably wouldn't be worth the trouble." Our drinks arrived and he sipped his.

"Why the beard?" I asked.

"It's an experiment. There's a Chekhov play coming up,

well it's actually a play about Chekhov. Bev knows the casting director and she thinks she can get me an audition."

"You see yourself as Chekhov?"

"Or just generic nineteenth-century Russian; they all had beards. Sure, I could do that."

"You have a lot of confidence in yourself," I said.

"Why shouldn't I?"

I swallowed half my bourbon glancing back at my friends in the booth. I could hear their sudden bursts of laughter, but I couldn't make out what they were saying. The room was dimly lit and smoky; they seemed far away. A green shaded lamp over the mirror cast threads of light on the reflection of Eve's golden curls, her rosy cheeks, as she reached across the table to snatch a cigarette from the communal pack. "That girl finds you very attractive," I said to Guy.

His eyes followed mine, but listlessly. "You're having a fine time here," he said.

"I am," I agreed.

"Are you fucking that TV actress?"

"Marlene? I wouldn't say if I were." Eve, feeling our eyes upon her, sent me a provocative smile, a wave, a wink.

"You're fucking that girl," Guy observed.

"Why are you interested?"

"I'm not interested," he said.

"What is it you want here?"

He smiled, but not at me. "You're not bad in that role," he said. "The hustler who thinks he could be a star. It suits you, eh?"

"Actually no. I'm acting."

This made him laugh which was never a pleasant sight. "Is that what you call it?"

"You're always ready with the critique," I said. "Who asked you to come here anyway?"

He took a beat, drawing down his eyebrows and upper lip in a mockery of serious consideration. "Madeleine," he said.

I didn't believe him, but I was curious. "Did she send you to check up on me?"

"It's too late for that, isn't it?"

"What is it about being asked a question that you don't get?"

"She's pregnant," he said.

This was a conversation-stopper. I took the opportunity to signal the bartender for another drink. Guy looked back at the table where the waitress was setting down two large pizzas. "That girl is pretty enough," he said, "but she's a terrible actress."

"Madeleine sent you to tell me this?"

"It's not as if she can reach you on the phone," he said. "And it's not the sort of news one puts on a postcard, is it?"

This was true enough, but still I didn't believe him. "Why didn't she come herself?"

"She doesn't have time."

"So you're the wicked messenger."

"I take it this is unwelcome news."

"When did you and Madeleine get so close?"

"We've been friends a long time; we have the same agent."

"And I've been away for two months."

He looked back at Eve. "You know, I think it's really a bad idea to have sex with an actress whose work you have contempt for. It coarsens you."

"So who's the lucky father?" I said.

"That's just what one can never be sure of, isn't it," Guy said. "Much has been made of that very problem in the theater."

"What's she going to do?"

He lifted his chin and tapped around the edge of his beard as if he was securing it to his face. "I think the question is: What are you going to do?"

"Is the beard real?"

"Sure it is," he said.

"I just can't believe Madeleine would send you to tell me this news." It was so unfair, I thought. Everything was going so well. "I'm going to have to think about this," I said.

"You wouldn't want to do anything impulsive."

"Exactly," I agreed, but then I realized he was attempting irony, which was a stretch for Guy. He couldn't get the inclusive fellow-feeling element that tempers the blade of wit. Instead of humorous prodding, his method was the full frontal sneer. My jaw and throat felt tight; I narrowed my eyes. I was angry with Madeleine. How could she put me in this intolerable position? She knew how I felt about Guy. And what if she was sleeping with him? I didn't trust either of them.

The group confined in the booth broke ranks and drifted toward the bar. Eve made a beeline for the stool next to Guy, engaging him at once on the question of what she should drink. This suited me; it gave me time to figure out what to say. My assumption was that Madeleine would want an abortion. She was far too ambitious and obsessed with her career to put it on hold to have a child no one really wanted. I figured she would know how to do whatever she wanted to do, but what she would need would be money. I had a little, not much. How should I send it to her? Should I give it to Guy or send a check in a letter? I wanted to help her without making any kind of commitment.

Guy was flirting energetically with Eve and she was eating it up. I heard the golden phrase "my agent" more than once and some disparagement of the reviewers who had courteously withheld comment about Eve's performance in our production. It was a rerun of the scene at Phebe's a year ago, when Guy had made a play for Madeleine, but this time I was wishing him success. If he spent the night with Eve it would prove something I wanted proved, though I wasn't sure exactly what that was. That Guy was a hypocrite? That he was heterosexual? Something along those lines.

But in spite of Eve's best efforts, Guy wasn't tempted. At length he turned to me and announced that he had to catch the last bus back to the city. "Walk over with me," he said. "And we can finish our conversation."

I followed him out into the street; my shoulders drooped, my feet shuffling like a reluctant child. The walk he proposed, which wasn't half a mile, stretched out interminably. I felt I'd been sentenced to a term at hard labor. After a block of this he looked back sharply. "Good grief," he said. "Can't you keep up?" I hustled along, allowing hostility to double for energy. Why did Guy always make me feel so tired and so shamed? I'd done nothing wrong. "So what do you want me to tell Madeleine?" he asked.

"I don't want you to tell her anything."

Again the close, deprecating look. "So I'll tell her you have nothing to say to her."

"Does she need money?"

"I should think so."

"Tell her I'll send her some money."

"You could just give it to me."

"No, I'll mail it."

"I'd rather you didn't do that."

"I don't get why you're in the middle of this," I said. "Why should I care what you'd rather I did or didn't do about Madeleine?"

"Because Madeleine doesn't know I'm here."

I stopped short. "So you lied?" I said.

"For a good cause."

I pressed the heels of my hands into my temples. "Who do you think you are?" I exclaimed.

"Would you come on," he said. "If I miss this bus I'll have to sleep on your floor."

This was a persuasive argument. I matched him stride for stride while he explained his mission. "I told her I would come talk to you, but she didn't want me to. She said you'd only sent her one postcard and it was hardly even friendly. You really hurt her with that. She figured you didn't care what happened to her and knowing she was pregnant would only make everything worse. But I thought you had a right to know."

"Did it occur to you that she doesn't want me to know because I'm not the father?"

"She's more than two months pregnant, Ed."

"That doesn't prove anything."

He grasped his beard in both hands and, without missing a step, tore it loose from his chin. "This thing is driving me nuts," he said.

"Does it itch?"

"Like fire ants," he said. "It's like having fire ants on your face."

The bus station was a bench and a sign in front of a newsagent's store and as we turned the last corner we could see a few people milling about in the bug-saturated light of the streetlamp. I wanted to close the conversation on a clear and final point. "The way I see it," I said, "is that it's up to Madeleine to decide who to tell and what to do. If she doesn't want me to know, so be it."

Guy stuffed the beard into his satchel. "The way I see it," he said, "is that Madeleine is a girl in trouble and you can't be bothered. Which is fine, Ed. I should have known. I should have known."

I reached into my pocket and pulled out all the cash I had, about fifty dollars. "Look, this isn't much, but give it to her. And I'll send you a hundred more tomorrow. Just say you're giving it to her; she doesn't need to know it's from me."

He took the cash and held it for a moment, as if trying to

make up his mind whether to keep it or throw it in my face. We were close to the stop and we heard the huffing of the bus before it lumbered into view. The waiting passengers formed themselves into a civilized line. Guy and I stood motionless, both transfixed by the folded bills he gripped in his fist. As the bus came to a halt, the brakes whirred and groaned and the wings of the doors flapped open with a breathy whoosh. Guy crammed the money into the pocket of his jeans. "You make me sick," he hissed, and he turned on his heel, leaving me on the curb.

I didn't know if I'd been repudiated or skillfully scammed. I stood there, watching the passengers file into the bus, until I was certain Guy was on it. Then, in case he got back off, I decided to wait until the doors were closed. After that it seemed the best course to be sure the bus actually pulled away from the curb and rolled off into the night. When I couldn't see it at all, I rubbed my eyes and looked again. Only then did a sensation of deep release and relief allow me to turn away and walk back to the boardinghouse where Eve, languidly rocking herself on the porch swing, waited for me.

The next day I wrote a check for one hundred dollars, leaving twelve dollars in my account, put the check in an envelope, and because I didn't know Guy's address, sent it to him care of his agent, Bev Arbuckle. I didn't want to do it, but I didn't not want to do it, either. Guy's melodramatic description of Madeleine as "a girl in trouble," which struck me as something from a '50s soap opera, stung me—you can't turn your back on a girl in trouble. But Madeleine wasn't some misguided teenager; she was an adult, perfectly capable of making her own decisions. Trusting Guy to give the money to Madeleine kept me from having to contact her directly. I honestly believed, I still do, that it was up to her to tell me what she wanted me to know, yet knowing what I now did, I wanted to help her. I liked the anonymity of my admittedly small contribution to her well-being. And I liked especially that she clearly had no intention of involving me in her predicament. I had another month in Connecticut and by the time I got back to the city, Madeleine would presumably be as she had been and we could go from there.

In the meantime, Marlene, by example and by design, was teaching me what I needed to be an actor. Interestingly it was a combination of egomania and complete selflessness. In the process of taking on a character, some essence of the self must remain intact. "Never lose yourself on the stage," Stanislavski famously advised. I saw in Marlene, day after day, something essentially unaltered that absorbed the character she played. She didn't become Alexandra del Lago, Alexandra del Lago became Marlene Webern. It's difficult to describe, it sounds abstract and absurd, but for me at that time, it was transformative, allowing for subtleties of interpretation and impression that had hitherto eluded me. Marlene watched me literally like a hawk; it was as if her eye was equipped with a zoom lens that saw straight into the heart of me. Especially when we were onstage together, I could feel that probing eye on me and it charged our time together with what reviewers call "electricity." Yet she was not, by any means, always focused upon me. Her eyes often wandered away, resting on some prop item or on her own hands. Sometimes she lifted her chin in my direction but let her eyes go maddeningly out of focus, with that inward smile of hers and an attitude of listening. When she wasn't watching me, she was intensely listening to me.

I became conscious of how rarely people actually look at or listen to each other in ordinary life, or if they do, how often it's with ill intent. Marlene's attention was nonjudgmental, curious, and serene, neither hot nor cold, and it was like that onstage and off.

One Sunday afternoon in the last week of the season, I found myself at loose ends after the children's production, in which I had a role as a wolf. Acting for children is relaxing; they're such an open, rambunctious audience, eager to go on the wildest flights of fancy, their little mouths open in helpless ohs and ahs, their eyes dancing with delight at each revelation of the simplistic plot. I'd taken off my wolf makeup and hung up my wolf suit for the last time, and I felt sad about that.

The others had all gone off in a rush after the show. It was a clear, hot day, one in a string of them, and they had planned an outing to the coast for a swim, an opportunity I had declined. I wasn't up for the beach just yet. As I stepped from the dark theater into the blazing sun the sensation of carrying a weight of gloom became so pronounced I owned it. "I'm sad," I said to no one, and sat down on the step. I fished in my pocket for a cigarette, lit up, and breathed in the pungent, lethal smoke. Soon I'd be back in the city looking for a job. I heard the creak of the screen door behind me, but I didn't bother to look up. The stairs were wide, I wasn't blocking the way. A pair of tanned feet in red sandals appeared on the wood next to my hip. "I thought everyone went to the shore," Marlene said. The sun was behind her and I squinted up at her. Her eyes were hidden behind her dark glasses, her hair was loose, her full lips were slightly parted; star power wafted from her like a breeze from another planet. How was it possible that I knew this extraterrestrial beauty? "I don't care for the beach," I said.

"I don't either," she said, smoothly dropping down on the step beside me. "All that sun is bad for the skin and sand is very unpleasant."

"You speak against sand?"

"It sticks to everything. It gets into everything."

I took another drag on my cigarette. "That's true," I said.

"You do look the picture of despondency," she observed. "Has something happened?"

"Not really."

"Romantic entanglement? Financial reverses?"

"I'm depressed because the summer is nearly over," I said, "and you're going back to L.A. and I may never see you again."

"It has been an excellent season. But you should be energized; you've grown as an actor."

"Have I?"

"Oh, immensely. Don't you feel it?"

"I feel it when I'm with you."

"We had a lot of fun with our play."

"I'll miss kissing you. I really love kissing you."

She laughed. "That's very sweet."

"No. It's not."

"You'll be kissing someone lovely on the stage in no time."

"It would help if you'd say you didn't actually mind kissing me."

She turned away from me, as if she heard someone approaching, but there was no one. "Actually those scenes were disturbing to me. You remind me so much of my son."

"Good God," I said.

"I didn't want to tell you because I thought it might inhibit you."

I hadn't given much thought to Marlene as a mother. When I'd heard about the son, I'd pictured a boy in grammar school, a little leaguer or soccer enthusiast. "How old is your son?" I asked.

"He's twenty."

"How is that possible?" I said.

"I was young when he was born."

"Do I look like him?"

"Not really. It's something about the way you move. Your gestures remind me of him. You're much more alive than he is. He's an unhappy young man, I'm afraid. Not very lively."

"Why is he unhappy?"

"Probably because his mother is an actress."

"Is he in school?"

"No. He didn't do well in school. There were drug problems and he's very independent, he doesn't take . . ." she paused, searching for the right word, "direction."

"Does he want to be an actor?"

"Oh no. He despises acting."

"That's not great," I said, pointlessly.

Marlene drew herself up and removed her sunglasses. Her

eyes were moist, and her voice, when she spoke, quavered slightly, as from emotion. "I'm worried. Tell me, what is the matter with my son? Why is he so sad and so austere?"

"Chekhov, right?"

She slid the glasses back into place. "Very good," she said. "It's Arkadina in *The Seagull*. I'll be doing it in the spring in Pasadena. So you see, everything is of use."

"You're always working."

"Yes," she said. "I've been fortunate. But you will be too."

"Not if I don't find an agent."

"I thought you had one."

"No. I don't."

"I'll send you to Barney. He'll be perfect for you and you for him." She opened an absurdly small purse and took out her wallet, not, I noted, the one I'd snatched from the bag in the immortal improv. She extracted a card and wrote a name and phone number on the back. "Call him when you get back," she said. "Tell him I sent you. And I'll call him to tell him about you. He'll be expecting you."

I took the card and studied the name, Barney Marker. "You're something with these cards that change my life."

"You're very talented, you should be encouraged. But I want to advise you about your training. Sandy is a wonderful teacher. Listen to everything he says, but don't take his criticism too much to heart. There's a coldness in you that he'll take offense to, he'll try to root it out of you, but I think ultimately it will be your strength."

"You think I'm cold?"

"Part of you is. Yes. The other part is very hot, very passionate. It's your temperament, and it's a gift. Not many actors can stand still the way you do."

"Are you like that?"

"Like what?"

"Hot and cold."

"I was. These days I'm mostly weary. But when I'm working, I'm all right."

"I think you're brilliant," I said.

She rested her hand on my knee sending a bolt of liquid heat straight to my groin. "I know you do, Edward," she said. "And that's very gratifying to me." My brain, joining in the excitement in my groin, was churning out torrid images.

"Could I ask you something?" I said.

"Of course."

"You know that photograph you had in your wallet that first time, at school? When we did the improv?"

Her eyebrows knit over the glasses. "No," she said. "What photo?"

"The one of you, on the couch."

She drew her hand away and pressed her fingertips against her lips in an expression of deep puzzlement. "A photograph of me?" she said.

"On a couch."

"My driver's license is in my wallet. But I'm not on a couch."

"You're acting," I said.

"In the photo?"

"No. Now. You're having me on."

She fumbled with the bag. "Would you like to see my wallet?"

"No," I said. "It's not the same one."

She opened the purse and closed it again, emanating mystification from every pore.

"Forget about it," I said, stubbing out my cigarette next to my shoe.

So I was never to know anything about the photograph and Marlene was such a good actress that I suddenly doubted whether I had actually seen it.

"I must be off," she said, glancing at her watch. "I'm lunching with the board."

I slipped the card into my shirt pocket. "Thanks for this," I said. "It means a lot."

"Let me know what happens. My address is on the front."

"I will," I promised, and I did. When I got back to the city the third call I made was to Barney Marker. "Mr. Day," his assistant said. "Yes, Ms. Webern spoke with Mr. Marker about you. Can you come in on Wednesday in the afternoon?"

The second call I made was to Teddy.

"You're back at last," Teddy said. "Come over at seven and we'll go get dinner somewhere. I've got a lot to tell you."

The first call was to Madeleine. I left a message with the service. "Tell her I'm back," I said. "She knows the number."


"Oh my God, you're a blond," Teddy cried when he opened the door. "It's a totally new you."

"Not for long," I said as we exchanged an awkward hug. "Getting it done is torture and it fries your hair." I followed him into his kitchen where he immediately began pouring out glasses of Scotch.

"Let's have a drink before we go out," he said.

Teddy looked different too, though just how I couldn't say. He seemed lighter, more buoyant. He was wearing a stylish beige linen jacket, expensive, definitely Italian, which was odd, because Teddy was generally indifferent to fashion. His ironic woebegoneness, partly attributable to his face and partly to his disposition, was in place, but there was a brightness about him I'd never seen before. His habitual lethargy had been replaced by something more sinuous and expansive. "You look great," I said.

"Did I look bad before?"

"I don't know. You look happy."

"I am. I really am."

"Do you have a job?"

This made him laugh. "Not exactly, but in a way yes, I do. Or maybe not." He handed me a glass and we went out to the sitting room. There was a large painting I hadn't seen before hanging over the fake fireplace, very dark with dots of bright color that made me think of lights on a bridge at night.

"That's new," I observed.

"It is," he said. We sat in the armchairs which had been turned to face the painting. "So how was it? Were you a success?"

"I was," I said. "It was great. It changed my life."

"I've had a transforming summer myself."

"So what do you mean about the job? Do you have one or don't you?"

"I do. It's a new part for me. I'm in love."

"That's not true. You're always in love," I said.

"But this time it's different."

"It's requited," I suggested.

"It is so requited." He sipped his drink, his eyes alight with amusement.

"Is it Jasmine?"

"No. But that's a good guess. It is someone in her family."

"She has a sister?"

"No. She has a brother, no sisters."

"It's not Mrs. Lee!"

He sputtered with delight. "No, no, not Mrs. Lee."

"You look like you're going to pop," I said. "Who is it?"

"It's Jasmine's brother," he said. "Wayne."

"You're joking," I said. And it was a good joke, but I failed to see the point of it.

"I've never been more serious in my life."

My jaw went slack with amazement. "I see you've been keeping something from me," I said.

"I've been keeping something from myself. And it's been killing me. Slowly, slowly, year after year."

"I'm dumbfounded," I said.

"I know you are. I was too."

"Give me a little more Scotch for the shock and tell me exactly how this happened," I said.

"I can't wait to tell you," he said, passing the bottle. I settled in my chair, ready for a story packed with my favorite subject, unexpected and powerfully conflicted emotions.

"You know Jasmine and I hit it off that night we met her at the restaurant, and after you left we went out a few times. Mindy was giving me such a hard time and Jasmine is a sprite and so undemanding it was a relief to be with her. One night she invited me to dinner with the family—to taste real Chinese food, she said—though I think she'd already figured out more about me than I knew about myself The inscrutable Chinese, you know. We don't get them but they see right through us.

"So I went down there and it was her parents, the aunt, Mrs. Lee, who you met, and her husband—he doesn't speak English—and Jasmine's brother, Wayne, who was in the kitchen when I arrived. He's an incredible cook. I was sitting at the table with the family when he came in carrying a tray of the most fabulous dumplings and when I saw him my heart just stopped. All I thought was, What a handsome man. Jasmine introduced him and I stood up to shake hands, and I tell you Ed, the look he gave me went through me like a skewer through a hot dog. Then we all sat down and pitched into the dumplings and everyone started talking half in Chinese and half in English. This went on for about six courses. At one point Wayne was bringing out a platter of noodles and he lowered it to the table from behind me. I said something idiotic like 'I love noodles,' and he laughed. Then he put his hand on my shoulder, just the lightest squeeze and he said, 'So you like Chinese noodles,' and everyone laughed hysterically. They're very giddy, that family; they laugh a lot. So different from dinner at the pater's; I can't tell you.

"The evening wore on and I learned that Wayne was a painter and he's even had a few pictures in shows. He works in a gallery in SoHo and has a studio in the East Village, and everyone in the family knows he'll be a great painter and they're proud of him. Again, the opposite of my experience."

"East meets West," I said.

"It was just mind-boggling. I kept drinking rice wine and trying not to look at Wayne, but it was hopeless. And I was having a good time. Jasmine was being enormously sweet, and the mother wanted to know all about Stella Adler—she thinks Jasmine should study with her. The mother is completely informed about theater, which is astounding. Anyway, somehow I got through it without fainting away, and as I was leaving Wayne said I really should come by his studio to see his work. I said I'd be very interested in that, and he said, 'Come tomorrow,' which was a Sunday. 'I'll be there all day.' So I said I would come around four and he told me the address and that was that."

"So you went to the studio," I said.

"I did. But first I came home, of course, and tried to make some sense of what had happened to me. I sat in this chair and drank a big glass of Scotch and halfway through I started crying."

"You felt sad?"

"I felt scared. I was scared to death. I decided not to go. I couldn't deal with it. Then I'd think of that little squeeze on my shoulder and I knew I had to go, and that made me cry harder. I cried all night. I hardly slept at all. On Sunday I just read the paper and drank coffee all day, trying not to know what was going to happen. I told myself he was just a friendly Chinese man and I'd go see the pictures and we'd have a nice chat about the art scene. The hours dragged by; I think I read every single line of the entire Sunday *Times*. Then, at last, it was time to go. I was wired to the limit from no sleep and the tears and then all the coffee; I'd eaten one piece of toast. I arrived at the door— it's more like a garage door, it slides open—and I rang the bell. There was this sound like the gate of a prison rolling back and there he was.

"We went inside and he offered me some herbal tea which was really welcome. We started talking about the dinner and the family and what Jasmine should do about her career. I felt completely comfortable. I took my tea and he showed me around the studio—it's pretty bare, very Zen, though Wayne's not a Buddhist—and I walked around looking at the paintings everywhere. He's done a lot of work. Some were stacked against the walls and some were hung up. I went along admiring each one and I stopped at this one." Teddy looked up at the painting over the fireplace. "This fantastic picture."

"It's his?" I said needlessly.

"Oh yes. Do you like it?"

"Yes," I said. "I do."

"I stopped in front of it and I said something, who knows what. What did I say? My heart was just racing. Wayne came up beside me and he did the dearest thing; he just put his arm around my shoulder and he said, 'You like this one particularly?'

" 'I do,' I said. He took the teacup away from me and put it on the floor and then he stood between me and the picture and put his arms around me and kissed me. And all I could think was, God help me, I'm in love with a Chinese man." Teddy paused, allowing me to savor the moment.

"Amazing story," I said.

"It is," he agreed. "I've been waiting for you to get back so I could tell you."

"Does anyone else know about it?"

"Oh yes. But not the details. And of course my family knows nothing about it yet. The pater will disinherit me when he finds out."

"That's big."

"It is. But there's nothing to be done about it." He said this frankly, without self-pity, as if he was describing an approaching weather system.

"So," I said. "You're out of the closet."

He frowned. "I've never liked that expression. But it's apt, I guess. That whole business about being in a closet, it irritates me. I always picture this absurd fag standing just behind the door, stripping down to his briefs and then—BAM—he kicks that door open and leaps out singing, 'I Gotta Be Me.' " He sang this line in a thin falsetto that made me laugh.

"But I wasn't just behind the door, Ed, I was way, way back in the darkest corner of the closet, behind the coats and the old badminton sets, and the snow boots, just crouched back there like a little mouse nibbling on crumbs I found in the coat pockets, and it was dark and I was scared, and also sad. I've been so sad for so long."

I considered this confession. "It made you kind," I said. "And it made you an actor."

"But not a *good* actor. That's one of the things I've been sad about. And here's a really funny part. A few weeks after that kiss, I had to do a scene for Ms. Adler and I just ripped right through it; I felt absolutely confident and powerful as I never have before, and when it was over she said, 'Well, Mr. Winterbottom, I see that I am a very talented teacher.' Poor old lady, she thought it was her teaching that finally got me to some kind of breakthrough, but it had nothing to do with her. It was my wonderful, beautiful Wayne who led me out of that suffocating darkness I'd been trying to thrive in and into the glorious light that is just pouring over me now, just blinding me with the joy and the freedom of it. When I think of how close I came to marrying Mindy Banks my blood runs cold. My God, Ed, I wake up in the morning feeling absolutely great. I can't wait to jump out of bed and spend another day basking in this wonderful, wonderful light."

He'd gotten out of his chair at some point and finished his aria standing beneath the painting, his arms opened wide to embrace his new self. It occurred to me that he'd probably bought the picture from Wayne. Teddy was, after all, rich, at least temporarily, and Wayne was surely poor. "That picture is actually rather dark," I observed.

Teddy smiled beatifically down upon me. "It is, isn't it?" he said and we both laughed.

"How did Mindy take the news?"

"Not well. She thinks Wayne will break my heart and I'll come crawling back to her."

I thought so too, but I wasn't going to tell Teddy; it would have been cruel. The whole idea of Teddy's Chinese man gave me the creeps. I imagined Jasmine had figured out Teddy was rich and ripe for exploitation by her brother. The whole family may have been in on it. But whatever happened, Teddy was visibly, seriously altered, and I believed what he said about his acting having been hampered by the denial of his sexual attraction to other men. That part made sense. "It's not going to make your life any easier," I said. "But it doesn't look as if you've got any choice."

"Are you shocked?"

"Of course, I'm shocked. But we're still friends, I hope."

"I want you to meet Wayne."

I didn't want to meet Wayne. I wanted Teddy to get over Wayne and go back to being reserved, ironic, and up for late-night drinking sessions at the Cedar or Phebe's. "Let's just wait a little on that," I said.

He threw himself down in the chair. "No one is happy for me. I don't understand it."

"If you're happy, I'm happy for you. I just need a little time to get used to the new you."

"Everything's changing," he said. "The old crowd is pulling apart. You know about Guy and Madeleine."

The conjunction of these two names irritated me so much that I squirmed in my chair. "What about them?"

"They're married."

"You're joking," I said, because surely this was a joke.

"No. They got married a few weeks ago. They went to City Hall. Mindy was a witness."

"Is she out of her mind?"

"Mindy?"

"No, Madeleine."

"I don't think so. But there was motive for haste. She's pregnant."

"I know that," I said.

"She told you?"

"No. Guy told me."

"I guess it was an accident, but they seem pleased about it. Guy especially."

"So they're living together."

"They are, at his old place. But they're looking for something better, for when the baby comes."

Physically speaking, anger is a complex emotion. It takes many forms, depending upon the degree to which it is allowed to be expressed. In our society no one wants either to see it or own to feeling it, so it breaks out in all sorts of inappropriate hostility, particularly in the workplace. It can be slow in developing, gathering force over a long period of time. This is what we mean by the expression "the last straw." Or it can be quite sudden, full-blown, and overpowering, as in "I saw red." What I felt at Teddy's news was largely of this latter variety and I was at pains to conceal it, but there was also something of the slow simmer coming to a boil, something that had known from the first time I saw her that Madeleine would bring me to seeing red. "I can't believe this," I said.

"I see that," Teddy said. "You've gone pale. It looks like a bigger shock than my affair with Wayne."

"Jesus," I said. "Maybe it's the combination." But it wasn't. I hadn't felt much beyond surprise and interest in Teddy's confession; it didn't touch me. This news penetrated deep into my thoracic cavity, where my liver was briskly pumping out enough bile to digest a brick. The truth was bitter. I didn't want to marry Madeleine—I didn't want to marry anyone, the idea was appalling—but I didn't want anyone else to marry her and I most particularly did not want Guy Margate to marry her.

"Mr. and Mrs. Margate," I said sourly.

"Well," Teddy said. "She's not changing her name."

At dinner Teddy talked about nothing but Wayne. He was in the first giddy stages of infatuation, his ragged heart flapping on his sleeve for the whole world to see. I hardly knew what to say to him but it didn't matter because he wouldn't have heard me if I had. I pleaded fatigue and the necessity for an early wake-up call—I'd been laid off at Bloomingdale's and would have to scare up a new day job—and we parted after dinner, he to Wayne's studio, I to my apartment, which the Georgia peach had evidently spent the summer scrubbing down with bleach; even the dresser drawers reeked of it.

My brain was in an uproar. I paced up and down, muttering imprecations against Madeleine; how could she have done it, how brought herself to so low a pass? I dropped to the floor and did push-ups until my arms trembled. I put Jim Morrison on my record player and sang along with "The Crystal Ship" and "Back Door Man." At midnight I could stand my thoughts no longer and went out.

The streets were empty but for panhandlers and unsavory types, so I walked at a brisk pace down to Washington Square,

across to Broadway, and back up to Union Square, where there
was an all-night bar patronized by models and Hispanic drug
dealers. I had a quick drink there, exchanging pleasantries with
a beanpole of a model who called herself Vakushka, "You
know like in that movie."

"Verushka," I corrected her.

"No, I'm sure it's Vakushka," she replied. I set out again,
across to Fifth Avenue and back down to Washington Square.
The night was damp and progressively cooler. As I crossed into
SoHo a light rain began to fall and by the time I got to Spring
Street it was a downpour. I turned back toward the Village.
There was still a smattering of nightlife going on, people rush-
ing into and out of cabs and cars, lights flickering from the
open doors of a few bars and restaurants. I cut across toward
Bowery, thinking I might dry out at Phebe's if they were still
open. The street widened, light posts were farther apart, the
rain clattered, running off the gutters, puddling around the
plastic garbage bags lining the curb. A torn bag rustled omi-
nously as I passed and in the next moment a rat rushed out at
me. "Get away!" I snarled, revving up to a trot. At the corner I
turned north again, shielding my eyes with my hand to see
through the sheeting water.

A man sporting an umbrella appeared on the opposite sidewalk, moving swiftly, as I was, and in the same direction. For a
block he mirrored me. I could sense him there more than see
him, and at the next corner he crossed to my side and came up
behind me. The umbrella, a cumbersome and sensible accou-
trement, made me think he was unlikely to be a thief or a thug.
Phebe's lights glimmered in the near distance; he was clearly

headed there as well. I glanced as surreptitiously as I could over my shoulder, but all I could see was the umbrella and a loose jacket flapping open as its owner hastened along.

"Why don't you slow down and share my umbrella?" he said. "We've still got a block to go."

It was Guy. My first impulse, which was to run away, gave way to my second, which was a burning curiosity to find out something about Madeleine. "How did you know it was me?" I asked, as he extended the umbrella over my head.

"I knew it as soon as I turned the corner. You walk like a dog with your head down."

"Ever observant," I said. "Can you do an impression of me?"

"As a matter of fact I have a very good impression of you. I'll show it to you someday."

The thought gave me pause. Did he do an impression of me for Madeleine? Did she laugh? Did she correct him on certain intimate details? An unpleasant scenario played out in my head as we covered the last block and stepped in under Phebe's awning. The chairs were stacked on the tables but there were a few stragglers at the bar, waiting out the storm. We went in; I shook myself off and passed a handkerchief over my hair. As he folded his umbrella and propped it primly against the doorframe I took a closer look at Madeleine's husband.

He'd changed again. His face was haggard, his hair was greased and slicked back, his skin was sallow, there were dark circles beneath his eyes. Married life. The jacket was bomber style, not new, shiny, probably water resistant. The sleeves were too short. There was something seedy about him, but his good posture and bones combined to give him an air of shabby gentility. He knew I was examining him and allowed a moment before he turned to me, his expression flat as a foot, and said, "I could use a drink."

"Me too," I agreed. We went to the bar.

"Miserable night," said the bartender. "What will you have?"

We had bourbon. "I understand you're to be congratulated," I said, lifting my glass in a mini-toast.

"News travels fast," he said. "Who told you?"

"Teddy. I just had dinner with him."

"Did you meet Wayne?"

"No. But I heard a lot about him."

"Teddy's not serious," he observed.

"He says he's never been more serious in his life."

"Not about Wayne. About being an actor. He's not serious and Wayne is a way out."

"He says his acting has improved."

Guy snorted. "Do you believe that?"

"Well," I said, "if he's been repressing a whole part of himself and now he's not, it stands to reason he'll be a better actor. He has access to more of himself. I mean, before he was acting even when he wasn't playing a part. Now he's not, so there should be more truth to his work."

"You sound like Madeleine."

"Do I?" I said. Madeleine often carped about "truth" until I was stultified with boredom. "Maybe she's right."

Guy rolled his eyes dramatically. "There's no way around playing a part," he said. "There's no truth to be known. You make it up as you go along. If anyone should know that, it's you."

"Does Madeleine know you think like this?"

"Of course not. I'm not stupid."

So he had contempt for Madeleine too. "How is she?" I asked.

He swirled his bourbon in the glass and knocked it back. "She's asleep."

Of course, I thought. He knew when Madeleine was asleep and when she was awake. And when she washed her hair, and what brand of toothbrush she preferred, and how carefully she placed those cotton balls between her toes when she painted her toenails. What Guy must know about Madeleine depressed me. "So you're on the prowl," I said.

"I have trouble sleeping," he said. "I walk around at night. But you know that."

We all stayed up late and burned the candle at both ends, so it had not, until that moment, occurred to me that Guy was an insomniac. It was sleeplessness, he implied, that had drawn him out on the pier that night. He was searching for sleep and he'd found a drowning man. And now he'd left Madeleine alone in a dingy apartment somewhere because he was too restless to lie by her side. The longer I spent with Guy the more I wanted to talk to Madeleine, but he was between us now, like an ogre guarding a princess, and he couldn't even be counted upon to fall asleep long enough to get past him. All my anger against her had been washed out of me by the rain and I could feel the cold, wet shirt against my back, the squishy toes of my socks. I was a miserable wet dog in the manger if ever there was one.

"Is she working?" I asked.

"She's not acting, if that's what you mean. She's got a job at the bookstore with me. She gets tired out pretty easily; the doctor says she's anemic. She's not going back to classes when they start up again."

"I'd like to talk to her," I said.

He pushed a few bills across the bar, studying me with his dark eyes. "I'm sure you would," he said.

She doesn't love him, I thought. How could she? He'd caught her at a weak moment. She had no one else to turn to and he was there. He twisted his mouth into something like a smile and gave a quick chuck to my shoulder with the back of his hand. "She liked that photo I took of you," he said.

"What photo?"

"In Connecticut."

My brain contracted around this information like an octopus engulfing a bivalve. "But you told me she didn't know you were coming to see me."

"She didn't know then. But when I got back I told her. And I gave her the money you sent. She appreciated that."

"I asked you not to tell her it came from me."

"I'm not going to lie to Madeleine for you. She's my wife."

I rested my elbows on the bar and lowered my head into my hands. "Oh, man," I said.

Guy buttoned his jacket. "I'm off," he said. "Nice running into you, Ed."

"Oh, man," I said again. I didn't lift my head until I heard the door swing closed behind him.

He'd laid a trap for me and I'd waltzed right into it. God knew what he'd told Madeleine about our meeting in Connecticut. How could I talk to her? She clearly wasn't going to return my calls, she wasn't going to classes, and she worked in the same place as her husband. And even if I did manage it, what could I possibly say? *It's your own fault,* I upbraided myself. *You wanted to get away from her, you wanted a break, you welcomed it.*

*That's true,* I protested in my defense. *But it wasn't supposed to turn out like this!*

The next morning I went down to SoHo to see if I could get my old job back. I was welcomed by my employer like the prodigal son. He was shorthanded; two waiters had quit by simply not showing up. He offered me a flexible schedule, including lunches and enough hours so that I wouldn't need a second job. On Wednesday I met with Barney Marker, an avuncular, fast-talking hipster from Brooklyn who asked me a number of questions, the last of which was did I think I was up to Pinter. He knew the director for a production of *The Birthday Party* coming up at the Roundabout, which had recently moved from a supermarket basement to a theater on Twenty-third Street. It was Equity, reputable, and regularly reviewed. With a pair of glasses, Barney said, I would be perfect for the part of Stanley.

I bought the glasses and a few days after that I read for the part, got a callback the next day, and by the end of the week signed up for my first substantial role in New York.

I felt great; things were definitely looking up. I wanted to tell everyone; most particularly I wanted to tell Madeleine. But I realized that I didn't even know where she lived.

I called Mindy Banks. "I don't think she wants to see you," she said, but not coldly.

"I need to talk to her," I pleaded. "I don't know what Guy told her but I'm pretty sure it was all lies. She won't return my calls. I'll have to go where she is, but I don't know where that is."

"She works at a bookstore," she said.

"I know that, but where is it?"

Mindy hesitated, consulting some code of female fealty. "It's at Columbus Circle. She works on Monday and Wednesday night. They stay open late."

"Is Guy there too?"

Again she paused.

"Mindy, I'm desperate."

"He's not there on Monday nights."

"Bless you," I said.

"Do you see Teddy?" she asked.

"Only once since I've been back."

"Have you met this Wayne character?"

"No, I don't want to. Have you?"

"I've seen him," she confided. "I went by the gallery he works in. He thought I was looking at the pictures."

"What did you think?"

"I think he's a Chinese devil."

I laughed.

"It's not funny," Mindy said. "Do me a favor and take a look for yourself. I'm so worried about Teddy it's making me sick."

A surprising number of customers were in the bookstore, scanning the tall shelves and thumbing through the volumes on the display tables. The place was vast, wall-to-wall books, various niches and corners formed by free-standing shelves and an information desk that looked like a bar at the center where two clerks, neither of them Madeleine, dispensed helpful hints to the shoppers. I had no idea how she would feel about being accosted in her workplace and I was nervous. I glanced about, pretending to read the placards over the shelves: Science, History, Chess. At a checkout counter near the door a businessman unfolded his wallet before a youthful clerk, not Madeleine, dressed in the equivalent of a dashiki. A murmur of female voices drew me into the Fiction aisle but the two women who halted their conversation at my approach were bespectacled and white-haired. I passed them with a nod and entered Poetry, an impressive collection, just in time to see the heel of a black shoe and the flare of a red skirt disappear into Religion/Philosophy. I followed; she turned again into Occult. She was carrying a book, and as I came around the corner, she stopped before a shelf and, stretching up on her toes, carefully slid the volume into place. Her hair was pulled back in an ill-contained knot. She was wearing a cerulean blue cardigan I'd never seen before that made her eyes, when she turned them upon me, glisten like captured bits of sky.

"Madeleine?" I said, tentative as a schoolboy.

Not a pause, not a moment of reserve or recrimination, no weighing of options or just deserts; she came down on her heels, her lips parting in a smile of such warmth that I moved quickly toward her, holding out my hands. "Edward," she said, stepping into my embrace, her arms circling my neck, nestling her head against my chest. My heart swelled with surprise and then pity. What on earth had we done to ourselves? I pressed my lips into her hair, that familiar spicy fragrance, and tightened my arms around her back. "I missed you so," she murmured.

A theatrical "ahem," issued from a professorial type happening upon us in his quest for an essential tome. We separated, holding hands. She didn't look pregnant, I thought, and she certainly didn't look anemic. "When do you get off?" I asked. "I'll wait for you. I've got to see you."

"It's impossible," she said. "Guy comes to meet me at eleven; that's when we close."

Guy, I thought, Guy Margate. Her husband. How was it possible? "Can you leave now for a while? Can you make some excuse?"

"I could go out for a few minutes."

"That's no good," I said. "Where can we go?"

She gazed at the professor, flagrantly fingering book spines near the end of the aisle. A sly smile played at the corners of her mouth. "Follow me," she said softly, and I did, awash with desire, past Theater, through Nonfiction, which went on and on, to a door marked DO NOT ENTER. We entered. It was a narrow dark office with a desk, a chair, and a battered leather couch. Oh, blessed couch. We made for it without a word, pulling our clothes aside, eager and abandoned, just as we were that first night under the staircase on the Jersey shore, that night when Guy Margate saved my life.

It didn't take long. Madeleine was stifling laughter near the end; she'd told me before that she found the "state" I got into amusing, which was another thing I liked about her. We gasped for a few moments, pulling ourselves apart. "God, Madeleine," I whispered.

She sat up, demurely rearranging her clothing, but I was too whacked to bother. "I'm going to go out first," she said. "You can stay here a few minutes. No one comes in here at night."

"Don't go yet," I said.

"I have to. I don't want to lose my job."

"When can I see you?"

"I don't know. It's difficult," she said. She was feeling around for her hairpins, thrusting them into her hair.

"Can't you call me? Will you just call me, so we can talk? I don't know what's going on."

"I know you don't," she said. She stood up, brushing down her skirt. "It's so dark in here."

"Will you call me?"

She guided herself to the door by clinging to the edge of the desk. "When you go out," she said, "don't look for me. You should leave the store." Carefully she opened the door a crack and peered through it. A thin shaft of light dashed across the floor

and up the opposite wall. "I'll call you," she said. Without looking back she pulled the door just wide enough to pass and slipped
away, leaving me on the couch with my pants around my ankles,
satiated, stunned, and, as usual, completely in the dark.

For two days I stayed close to the phone and checked messages
when I couldn't, but there were no calls from Madeleine. I
called her service and left a message to call me at midnight. I
figured Guy would be out walking. I got back from work at
eleven forty-five and sat next to the phone, making notes on
my Pinter script. Pinter is an actor's playwright, there's a lot of
room in those loaded exchanges, a lot of choices to make, a lot
to do or not to do. I was finding it hard to concentrate; I kept
staring at the phone, which was an old dial model, ponderous
and obtrusive. Like Pinter it had a quality of menace. At twelve
thirty it rang. "Talk to me," I said.

"Were you asleep?" she asked.

"No. I'm studying my play and I'm waiting for you to
call me."

"You didn't tell me you had a job."

I laughed. "We didn't talk, sweetheart."

"What is it? Where is it?"

"*The Birthday Party,* Stanley, the Roundabout."

"That's incredible," she said. "That's fantastic."

"It is," I agreed. "I'm excited. When can I see you?"

"That's easier said than done."

This response irritated me. "Whose fault is that?" I
snipped.

There was a long Pinteresque silence which I steadfastly refused to enter. I listened to Madeleine's breathing. Was it un-
even? She was a weeper; was she weeping?

"Yours, actually," she said calmly.

The eruption of mutual recrimination that followed went
on for some time. It was unpleasant, but some errors were
cleared up on both sides. In the midst of my lame explanation
of the compromising Connecticut pub photo, she exclaimed,
"Stop, darling, I can't talk, he's here."

"When can I see you?" I pleaded. "Where?"

"Tuesday night," she said. "At nine. I'll come to you."

"I'll be here," I promised.

"I won't have much time." The line went dead.


What was I supposed to think of Madeleine? She was a complete puzzle to me, yet I felt, as I had during those weeks when
we were pounding the streets for work, a bond of goodwill between us. She was married and pregnant and there was nothing either of us could do about that. I wasn't excited about the
prospect of a baby, to say the least, and I wasn't looking forward
to seeing her swelled up in that awful, ungainly, explosive way I
find so disturbing. It would just get worse when the creature
was out in the world, mewing, spitting, and shitting; demanding all the attention in the room. I've always known I wasn't
cut out for fatherhood. What man is? It's a service role after all,
unless one decides to take prisoners and call it family life. I
wanted none of it.

But just to demonstrate how truly perverse human nature is, Teddy, having discovered that he was not biologically inclined to perpetuate the species, was in a nesting mood. "Come by," he said in his phone message. "I'm having a drinks party. Wayne is moving in and we're celebrating. Saturday. Anytime after eight."

Within the hour Mindy called. "Go with me, Ed," she pleaded. "I can't face this by myself."

To buck ourselves up for whatever was in store for us, Mindy and I agreed to have dinner before the party. We were determined not to be early, so we met at eight in a little place she'd chosen near NYU where the food was cheap. She was looking great. She'd lost weight and she was dressed to kill. I wanted to talk about Madeleine but Mindy wanted to talk about Teddy. She feared Wayne would be the ruin of him. So far he hadn't told his family about his mad affair, but this moving in together, which was so unnecessary, was bound to get back to them. His father came to the city regularly on business. Suppose he stopped by unexpectedly and the Chinese boyfriend answered the door in his kimono.

"He could just be a friend," I suggested.

"Wait until you see him," she said.

We split a bottle of not good wine and picked at our food, comrades in rejection. When I asked how soon after my departure for Connecticut Madeleine and Guy had become an item, she was evasive. "We were both so busy, I hardly saw her all summer," she said. "And then she called to say she was getting married and needed a witness."

"Did she say it was because she was pregnant?"

Mindy chewed a lettuce leaf, considering my question. "She didn't," she said. "I thought she was in love."

"So maybe she wasn't pregnant."

"I think she must have been."

"She doesn't look pregnant," I said.

"So you've seen her."

"Briefly," I admitted. "I went to the bookstore."

"That's good," Mindy said. "You two should be friends. I know she's very fond of you."

"Fond," I said.

"She cares about you."

I finished the wine. "Let's go meet the Chinese," I said.


A party, after all, is a kind of play. There are entrances, exits, sudden outbursts of emotion, affection, or hostility, lines drawn, tales told out of school, and there's a set. Many plays contain party scenes. Chekhov is fond of having them offstage, with characters drifting in and out and shouts going up from unseen guests. The eponymous birthday party that transpires in Pinter's play is a kind of anti-party, a grim affair that includes threats, seduction, and a nervous breakdown but there is a song, a sweet love long, in the midst of the general decline. I wondered how my director would see this moment.

Which brings me to the important difference between a party in a play and a party at a friend's apartment in Manhattan: at the latter there's no director.

Teddy's party was well under way by the time we arrived; we could hear the sound of laughter and the gaggle of conversation from the hall. A young man I didn't recognize opened the door and waved us in urgently, as if he was on a boat pulling away from a dock. "Drinks in the kitchen," he instructed as we came aboard, returning his attention to a short, pale girl dressed in a tie-dyed caftan. Mindy stuck to my side as we made our way through the crowd, which was composed of small groups that yielded like amoebas to let us pass. I saw Gary Santos near a window, and Jasmine, poised beneath her brother's artwork, in heels and a tight red dress, hollering into the ear of a seriously older man. I recognized a few others as actors, but most of the guests were strangers to me. "These must be Wayne's friends," I ventured to Mindy.

"He's over there," she said, rolling her eyes stagily to my left. I looked past her shoulder and spotted Wayne without difficulty—indeed he would have stood out in any crowd.

"Good God," I said.

"Don't stare," Mindy cautioned, prodding me on.

"He looks like Genghis Khan," I whispered.

Which was true. Wayne had an amazing face, bizarrely flat with black slits for eyes and a shock of stiff black hair that stood out in all directions. A Mongol face that made the word "steppes" leap to mind. One could picture him wearing a yak-fur hat and a yak-skin coat, astride a tough little pony. Instead he wore a gray V-necked sweater that looked like cashmere over blue-and-red-plaid bell-bottom pants and loafers without socks. He was tall, slender, elegant; his hands were as delicate as a girl's. I made these observations on closer inspection. In that first glance all I saw was that he looked completely foreign, not just from another world but from another time.

In the kitchen we found Teddy setting out bite-size dumplings on a plate. The counters were freighted with trays of brightly colored snacks. He looked polished up, bright, as a painting does after it's been cleaned; his colors were refreshed. "Here you are," he said. "Come try these before they get snapped up. They're fantastic." Mindy approached him tentatively, as if she expected a rebuff, but he passed his free arm around her waist, kissed her cheek, and popped a dumpling into her mouth. "How are you, dear?" he said. "I'm glad you could come."

"Good," she replied through the dumpling.

"It's delicious, isn't it?" Teddy said. "Wayne made them. He was up all night." He raised his arm in an introductory flourish. "Chinese party food!"

"One hour later you power hungry," I quipped.

"Now, Ed," Teddy chided, "let's not have any low ethnic humor."

I poured myself a Scotch. I felt uncomfortable and defensive, as if I was waiting for an audition. "Who are these people?" I asked.

"This is the art scene," Teddy said. "They're a fascinating bunch. Painters aren't like us at all. They have these funny things called identities."

"That sounds gloomy," I said.

"It isn't very playful," he agreed. "Wayne thinks it's hilarious so of course they're all in awe of him. Have you met Wayne?"

Though this was a simple yes or no question, Mindy and I exchanged perplexed looks. "You two look lost," Teddy said. "Grab a tray; go play waiters at a party."

I threw back my Scotch, took up a tray, and led the way into the scene. Clever Teddy had assigned me a role I knew I could play to perfection. A pod of guests opened before me and I lowered my tray skillfully before them. "Will you try one of these?" I offered. A lady with a prodigious nose snatched up a shrimp toast. "And here's a napkin," I offered. Our eyes met, I read her thought—what a handsome waiter! I raised my tray and moved on. Two hirsute young men, vacantly repeating the name "Cy Twombly" at each other, paused to load their flimsy napkins with treats. I looked past them into the kitchen where Mindy and Teddy still stood face-to-face over the dumplings. He was rubbing his hands together, his eyes cast down, his mouth slightly ajar. Mindy was talking earnestly, wagging her head with the force of her argument. Teddy took up a paper napkin and passed it to her. She dabbed her eyes with it, but she didn't stop talking. Poor Mindy. Teddy had tried to help her out, but she had refused the part.

My progress led me away from the painful confrontation going forward in the kitchen to the blithe and exotic author of that suffering. Wayne was leaning against a bookcase in conversation with a large blonde who pursed her lips skeptically when it was not her turn to talk. I eased my tray between them.

"You're Edward Day, aren't you?" Wayne said.

"No," I replied. "I'm just a waiter."

He narrowed his impossibly narrow eyes at me, lifting the corners of his mouth. "That's funny," he said.

"Why is it funny?" asked the pursing lady.

"Because we didn't hire any waiters."

"What makes you think I'm this Edward person?" I asked.

"Teddy has a photo of you, at the beach house."

"Ah," I said. "The beach house."

A surge in the conversational volume near the door caught Wayne's attention. I had my back to it but I recognized a too-hearty laugh, followed by a squeal that could only be Mindy Banks in the rapture of greeting an old friend. "Now I'm confused," Wayne said. "I think that could be Edward Day too."

"They do look alike," his large friend agreed.

I pulled my tray in close to my chest and turned to see Mr. and Mrs. Margate arriving at the festivities. Guy's head, visible above the company, swiveled from left to right, taking in the scene. He had cut his hair short and was clean shaven. All I could see of Madeleine was her hair; Mindy's fond embrace blocked the rest of her. "Take this, would you?" I said to Wayne, pressing the tray upon him.

"No, no," he protested. "I don't want to be a waiter."

"Just put it down," the large woman said testily.

I took her advice, ditching the snacks on a nearby coffee table where they were instantly decimated by ravenous artists. I made for the door where Madeleine, having been released by Mindy, stood facing me. She was dressed in an off-the-shoulder blue peasant dress with a black Mexican shawl, very flattering, but what I noticed next was that she looked ill. She was what my mother called "green around the gills." Her eyes, which had been so sparkling and mischievous only a few days before, were dull and sunk in dark circles. As I approached, she hunched over abruptly, pressing both hands against her abdomen. Her eyes closed, she took in a frantic gasp of air. I reached her side.

"Jesus," I said. "What's wrong? Are you OK?"

She clutched my arm and straightened, giving me a wan smile. "I'm not sure," she said. She glanced about at the cheerful partygoers, none of whom had observed her distress. "I guess I shouldn't have come. Guy tried to talk me out of it, but I wanted to see Teddy and his friend."

"Have you been sick?"

"I was throwing up this morning, but that's not unusual. I had a terrific headache last night. Now it's gone but I'm getting these sharp pains. I don't know what it is."

I laid my palm across her forehead; it was much too warm. "I think you have a fever. You need to lie down."

"It would be good if you get me to the bathroom," she said.

"This way," I said, passing my arm around her shoulder. It was at this point that Guy desisted from ogling his potential audience and turned his attention to his wife.

"Hello, Ed," he said, encroaching upon us as we edged along the wall. "I thought you might be here."

"Madeleine's sick," I said. "She should be in bed."

"What?" he said. He squeezed himself in on her other side, bending over her so that his mouth was close to her ear, "Sweetie, are you feeling punk?" he whispered. It was so close to baby talk my hackles went up. Madeleine leaned into him and I was forced to loosen my hold on her.

"I just need to get to the bathroom," she said. This destination was nearby and fortunately empty when we arrived, cosseting Madeleine between us.

"Should I come in with you?" Guy offered as she opened the door.

"No," she said, waving him away. "I'll be fine. Just wait for me."

Guy and I stood on either side of the door, like fresh recruits in the Royal Guard, while the sounds of Madeleine retching, running water, flushing the toilet, and retching again drifted through. Word got out that a guest was vomiting in the bathroom and Teddy appeared, emanating concern. "What can I do?" he asked.

"Nothing," Guy replied with an air of sufferance. "It can't last much longer. She hasn't eaten anything all day."

"Why did you bring her?" I snarled. "You can look at her and see she's sick. She has a fever."

"I'm sure you know all about it," he said.

Another round of heaving and flushing sounds issued from the inner chamber.

"Honey," Guy addressed the door. "Can I do anything?"

We heard the sound of water running, then silence. We men looked at one another, wide-eyed and helpless. Jasmine appeared, all competence in spite of the red dress. "What's going on?" she said.

"Madeleine's sick in there," Teddy said. "We don't know what to do."

Jasmine tapped the door. "Madeleine," she said. "Do you need help?"

No answer. No sound at all.

"Is it locked?" Jasmine asked, trying the knob, which turned easily. She opened the door a crack, peered in, then, casting us a look of frank dismay, slipped inside and closed it behind her.

Wayne's large blond friend bustled up, wanting to use the facility.

"You'll have to wait," Guy informed her. "My wife is very ill."

She backed away, screwing up her mouth in her habitual moue, scrutinizing Guy and then me. "So which one of you is Edward Day?" she asked.

The bathroom door opened narrowly and Jasmine's head appeared in the gap. "Teddy," she said. "Call 911. And then bring me some towels."

This was too much for me. "I'm coming in," I said, pushing past Jasmine, who offered no resistance. She closed the door and leaned her back against it. Madeleine was slumped on the floor, propped against the cabinet, holding a blood-soaked towel between her legs. Another one, wadded and cast aside, was so saturated it had formed a thick brownish pool at the edges.

"Oh, darling," I said, kneeling next to her.

"My shoulder is killing me," she said weakly, lifting her eyes to look at me. Her face was porcelain white, unearthly, her eyes unfocused, the pupils dilated. Jasmine opened the door again and Guy, bristling with importance, charged in.

"The ambulance is on the way," he announced.

At the sight of him, Madeleine burst into sobs. The room was too small for four people so I got to my feet, making way for Guy. We brushed shoulders as he dropped to his knees beside his wife. "Oh, oh," he wailed, "the baby, the baby." Madeleine moaned, leaning into the towel with both hands. I backed away. Jasmine was wringing out a washcloth at the sink.

"Is it a miscarriage?" I asked her.

"I think it's worse than that," she replied.

The turbulent intrusion of EMTs dangling stethoscopes and unfurling a nifty stretcher is reliably the death of a party. Barks of "Stand back" and "Out" were the extent of their contribution to the festive repartee, and they didn't stop to sample the dumplings. Guy, who was still on his knees on the bathroom floor, was the object of the second command. "What is it?" he whimpered as he backed out the door. "What's happening to her?" I was standing just outside and I could see Madeleine, collapsed sideways, eerily still, her eyes glazed, the greenish tinge around her mouth definitively shifted to blue. "She's going into shock," the female of the rescue team informed us, and before you could say "hypovolemic" they had her on the stretcher and were heading for the street. "I'm her husband," Guy repeated, escorting them, like Moses, through the parting sea of wide-eyed guests. "Come with us," Ms. Medic ordered and they were out the door. A dazed group, myself among them, spilled out into the hall, clutching our drinks and watching mutely as the rescued and the rescuers disappeared into the elevator. Teddy put his arm around me. "That was awful," he said.

"Where will they take her?" I asked.

"St. Vincent's, I guess. It's the closest."

"Where is it?"

"Twelfth and Seventh Avenue."

"That's good. I can walk over."

"Maybe you should wait a little while so they can get her admitted," he advised. "They don't encourage you to visit the emergency room unless you have to, if you see what I mean."

"I see what you mean," I said. The guests filed back inside, several making straight to the kitchen for refills. The talk was about who had seen what part of what had just happened. One claimed he knew nothing until the medics burst through the door and he thought, at first, it was some kind of raid. Another had noticed an odd gathering of concerned faces near the bathroom door and concluded the toilet was overflowing. Jasmine, looking like some fetishist's fantasy, passed through the hall in her red dress and high heels hoisting a mop and a bucket full of bloody towels. "I'll put this in the closet for now," she said to Teddy. "We can deal with it later."

As his sister passed with her grisly trophy, Wayne, who was driving a corkscrew into a bottle of wine, lifted his upper lip in a sneer of disgust. "Just get it out of sight," he snapped, thereby earning my eternal enmity. The cork came free with a cheery pop. "Let's get back to the fun part," he said, nimbly dispensing the golden liquid among the glasses pressed upon him.

I set my glass in the sink. When I looked up I saw that

Teddy was watching me and that he had deciphered my feelings about his paramour. His brow was furrowed, his eyes full
and sad, his lips pressed in a thin line, as if to keep in words that
might best be reconsidered. He was a social creature to his
bones and it was important to him that his friends accepted his
new love, his new life, his new self. He looked uncomfortable
and on edge, whereas Wayne was having a fine time and appeared perfectly at ease. No good will come of it, I thought,
ducking back into the living room. Wayne's paintings now
covered most of the wall space and made the room feel dark
and cramped. The partygoers were trying to get back in the
swing of things, but it was heavy going. I picked up a dumpling
from a tray near the door on my way out.

Difficult as it is to imagine now, nobody had a computer in
those days, so finding someone in a hospital involved a lot of
phoning and consultation with charts attached to clipboards.
At length I was informed that Madeleine was on the fifth floor
and directed to an elevator which would take me to a desk
where I could make further inquiries. At this stop, a space station manned by aliens, I was told that Madeleine was in surgery. If I wished, I could proceed to the waiting room down
the hall, first right, then straight ahead. I did so wish. After a
longish stroll, past many doors opening upon scenes of human
suffering unfolding in front of televised scenes of human suffering, I came to a glass-fronted room in which Guy Margate was
pacing manically up and down.

"I don't know what's going on," he announced upon my entrance. "It's making me crazy. Do you have any cigarettes?"

I had, in fact, an unopened pack. "I'm trying to cut down," I said as I tore off the cellophane wrapper and pulled out the bit of foil.

"Now is not the time," said Guy. He produced a flip-top lighter and we lit up companionably.

"So what *do* you know?" I asked.

"She needs a blood transfusion. I picked that up from the medics. I haven't seen a doctor."

"That sounds bad."

"Have you ever ridden in an ambulance?" he asked. "It's totally weird."

"No," I said.

"It's completely weird."

"It must be," I agreed.

He puffed at his cigarette, paced to an ashtray on a couch-side table, and tapped off the ash. "What did Teddy say?"

"He said it was awful."

He charged back to the door, looking out at the empty hall. "I can't stand this," he said.

"Just keep walking," I said.

He headed for the water fountain. "You're calm. Why is that?"

"I'm not calm," I said. "I just don't find walking up and down like a caged animal helps much."

"You should try it."

I stalked to the door and back to the couches, crossing

Guy's path as he went from the fountain to the wall. "No," I said. "This doesn't work for me. I'm going to sit down and jigger my leg." Which is what I did.

"Be my guest," Guy said, moving on.

"Was she conscious?" I asked.

"No. I think they knocked her out in the ambulance."

"And they didn't say anything about what was wrong."

"They said she'd lost a lot of blood."

"I'll say," I said.

"I had to sign papers, releases, you know, about how they're not responsible if she dies. But she won't die. I'm sure she won't die."

"Don't even say that."

"You're right. That's bad luck. She's strong."

"She is."

"But she's anemic. That means not enough blood."

"It means not enough red blood cells. But there's the same amount of blood."

"So she has a normal amount of blood."

"I would think so."

He stubbed out his cigarette. "I feel helpless. That's what's making me crazy."

"Have another cigarette," I said, brandishing the pack.

"Thanks," he said. "Thanks for coming."

"Wouldn't have missed it," I said. Guy pulled out his lighter and we lit up again.

By the time the blood-stained doctor from Mars opened the door, we were down to three cigarettes. He stepped inside, rested his hands on his hips, and looked from Guy to me and back again. "Which one of you is the husband?" he inquired.

"That's me," Guy replied, whirling upon him. "For God's sake, tell me she's not going to die."

"She's not going to die," he said firmly.

Tears sprang from Guy's eyes. "Thank God," he said. "What happened to her? What did you do?"

What happened to Madeleine, the doctor explained, was an ectopic pregnancy which—Jasmine was right—is a lot worse than a miscarriage. I now know it means the fertilized embryo has lodged in the fallopian tube instead of in the uterus where it belongs, and if you are a pregnant woman and you have bleeding, abdominal pain on one side, and, for some strange reason having to do with nerves, severe pain in one shoulder, get yourself to a hospital pronto. Madeleine, our medical expert informed us, had nearly died. Sometime between her upright entrance at Teddy's party and her prostrate exit on the stretcher, the fallopian tube had burst. "Of course we had to terminate the pregnancy," the doctor explained. "It was a mess in there. The tube was destroyed, fibroids all over the place; I saved the ovaries, but I had to take the uterus. She won't be able to conceive again."

"Oh no," Guy whispered at this news. "Oh, that's terrible. Did you hear that?" he said, turning to me.

"I did," I replied.

The doctor agreed that it was too bad. But, he assured us, the surgery was successful, the patient was young and strong, and in a few weeks she would be fine. She was stable though still unconscious and Guy was welcome to sit in the room with her until she came to.

"Let's go," Guy said, breaking for the door. The doctor raised his eyebrows at me and followed the eager husband. "I'll phone you," Guy called back to me as he and the doctor disappeared down the hall.

I went back to the couch, sat down, and broke into a cold sweat.

What actors know about emotions is that they come in pairs, often in direct opposition to each other. That's what it is to be conflicted. We want what we should not want and we know it. We desire that which is dangerous or forbidden and might cause us to suffer. We fear success, embrace failure. We strive to be independent, longing at the same time to surrender to a burning passion. We hold ourselves aloof from the people we need and seek the approval of those who have no use for us.

Or at least I do. I was sweating with relief as well as anxiety, relief that Madeleine would recover and be herself again, anxiety that she would be different, that she would decide to leave me out of her life and cleave to her husband. There was an element of incredulity and anger that she might do that, for I couldn't persuade myself that she was in love with Guy. Now there would be no other reason for her to stay with him. I thought there was a possibility that she would continue to play us somehow, that we were sport to her, which made me anxious, but also relieved, because then I wouldn't be responsible for anything, for any of it. I confess that I had felt only relief at the news that she would not be able to have a child, which was enormously cruel and selfish of me, but there it is. I felt that. But I was also made anxious because I feared she would respond to her condition recklessly; it might make her bitter and angry and she might detect my indifference to the matter and hate me for it.

I took out a cigarette, examined it closely, and put it back in the pack. I recollected the shocking vision of Madeleine huddled on Teddy's bathroom floor, pressing into the mound of bloody towels between her legs, and another of her glazed eyes and blue lips as the medics descended upon her and the art scene outside yielded briefly to the life-threatening-emergency scene. It had all happened so quickly; I'd felt side-lined, a voyeur. Guy had been at the center of the action, forcefully taking his rightful place, which galled me, yet I had not wanted to be in the ambulance, was relieved to be left behind.

Marlene Webern's steady voice came to me: "There's a coldness in you."

She was right, I thought. Guy had accused me of being calm, and I had replied that I was not, which was true, I was beyond calm. He had his act down: he was nervous, erratic, abrupt, he couldn't keep still, he couldn't stop speculating about what might go wrong or right, he was frightened and hopeful by turns. When the news finally came, he was tearful. But all I had felt throughout the ordeal, and what I felt then, alone in that chilly room designed to accommodate desperate people in the throes of powerful emotions, was a generalized sadness and a humbling conviction that somehow I had been exposed and that everyone concerned now knew I was entirely unequal to my part.

———

It was a long time before I saw Madeleine again. Guy didn't call me from the hospital. Instead he called Madeleine's mother, with whom she had a difficult relationship. Madeleine, too weak to argue, agreed to go home to Cleveland.

I was absorbed in rehearsals for the Pinter and then in performances, so the only information I got about Madeleine and Guy was through conversations with Mindy. It was partly from her and partly from idle gossip, some of it in the pages of *Back Stage,* that I followed the ensuing roller-coaster ride that was Guy Margate's career.

While Madeleine was in Cleveland, Guy was offered a job as assistant stage manager and understudy to the lead in a Broadway-bound play that was going into tryouts in Philadelphia. He expressed mixed feelings about this prospect to everyone who would listen, but was eventually persuaded by Bev Arbuckle that it was a good option, as he had nothing else going and was desperate for cash. The lead, a talented actor named Marc Trilby, took a dislike to Guy from the start. Early in the rehearsals, the story went, he announced that Guy would never get a chance to play the role for an audience, not once, so he should just forget about it. In the meantime Madeleine, her health improved, frantic to get away from her mother, and determined that, as she could not have a family, she would have a career, joined her husband in Philadelphia, where she quickly landed a role in a revival of Shaw's *Heartbreak House* at a regional theater.

Guy's play opened to excellent notices. Marc Trilby was

particularly well received and the producers, buoyed by their success in the provinces, prepared to move the show to Broadway. At the end of the Philadelphia run the actors, all save Guy, were euphoric to have a hit on their hands. They arrived in town and immediately began their rehearsals on the new stage.

A few nights before the opening, Marc Trilby was having dinner with well-heeled friends in a new Italian restaurant on the Upper West Side. It was a tall, narrow building with dining rooms on two floors, the kitchen and bathrooms tucked away below street level. In its previous incarnation there was a dining room on the third floor, but in the renovation this space was consigned to storage. Late in the evening, Marc Trilby, well lubricated by alcohol and the praise of his fellows, excused himself from the table and wandered off in search of the men's room. Somehow he persuaded himself that it was up one flight instead of down two. He climbed the carpeted stairs, crossed a dimly lit landing, opened a likely-looking door, stepped into an open shaft that had once served as a dumbwaiter, fell through two floors, and landed, to the astonishment of the line chef, on a prep table in the kitchen. Both of his legs were broken in the fall.

Two nights later, Guy Margate made his Broadway debut.

The New York critics were unanimous in their contempt. The script, the direction, the acting, were variously disparaged, but one thing all agreed upon was the inadequacy of the lead, one Guy Margate, who, it was acknowledged, had leaped into the fray because of an unfortunate accident to the estimable Marc Trilby. Audiences, so warned, stayed away. In two weeks the producers were forced to admit the failure of their enterprise and the play quietly closed.

I didn't see it—it was during my Pinter run—but Mindy did and even her charitable heart could find nothing kind to say about Guy's performance. "He's just not right for the role," she concluded. "And, of course, the reviews have been so brutal he's terrified and it shows."

Did Madeleine witness her husband's humiliation upon the boards? I didn't know. I'd heard not one word from her since the night she nearly died. I didn't know how to reach her, but she knew where I was, so I concluded, not unreasonably I think, that her silence was purposeful, and that I'd lost her one more time.

# Part III

I'd like to skip ahead six years to the winter of 1982, but having
so carefully detailed the events of a short period I fear my readers will require a summary of this gap. For myself, I can do it in
two words: I worked. The Pinter was a success, my Stanley
hailed as "hilariously punchy," "as startled and startling as a deer
in the headlights" (I loved that one), and "sheer madness fueled
by paranoia and delusions of shabby grandeur." I was nomi-
nated for an award that William Hurt won. Barney had a good
strategy which kept me busy, and I was lucky—or so my friends
thought. Gradually I had to phase out my waiter's job because I
was acting too much to keep it. Not that I was making any
money. The explosion of Off and Off-Off theater in the '70s
put a lot of actors out there, but the exciting new work was often at non-Equity theaters which paid less than union wage. A
common practice was to use a pseudonym, wrapping, in effect,
an actor who wasn't in the union around an actor who was.
Mine was Dale Edwards, not terribly original, I admit, but I've
never wanted to get too far from myself. It was a heady but
discouraging time; I was in a production with an elaborate
$20,000 set where the actors were paid literally nothing but the

honor of working with that scenery. Another short run in a tiny midtown theater paid $50 a week. At the Roundabout, when the paychecks arrived, the techies put down their hammers and saws, left the lights on, and marched off to the bank in a herd, because they knew if they waited until the following morning, the checks would bounce. Many fine actors, reduced to doing commercials, driving cabs, or juggling temp jobs, gave up and went to California. Some tied themselves to regional companies where they had job security of a sort. My way was slow, but it was steady. I was single and parsimonious, and my apartment was rent-controlled. Others had it a lot harder. Al Pacino, famously, slept on the stage in a ratty theater on the Lower East Side.

I saw Teddy rarely, usually backstage, because, stalwart friend that he was, he attended every play I was in, no matter how small the part or tattered the venue. Wayne was never along. As it turned out, Wayne had no interest in theater, but Teddy maintained this didn't affect the amatory bliss of their cohabitation. What did put a strain on it was, as everyone had predicted, Teddy's father, who had gotten wind of his son's attachment and recalled him to the family manse for a serious talk. "He told me he'd always known I would disgrace the family," Teddy confided, "but he said he was impressed by the originality of my failure, and how many parts it had to it: first the acting thing, which was pathetic, then the homosexual thing, which was disgusting, and then the Chinese thing, which was so appalling he didn't want to speak of it."

"Did he cut you off?" I asked.

"We're in a standoff," Teddy explained. "It's all very Oscar

Wildesville, except Wayne has no fortune to lose. The pater has agreed to continue my allowance for the meantime. It actually comes from my grandfather's estate so he would have to make an effort to hold it back and I could conceivably sue and win."

"You've consulted a lawyer?"

"Wayne did," Teddy said. "I can't be bothered, frankly."

I considered the implications of this last revelation to be of the worst sort possible.

Back to the deep freeze of December 1982. An actor was in the White House and all was right with the world. I had auditioned for the part of Jean, the valet in Strindberg's *Miss Julie*, which was being revived at a now extinct theater in the East Village. It's a delicious role, full of menace, subtle seduction, and all manner of imposture. Jean is a valet who takes total control of his vivacious and temperamental mistress; in the end she is so completely under his spell that he persuades her to kill herself. The theater was Equity and with good reviews might support an extended run. I read for the callback with a beautiful actress, Sylvia Brent, who went on to have a career in a long-running soap opera, a fate she didn't deserve. She wasn't brilliant, it can't be denied, and I could tell she was nervous, so I played into her insecurity and we came off strongly. I got the part, she didn't.

We opened in icy January to good notices and receptive audiences, all pleased to be warm for a few hours in a darkened theater while class warfare played out convincingly on the stage before them. Our six-week run was extended an extra two, though it was clear that we wouldn't be sustainable beyond that, the Strindberg ceiling being understandably low. One dark Sunday afternoon in February, when the streets were glazed with ice and the wind was rattling the windows so forcefully one expected to see Catherine Earnshaw peering in looking for Heathcliff, I was in the dressing room after the show, dreading the gauntlet to the subway. We'd played to a diminished audience of committed Strindberg enthusiasts and stalwarts from the sticks. *Miss Julie* is a three-person piece, just the valet, Jean; his mistress, the eponymous Julie; and the kitchen maid, Kirstin, who may or may not be Jean's fiancée. Our trio shared a comfortable, old-fashioned dressing room/ greenroom with a mirrored counter, a screen, a couch that sometimes served as a stage prop, a coffee table, a sink, and an impressive British-style electric kettle. The ladies had gone, having agreed to share a cab, as they both lived midtown. Feeling mildly depressed by the low turnout, I had prepared myself a mug of tea and settled on the couch. The play was in its last week and I was, as always, uncertain about what I would do next. I knew what I wanted to do, however, and I was on the very cusp of doing it. I had an audition for the part of Astrov in a new production of *Uncle Vanya* scheduled at the Public Theater, a part I wanted more than I cared to let myself know. The casting director had seen both my Stanley and my Jean. She had called Barney and invited me to audition, so my hopes were perilously high.

To appear at the Public Theater in a Chekhov play would qualify as an enormous coup, but it was also a dangerous gamble. One could still be flayed alive by the critics, but it would never be the fault of the play—one would have failed to come up to the standard of an acknowledged genius.

I was reading, for the hundredth time, Astrov's prophetic speech about the deforestation of the district, and his despair of saving the natural habitat that once flourished and provided food and shade and spiritual sustenance for the peasants who, deluded by the siren call of progress, relentlessly cut down trees and cleared land. In two of Chekhov's plays, *The Cherry Orchard* and *Uncle Vanya,* the fate of trees is of nearly as much interest as the fate of the characters. *The Cherry Orchard* ends with the clanging of the ax, and the audience experiences this sound as dread.

There came a light rapping at the dressing-room door; nothing like an ax, but startling nonetheless. At first I thought it was the wind, effecting some structural creaking—the theater was old and full of complaints—but then it came again, a light drumming as of fingernails against the wood. "Come in," I said.

At this point I hardly need tell you the name of the actor who entered the scene. But I will remind you that I hadn't seen Guy Margate in six years, so, though you may be feeling very smug, I was taken completely by surprise. Guy, as was his habit, came on in medias res.

"I've got to hand it to you," he said, "when it comes to playing the brute with women, you're totally credible."

I closed my script and laid it on the coffee table. "Guy," I said. "I can hardly believe it. I thought you were in Philadelphia."

He stepped into the light, taking in the furnishings with his ever critical eye. "Isn't this cozy," he said. "You could practically live in here."

"It is," I said. "Have a seat. I can offer you a cup of tea."

"That would be fine," he said. I got up to tend the kettle while he stood there awkwardly, trying to decide whether to sit on the couch or pull up a stool from the counter.

"What brings you to town?" I asked.

"We're transitioning back to the city. Philly's just not what Maddie needs at this point. She has an important audition that could make the difference. She was too nervous to come alone, so I came with her."

"Black or herbal?" I asked.

"Black," he said.

As I busied myself with the tea, I sneaked brief glimpses at my unexpected guest. He'd gone through a fairly marked physical transformation. There was less of everything, less hair, less weight, less color. He looked as though he'd been laundered once too often. His eyes were odd—they bulged in a way I didn't remember—and his lips were dry and chapped. He was clean shaven, his hair was short, the hollows in his cheeks were deep, and there were two grooves, like quotation marks, between his brows. He looked older than me, and I wondered if he actually was. He wore a heavy green wool coat, too wide in the shoulders, too long at the sleeves. "Take your coat off," I suggested.

He shrugged off the garment, glancing about for a place to put it.

"There's a hook on that screen," I said.

"It's bitter out there," he said, hanging up the coat. He'd developed a slight stoop, as well as a corrective habit of lifting his shoulders and rolling them back and down.

"How did you know I was here?" I asked.

"Teddy told us. We saw him last night."

"But Madeleine didn't come with you."

"She's off with Mindy somewhere."

"Did she know you were coming to my show?" The water was bubbling and I handed him a stained mug with a tea bag in it, which he looked into ruefully. "It's just tea stains," I said.

"No. She doesn't know I'm here," he said. He held out his cup. As I filled it with boiling water, the old familiar distrust and physical revulsion was aroused in me, sharp and pungent as a scent, and I drew away from him.

"How is she?" I asked.

Guy pulled out a stool and propped himself upon it, letting his long legs splay apart and cradling the warm mug between his hands. His pants legs hiked up over the top of his well-worn boots. Horrific argyle socks clung to his thin shanks. I looked away. "She's good," he said. "Well, you know Maddie, she's good and she's not good."

"You call her Maddie."

"She doesn't mind. She likes it, actually. You were wrong about that."

"So what's not good?"

"Her nerves. She's working a lot. Her career is really taking off. In fact, I've pretty much had to put my own on hold because even though she's working, she's not making much

money, of course, she's an actress, and we have to live somewhere and we have to eat and someone has to put food in front
of her or she won't eat."

"So you've got a day job."

"At a bookstore. I've been there a few years. I'm a manager
now."

I didn't entirely buy this tale of husbandly self-sacrifice.
Rumor had it that after the Broadway disaster Guy had tried
out for a lot of roles in New York and Philadelphia but no one
had any use for him. There was a particularly cruel bit of gossip, put out by an actor who should have known better, that a
playwright impressed by Guy's audition was warned by the director, "Forget it. What you just saw is all you're ever going
to get."

This vicious tidbit came to mind as I watched Guy sipping
his tea. "Well, that's good," I said.

He swallowed, craning his neck and doing the thing with
his shoulders. "Really," he said. "What's good about it?"

"Well, that you're a manager."

"I'm killing myself," he said. "Managers don't get overtime
and work twice as many hours. It's a trap."

"I didn't know that."

"I have to do everything, the shopping, the cooking, pay
all the bills, keep Maddie calmed down. I never sleep."

I recalled the arduous business of keeping Madeleine
calmed down. "But her career is taking off."

"Regional stuff, but solid roles. Shakespeare, she did Desdemona last year. Rave reviews. She went up to Yale this fall

and did a new play. There was a write-up in the *Times*; you probably saw it."

"No," I admitted. "I missed it."

"He said the play was a bomb but Maddie was a star."

Every time he called Madeleine "Maddie" I flinched and he noticed it. I had the sense that he was doing it on purpose to irritate me. I imagined how persistent he must have been to wear her down to the point where she accepted this diminutive, because I knew she hated it.

Guy sipped his tea, watching me over the rim. What was he up to? What did he want from me? Was it money?

"You've been doing OK, I hear," he said.

Money, I thought. "I've been working. I don't get paid much, but I scrape by."

He took this in without comment. I pulled out a stool and sat facing him. "So, what's the audition?"

He rubbed his chin between his thumb and forefinger, pulling the flesh in to a wedge. "Bev thinks it could be the turning point for her," he said. "I do too. She's got a good shot at it. The director saw her at the Yale thing and liked what he saw."

"What's the part?"

"It's Elena in *Uncle Vanya*. A new production at the Public."

"Wow," I said.

"She would be fantastic in that part."

"She would indeed," I agreed. My heart rate increased to keep up with my careening brain. Madeleine as Elena, me as

Astrov, it would be a triumph of casting. The electricity would dim the houselights. The play depends on the audience's apprehension of the intense physical attraction between these two characters. Elena is a difficult role. She's a prisoner of her own beauty, she has no ambition, no life force, but she drives everyone around her to the limit of endurance. Psychologically she's opaque and she's made a decision no one can understand; she's married an old man and not a rich old man, either. Madeleine had just the right quality of unexamined stubbornness. The role would be a natural fit for her. And she was so lovely and she was so hot. As I sat there, with Guy's eyes probing me, I was filled with such a physical craving to see her, to be with her, that I got up, pretending I needed to refresh my tea. Other anxieties crowded in, one of which was the copy of the script I'd left on the coffee table. I didn't want Guy to see it. I didn't want him to know. When my back was to him, I shot a glance at the table. Yes, there it was and I had laid it facedown.

"It's a great play. A difficult play," Guy observed.

"Chekhov is always a challenge," I said, pouring water into my mug. Why should I tell him? After all, I might not get the part. A piquant moment of silence passed between us.

"I know you have an audition for Astrov," Guy said.

So that was it.

"Who told you?"

"A little bird." He said this slowly, mocking me.

"Teddy?" But I knew I hadn't told Teddy. I hadn't told anyone.

"I don't have to say."

"Well, it's true," I said. "So what."

"So I don't think it's a good idea."

"I'll certainly take that into account," I said.

"I think you should," he said, giving me a meaningful look.

"OK, I'll bite," I said. "Why is it not a good idea?"

"Maddie's feelings about you are complicated," he said. "Now is not the time for her to be forced to . . . explore all that. There's too much at stake for her in this project and she's going to need all her concentration to get through it."

"Bulletin, Guy," I said. "Madeleine is an actress. She's a professional. And so am I. That's what we do."

"You like to talk to me as if I don't know anything about acting," he said. "You've always done that. I may not be working right now, but I'm an actor."

"Then act like one," I said. "Or better yet, act like a man."

"I'm acting like a husband," he replied. "And one who cherishes his wife. You haven't given Maddie a second thought for six years, but I've spent every minute of that time taking care of her. She's a talented, brilliant actress, there's nothing she can't do, but she's fragile, she's a fragile woman."

Everything about this eruption of drivel offended me, but particularly egregious was the assertion that I'd given no thought to Madeleine over the intervening years. I thought of her all the time. I was like the guy in the Dylan song, I'd seen a lot of women, but Madeleine never left my mind. I felt I knew her better than Guy, and I was sure she saw right through his absurd posturing which was designed to disguise the obvious fact that she could act circles around him. At that moment I felt Guy's presence in my dressing room was an outrage against her. What would she say if she could see him, suited up as Guy the

Protector, with his bulging eyes and his ultra-earnest manner? I rapped my mug down sharply against the counter. "My God," I said, "she must be sick of you."

This surprised him. "That's not true," he said. "Maddie loves me."

"You're so fucking insensitive you call her by a babified name she hates and you tell yourself she likes it."

"You know nothing about it," he countered. "You've never had a loving relationship with anyone. All you think about is yourself; you can't be relied upon for anything, and believe me, no one knows that better than Maddie."

"What are you talking about?"

"Don't pretend you care about her. You used her when it was convenient, and when it wasn't, you couldn't be bothered."

"Did she say that?"

"She doesn't have to say it. I was there."

"That's right," I said. "You were there and that's why I never got a chance to do anything. You took over, that's what you do. You butt in where no one wants you and you take over. That's what you're doing right now. If Madeleine knew you were here, she'd be totally humiliated."

He blinked at me as if he couldn't focus, rolling his shoulders up and back. "So you insist on doing the audition," he said.

"Relax," I said. "I might not get the part. Or she might not. You've got odds, if you can figure out what they are."

"I think I have a fair idea of what the odds are," he said.

A heavy odds-calculating silence fell between us. Guy got

up, slid his mug onto the counter, and sat down again. I ambled over to the couch where, just to irritate him, I picked up the bright-yellow script and stood solemnly leafing through it. I was a bit young to play Astrov, the only thing I had against me. Astrov is thirty-seven. He fears his life is over, he's lost his looks. I'd have to feel forty. Madeleine was actually a little old to play Elena, but I didn't think that would be a problem, not with her slim figure and flashing eyes. Of course I hadn't seen her in six years, in which time her husband had lost half his hair. Guy sat pressing his fingertips to his eyes, rubbing hard. "I'm just exhausted," he said.

"Why don't you take sleeping pills?"

"I do, but they don't work for me." He dropped his hands to his lap and took in a long, slow breath, such as one takes before the commencement of a disagreeable task, a breath in which I sensed the drawing out of a tide between us. He exhaled through his nose, pressing his lips together and meeting my eyes coldly. "I should have let you drown," he said.

Here it comes, I thought. "I didn't ask you to save me," I said, which was a stupid thing to say. Guy pounced on it. He flashed his predator smile and then he did something profoundly unnerving: he flung his arms into the air and cried out in my voice, "Help, help, don't leave me."

It wasn't just my voice, it was my inflection, my manner, my peculiar combination of actuated facial muscles, my eyes wide with terror, my mouth trembling with fatigue, it was me, drowning, but only for a moment, and then it was Guy again, chuckling at his own cleverness.

"Very funny," I said.

"Very funny," he echoed. It was eerily like looking in a mirror.

"So you think you should have let me drown, but you didn't. What should I do, kill myself?"

"I'm not asking you to kill yourself."

"Not yet."

"Though in some cultures I do have that right."

"You've been doing research."

"I have. In the Eastern view, I'm responsible for you. Because I saved your life, I'm required to look out for you. But here in the West, you owe me your life. Basically, you belong to me."

"Any place where it's just a happy accident not necessitating a further relationship?"

"You'd like that, wouldn't you?"

"I think a case can be made for it."

He looked thoughtful. "I'm afraid not. It's universally understood that our relationship is special. It's mythic, actually. You were supposed to die that night, you were a goner, and I had to rob death to save you. At some personal risk, I might add, though you seem to discount that for obvious reasons."

"I don't discount it," I said quietly. He'd brought it all back with his cruel impression of me and his talk of robbing death. I remembered how I had struggled with him in the water, how certain I was that death had a grip on me and there was no escape, yet how desperate I was to be saved. I had no lucid thoughts, only terror and a belligerent conviction that I was too young, too vital, that it was unfair. How could death be indifferent to the injustice of it? And not just indifferent, but avid, pulling me down again and again, gagging me with gallons of water, wearing my will down to a fine thread of naked resolve. It was just at the moment when that thread snapped, when the waters closed silently over my head and I gave in to my fate, that Guy thudded into me in the darkness, his arms tightening around me, lifting me, while I squirmed and sputtered, dragging me back into the world.

"This seems like such a silly demand," I said. "It doesn't have enough gravity. I mean, it's serious, I really want to do this audition, but why would you insist on something so . . . I don't know, so personal? It doesn't seem fair."

Guy emitted a series of breathy clicks through his nose which I took to be laughter.

"This doesn't have anything to do with Madeleine, does it?" I asked. "That was just a cover."

"It was a test," he said. "And you failed."

"So if I back out of the audition because I think it's best for Madeleine, I pass the test, but since I failed the test, I have to give up the audition because you saved my life."

"I couldn't have put it better myself."

"It's crazy," I said.

He stood up, shaking down his pants legs over the appalling socks. "I know you got good reviews for this Strindberg thing," he said. "But I just don't get it. You're way off, there's no subtlety, it's a totally wooden performance. Everybody says you're up and coming, but Astrov is a complex role. It's not like this nasty valet thing. You're not ready for it; that's what I'm worried about. And Ed, you don't want to flop at the Public in an important role, take my word for that. It could be the end of your career."

"Jesus, Guy," I exclaimed. "Where are you from? It's hell, isn't it? It really is hell."

He wrested his coat from the hook, wrapped himself inside it, and fussily fastening every button, turned on me a sympathetic smile. "You're hysterical because you know I'm right. Think about that." He ambled to the door. "I've got to meet Maddie," he said. "Thanks for the tea."

"Wow," Teddy said. "He really worked you over."

This was true. I felt bruised by the latest scene with Guy and I'd run to Teddy for moral support. "Did Madeleine seem like a crazy person to you?" I asked.

"It's hard to say. She's a good actress. Now that I think about it, she didn't talk much. Maybe she was a little tense. Guy went on and on about the audition. He was more excited than she was."

"Did you talk about me?"

"I did. I told them about the Strindberg. But I didn't know about this audition. Why didn't you call me?"

"I didn't call anyone. I'm superstitious about this one, it feels big. I'm almost afraid to talk to myself about it."

"How did Guy find out?"

"That's what I'd like to know," I said. "Jesus, what am I going to do? I'm wrecked now. I'm completely unsure of myself."

"You're seriously thinking of backing out?"

"Barney will murder me."

"Is it because of what Guy said about Madeleine, or what he said about your acting? Or the other thing?"

"The debt?"

"The debt," Teddy said.

"Do you think he has the right to ask me to do this?"

"He wasn't exactly asking."

"That's true. He never asks. He doesn't think he has to."

Teddy said nothing, gazing into his Scotch, letting me work it out for myself.

"Is there some kind of cosmic thing that will backfire on me and ruin my career if I defy Guy Margate?"

Teddy dug into the ice bucket on the table and added a few cubes to his glass. The spirit of Wayne hung over the room; every inch of wall space was covered with his paintings. We were munching Chinese rice crackers. All agreed, it was impressive that Teddy and Wayne had stayed together so long, though Mindy maintained their longevity was the result of Teddy's willingness to support Wayne in a style to which he had quickly become accustomed. I thought it had more to do with Wayne being exotic, the lure of the East and all that distantly smiling serenity. I recalled Guy's description of the Eastern view, that because he had saved me, he was obligated to look after me. Was it possible that in his mixed-up brain he thought that was what he was doing? "Do you think he's trying to save me from myself?" I said.

"When's the audition?" Teddy said.

"Thursday."

He rubbed his cheek with the palm of his hand, ruminating upon my case.

"There's no guarantee I'll get the part," I said. "Especially now, since I'm going to be completely conflicted about it."

"I can't tell you what to do," Teddy said.

"I know."

"But I can tell you that what Guy said about your acting isn't true. You're a gifted actor; everyone knows it."

"Thanks."

"I envy you. So does Guy. That's what this is about."

I nodded, stuck for something to say. Teddy had left Stella Adler years ago and gone to Meisner for a while, then he tried Uta Hagen and then Julie Bovasso; he was a connoisseur of acting teachers, evidently unwilling to give up being a student. His performances were in showcases and rare at that. I'd seen him a few times over the years, always in small parts that he made the best of, but there was something inhibited about his work. I recalled how certain he'd been at the dawn of Wayne that the acknowledgment of his sexual identity would have a liberating effect on his acting, but that hadn't happened. If anything he was less confident, more tentative. Wayne's complete indifference to what was, after all, Teddy's art didn't help. Before Wayne, his friends were all actors, comrades-in-arms; now he spent his time at gallery openings, where painters sniped at one another, or at gay bars where one's professional aspirations were not the subject. He stayed in acting classes because it was the only way he could still fancy himself an actor.

"I've been lucky," I said.

"You have in some ways," Teddy agreed. "Though not in love."

"I'd sure like to see Madeleine," I said.

"Best wait until this audition thing is behind you both."

"That's true," I agreed. "I don't want to muck up her chances. How does she look?"

"She's more beautiful than ever," Teddy said.

"How could she have married that guy?"

"Guy," Teddy said. We smirked.

"He looks terrible," I said. "What's with his eyes? Is he on drugs?"

"He's on desperation," Teddy said.

"It's so unfair," I said. "If I had to drown, I don't see why someone decent couldn't have saved me. Why couldn't *you* have saved me? I wouldn't mind owing you my life for a second."

Teddy's expression was wistful. "I can't swim," he said.


I left Teddy in a mood as black and bitter as the frigid streets I walked through. I had to make a decision but I didn't want to think about it: I knew thinking wasn't going to help. Guy had attacked on three emotional fronts: my feelings for Madeleine, my personal sense of obligation to him for saving my life, and my insecurity as an actor. I might rationally decide that I would or would not undertake the audition, but emotionally I was a shambles.

It wasn't late, but the streets were quiet. A taxi whooshed by, ferrying a lone, pale citizen swathed in fur. A few pedestrians hurried from building to building, paddling the air with their bulky arms, simultaneously urged to speed by the cold and to caution by the ice. The Village was just entering the long period of gentrification which would not end until all but the most litigious of its residents were driven to points east and south. My building, which had so far escaped even a cosmetic coat of paint, huddled before me, the shabbiest on the block. The windows were dark, save the third-floor front, where an impoverished novelist, who would later enjoy a small but respectable following, scribbled into the wee hours of morning. I grasped the stair rail with my gloved hand and mounted the sticky, salt-strewn steps to the front door. Like most New York apartments, mine was overheated, and I was looking forward to the blast of warm air that would greet me after the long haul to the fourth floor. Somewhere between the first and second landing a memory eluded the thought police and burst into the full sensory-surround screen of my consciousness. It was Madeleine leaning into me on this staircase, her arm wrapped around my back, her hand resting on my shoulder, her eyes and lips raised to mine, that night after we'd come back from the Jersey shore, when I'd outwaited and outwitted Guy at the bar. How long ago that was; it seemed another world, though the truth I didn't know then was that I hadn't changed at all. I would change later.

As I trudged ever upward with this ghost of Madeleine clinging to my side, regret and anger percolated in my gut, while fatigue closed down various circuits in my brain. I flipped the locks on the apartment door and headed straight for bed. Madeleine was everywhere I looked, but especially behind my eyelids. As I drifted into sleep I heard her voice guiding me. "This way, Edward. This way." I thought about the scene at the bookstore, that night before the last night I'd seen her. "You shocking girl," I said, feeling pleased with myself. I knew I would dream of her and I did.

This was my dream. It was so odd that in the morning I wrote it down, so the details are exact. Madeleine and I entered a bedroom that looked a bit like a stage set. The furniture was oversized and crowded together; there were two doors, stage right and left, and upstage a heavy maroon curtain covered the entire wall. The bed was unmade, the sheets rumpled, a wadded quilt, resembling a dead body, hung over the foot. Madeleine turned to me and we kissed. I was eager to get her into the bed, but enjoying the deep openmouthed kiss too much to break it off. At length she pulled away and said, "Are you hungry?"

I knew then that I was famished. "Yes," I said. She stepped behind the curtain, reappearing almost at once with a plate of roast turkey balanced on one open hand, a knife, fork, and white napkin in the other. All this she arranged on the dressing table, motioning me to take a seat on the poufy stool in front of it. "I have to get ready for bed," she said. "Eat this and I'll be right back."

I settled down to the repast. Dream efficiency supplied a glass of cold white wine. As Madeleine went off behind the curtain, I took up the knife and fork and began to eat. The turkey was superb; I was certain I'd never had better. It was tender and moist, warm and flavorful. It's not easy to cook turkey this well, I thought. It's usually dry and stringy, like chewing a wrung-out mop, but this meat fairly melted in my mouth. Sleeping or waking, I know I've never come across a better bird.

As these cheerful observations passed through my brain, and the turkey disappeared down my gullet, I heard a shuffling outside the stage-right door. I put down my cutlery and stared at the door's reflection in the mirror of the dresser, moved by a dim premonition of what was about to happen. Abruptly the door flew open and Guy Margate stepped in. "What?" he exclaimed, observing me on my pouf. "You here?" Our eyes barely crossed in the mirror. He went to the bed, pulled his sweater off and tossed it on the floor. Then he did the same with his T-shirt, belt, pants, socks, and underpants. I watched him in the mirror as I finished the remains of the turkey. It made me uncomfortable, especially the girlish grin he sent me as he stripped off his underwear and dropped them, with a flourish, onto the pile, but I wasn't going to give him the satisfaction of ruining my meal. Naked, he fell to rearranging the pillows, straightening the sheets, shaking out the quilt. Then he slipped under the covers and turned his back to me.

I drained my wineglass. I could hear Madeleine behind the curtain, running water, brushing her teeth. "I'll be right there, darling," she said. Guy didn't move. The curtain rustled and she appeared, dressed in a scrumptious negligee, her hair falling loosely over her bare shoulders. She passed me without speaking and climbed into the bed, scooting close to Guy and press-

ing her lips against the nape of his neck, his back. "Darling,"
she said.

She thinks he's me, I thought.

Guy flipped over like a fish tossed on a dock, kicking off
the quilt. Madeleine screamed. She jumped up on her hands
and knees and crawled to the side of the bed. At last she saw
me, my back was to her, and I watched her in the mirror as she
swung her legs over the edge, covered her face with her hands,
and burst into sobs. Guy, very still now, eyed her coldly. It
struck me as funny; I don't know why. I laughed and Guy
laughed. We laughed together at poor Madeleine, who wept
inconsolably. I woke up.

What a ridiculous dream. I didn't even get to have sex
with Madeleine; all I'd managed was a kiss. And why the
turkey? What was the significance of the turkey?

I don't put much credit in dreams, but Madeleine always
did. When we lived together she liked to hear my dreams and
to speculate about the meaning of their random components. I
have such odd ones—sometimes they're more like stories and
I'm not even in them. Madeleine had a book she'd picked up
somewhere, a dictionary of dream symbols, which gave the an-
cient prophetic interpretations of an astonishing array of terms.
Once I'd had a dream in which I struggled with an enormous
piece of tree bark. "Tree bark," Madeleine read. "A danger-go-
slow warning in regard to the opposite sex." We both shouted
with laughter, for it was the night after she'd moved her records
and books into my apartment. "Too late," she said. "Poor Edward, it's too late to go slow now."

Another night I'd spent my dream time trying to warm myself by a cold radiator. "Remorse over an alienated friend is signified in a dream of a cold radiator."

"What could the ancients possibly have known about radiators?" I scoffed.

"The Romans had hot water," she correctly observed. "They had steam heat."

Thus my memory of Madeleine on the stair provoked a foolish dream and now the dream led me to recollections of daily life with Madeleine. I sat up in the bed and regarded my impressive erection. The erotically charged atmosphere of the dream had not yet dissipated: the kiss, then the turkey, then Guy's surprise entrance. He'd taken my place in the bed, but it didn't do him any good because it was me Madeleine wanted. The sight of him made her scream.

To act or not to act; that was the question.

My eyes fell on the Chekhov script I'd left atop my clothes piled on the floor. *You're a sly one,* Astrov says to Elena, when she quizzes him about his feelings for poor, plain Sonya. *You beautiful, fluffy little weasel . . . you must have victims.* I picked up the script and turned to that confrontation. Was it *"you* beautiful weasel" or *"a* beautiful weasel"? It was *a.* At the end of the speech Astrov folds his arms, bows his head. *I submit,* he says. *Here I am, devour me!* It's a declaration rich with irony, he's teasing her, but it's not entirely a jest. Astrov is a sensible man, a doctor, and a botanist; he cares about what future generations will think of his generation. He has little hope that the destruction of the local environment can be stopped, but he has to try, so he plants trees. His attraction to Elena, a lazy, selfish, desperate, beautiful siren who enchants him from the first moment he sees her, is serious. He knows this passion could be the wreck of him, yet he can't resist it.

I put down the script and stood up, thinking of myself as Astrov and Madeleine as Elena. How would she play her response to my plea to be devoured? Her line is simple: *You are out of your mind!* Does she believe that? It would depend on what I gave her. I crossed my arms and announced to the dresser: "I submit, here I am." I dropped to my knees, opening my arms, offering my naked plea: "Devour me!"

Then I got up, felt around for my slippers, and padded off to the bathroom. "Elena, you vixen," I shouted. "Your Astrov is coming to save you."

That was how I reached my decision—lightly. Playfully, as an actor, not as a friend of one or a lover of the other, not in defiance or in anger, but as one who is offered a prize and reaches out to take it. The audition was the following afternoon. I had purchased a bottle of dye to add silver at my temples and a tin of shadow to darken the light creases under my eyes. As I applied it, I thought of how much older Guy appeared than me; his looks, like Astrov's, were ruined. I raised my eyebrows to bug my eyes out like his, but that wasn't right. Astrov was exhausted, not tense. I recalled the stoop of Guy's shoulders, his tic of correcting it. I'm tall; I carry my shoulders back and low. I practiced at the mirror, trying out various degrees of slouch. I discovered it wasn't only at the shoulders; it started at the diaphragm. The belly was slack. I stepped back from the mirror to get a longer view. Years, I thought with satisfaction. It added years.

I read with the stage manager, a compact middle-aged matron who fed me my lines crisply, like sugared wafers. The director asked me a few personal questions. I was lucid and friendly, like Astrov, ironic and curious about the world around me. I got the callback the next morning. This time I read with Rory Behenny, a fine actor who had just finished a successful run at the fledgling Brooklyn Academy of Music. Rory was the reason our director had decided to take on the play. We did the scene in which Astrov and Vanya argue about a missing bottle of morphine. Vanya is suicidal; Astrov scoffs at him. Rory was like a quick fox, daring me to catch him. We had a lively skirmish and at the end our little audience of professionals gave us a lusty round of applause.

Barney called me the next morning, sounding glum. "Well," he said, "they've cast the Chekhov."

"And?" I said.

There was a pause, but I didn't hang on it; I was that confident.

"Rehearsals start Monday," he said.


Yesterday, as I was cleaning out the attic of our house, I came across a box of Madeleine's books. It had been hastily packed for the move from Philadelphia to New York, unpacked in the East Village apartment where Guy and Madeleine briefly lived, then packed again, by me this time, and shipped to Connecticut. At first I imagined that Madeleine might ask for her books, but it soon became clear that she was unlikely to do that, so the box became a disheartening reminder of all that I had

lost, and I stowed it away. It wasn't a large box. It occurred
to me that there might be something in it of use in composing
this memoir; at least it would refresh my memory of what
Madeleine was like then, what she chose to take with her on
what was to be a harrowing trip to oblivion. I brought the
box to my crowded study under the eaves and cut the tape with
a utility knife. One by one I unpacked the books. A dictionary,
a Bartlett's quotations, a complete Shakespeare, a complete
Chekhov, three plays by Ibsen, a stack of the bright-yellow
scripts Madeleine had collected for auditions, or just because
she was curious about something new and a script was cheaper
than a ticket. Stanislavski's *An Actor Prepares,* several nineteenth-
century novels, Hardy, Eliot, *Middlemarch*—she loved *Middlemarch.* Shurtleff's *Audition*—every actor had that one then and
I've noticed it's still in print. The collected poems of Yeats and
Blake, and, of course, the *Dreamer's Dictionary.* Serendipity! I'd
just been writing about it. I took it up and flipped through it
gingerly, with the creepy sensation that someone was watching
me. A musty odor arose from the pages, long cooped up and
eager to interpret those vagrant dreams. All right, all right, I
thought. What have you got for turkey?

Honestly, I didn't expect to find anything; turkey is a New
World bird, after all, but there it was, a longish entry between
"tunnel" (an obstacle dream) and "turnip: see vegetable(s)." For
all you dreamers of poultry, here's the entire scoop on the gob-
bler that was beat out by the eagle for the role of our national
bird. If you see a strutting turkey in your dream it portends a
period of confusion; a flock of turkeys predicts public honors; if
you kill a turkey, expect a stroke of good luck; if you cook,

dress, and serve the bird, you'll enjoy a period of prosperity. However, if you do what I all unknowing did, if you eat the turkey, "you are likely to make a serious error of judgment, so be very careful regarding any important matters which may be pending."

I snapped the book closed and dropped it back into the box.

I admit, as prophecy, the turkey dream isn't exactly Birnam wood, but as I piled the other books back on top of the malevolent dictionary, I had a sense of my fate having ambushed me with a spitefulness I could never have anticipated.

Not much happens at a first rehearsal, but the atmosphere is fraught with tension. The action largely consists of what un-clever people call a meet and greet, followed by a reading of the play. Our *Vanya* cast assembled at a rehearsal stage at the Public Theater, a large room with low ceilings, bare white walls, and a polished wooden floor. A few straight-backed chairs were scattered around, an upright piano loomed in one corner. There was a side table set up with coffee urn and pastry tray, and, at the center, a long rectangular table on metal trestles with ten green plastic chairs drawn up to it, the setting for our first run at Anton Pavlovich Chekhov.

Repertory actors have an easy time; they're like a team of draft horses accustomed to pulling heavy loads in tandem. They just want someone to point out the road and off they go. They may even genuinely like one another. But a cast of actors cho-sen through auditions are more like chickens in a coop, each actor strutting the length and breadth of the limited territory, secretly terrified yet determined to appear nonchalant. We have our parts; that's not the problem. It's the pecking order that needs establishing and that's going to be up to that big, mysterious rooster, the director, who grins and grins as we come in one by one, his eyes like black beads in which we see ourselves reflected in ludicrous miniature. A consistent first-rehearsal behavior I've observed over the years is this: if there is a window in the room, within fifteen minutes of arrival every actor will meander to it and stand looking wistfully out.

I arrived in turmoil. I knew it was going to be impossible for me to concentrate on anything but Madeleine, and I was vexed that this public setting was to be the scene of our first meeting in so many years. I had hoped that she would call me, that we might even manage a brief meeting, but no such luck. Now I would be forced to make lighthearted, self-aggrandizing chatter with my fellow actors and pretend I was, like them, absorbed in the business of the first read, when all I really wanted was to get Madeleine alone and talk to her. Seriously. I just wanted to talk to her.

When I joined the company she hadn't yet arrived, so I had a few minutes to take part in the jovial introductions. Here was Gwen Post, a mad, wild-eyed bag lady who would play Marina, our dear old Nanny; here was a gloomy, intense collection of outraged nerve ends named Sally Divers, who was our Sonya, the girl who cherishes an unrequited passion for Astrov. Rory Behenny, the eponymous Uncle Vanya, who had read with me at the audition, ambled among us, dressed in a bizarre outfit, part tuxedo and part tracksuit. He pumped my hand and announced to all that he hoped I'd remember to bring the morphine. My enthusiastic response was without pretense; Rory was a truly gifted actor. He died a few years later of pancreatic cancer, which meant the stealth attack of lethally reproducing cells was probably under way as we stood in the rehearsal room joking about the pressing need for morphine.

Peter Smythe, our director, a combination of sprite and gremlin, with milky-blue eyes and bright-red hair cut in a bowl like the early Beatles, moved among us making introductions and encouraging us to help ourselves to the refreshments. Anton Schoitek, a hulk of a Russian with a head like a wild boar, perfect for the part of the faithful retainer Telyegin, came in with a roar and lifted Peter off the floor, hugging him to his massive chest and growling "Peter, Peter, Peter." As we were laughing at this spectacle, the door opened again and Madeleine slipped into the room.

One by one the company focused on her. Peter slid down the front of the Russian, announcing her name. I was leaning on the piano, not directly in her line of sight, and I watched as her eyes passed among the others and lit at last upon me. Lit is the correct word; I felt as if I was standing in a single spot, with the rest of the stage and all the people on it cast into darkness. Peter, running through the names, arrived at mine. "Ed Day," he said. "Our good doctor Astrov."

"We've met," Madeleine said, smiling modestly.

Rory, who was next to me, sent a sharp look from Madeleine to me and back again, making a show of being caught in an electric charge. "I'll say," he said, and everyone laughed.

I'm an actor; I don't get caught out by my emotions, but it took a conscious effort to hold myself in check. My impulse was to cross the room and fold Madeleine in my arms, and I could have done it, in actor-display mode. No one would have thought a thing about it. But I didn't move. Nor did she. Our eyes met and I drank in her presence, detecting the subtle changes in her that only I could see. She was a little thinner, which made her seem taller. Her abundant hair was tied back; the front cut short, curling over her brow cherub-style, which contrasted interestingly with her high un-cherubic cheekbones. She was wearing a lavender sweater that shifted her changeable eyes toward gray. Her eyes were different. That was what kept me from moving. The brows were drawn slightly down and together. She regarded me from farther away than the actual distance between us. Indeed so defensive was her expression that her head was drawn back on the pale column of her neck. Her upper lip lifted slightly, revealing the line of her teeth. In the next moment she blinked and turned her attention to our director who directed her to consider the delights on the refreshment table. But I knew what I'd seen in her eyes, and it unnerved me: it was fear. Why should Madeleine ever be afraid of me?

Another actor arrived, I don't remember who, and then another, and then our company was complete. We were invited to carry our coffee and rolls to the table where the business of the play would begin. Peter assigned our seats and asked us to take out our wallets, a request I thought very odd, but it turned out to be an introductory exercise in which each of us chose something we carried with us, a photo or card or memento, and told a little story about why we kept it with us. I remember little about this process except that I had nothing more personal than my Equity card, a fact I described as "sad" to the amusement of the group. Only the Russian came up with less. He had nothing in his wallet but a twenty-dollar bill. "This is America," he said. "Who cares who you are, only money counts."

What was it that Madeleine always carried with her? I don't remember. The afternoon passed in a blur of distraction. My brain came up with various clever ways to disguise the fact that I wasn't entirely there. Peter wanted a cold reading, which was a relief. I couldn't have interpreted a nursery rhyme. Madeleine was sitting two chairs down from me so that I couldn't see her. Her voice, so rich and so familiar, vibrated in my ear. It was music, and I closed my eyes to take it in.

At last it was over and we were free to pull on our boots, coats, hats, scarves, and gloves and go out into the cold. I sidled next to Madeleine and waited for her to finish an exchange with Rory, who had worked with the director of a play she'd done at Yale. He asked if she shared his opinion that the guy was impossible.

"My audition lasted three hours," Madeleine said. "He kept asking for more and more personal stuff. He wanted to break me down. I was so angry that I started to cry and I figured I'd lost the role. But that turned out to be just what he wanted."

"He's a sadist," Rory said.

"He is," Madeleine agreed.

While Rory occupied himself with wrapping a long multi-colored scarf around and around his throat, Madeleine turned

to me and, with commendable calm, said, "How are you, Edward?"

"I'm fine," I said. "Where are you staying?"

"At a hotel," she said. "They put me up. It's just a few
blocks."

"Can I walk you over?"

"Sure," she said.

We didn't speak again until we were on the street and out
of earshot of our dispersing colleagues. "Is Guy with you?" I
asked.

"Not yet," she said. "He's coming in on the train late
tonight."

I took her hand and we walked another block in silence. At
the light I put my arm around her shoulder. She was trembling
so violently her teeth chattered. "Are you cold?" I asked.

"No," she said.

The hotel lobby was a dreary hall with a dim chandelier, a
faded carpet, and a single bored attendant at the desk. We
passed without greeting and stood in front of the elevator for
an eternity.

"This elevator is really slow," Madeleine observed.

"I read an article," I said. "Some guy did a study. The aver-
age time it takes until a person waiting for an elevator shows
visible signs of agitation is fourteen seconds."

"Fourteen seconds?" she said.

"Right."

"I'll remember that." The elevator dinged and the doors
shuddered open upon a blood-red interior. We stepped inside.
Madeleine pushed the button for the seventh floor. "At last," I

said when the doors had closed. She turned to me, raising her arms around my neck, and the kiss of seven floors began. When the doors opened I kept my hand on her waist and we hurried down the empty hall to the room door. On the way Madeleine loosened her scarf and unbuttoned her coat. She had trouble with the key, turning it left and right and then left again, but nothing happened. I nuzzled her neck, peeling the collar of her coat away with my teeth. "Too slow," I whispered. She laughed. "I know," she said. The mechanism clicked and the door drifted open. I pulled her in for another kiss, which we held on to as I backed her inside and kicked the door closed behind me. It was a tiny, hot, dark room filled by a double bed, which was fine with us. Madeleine unbuttoned my coat; I pushed hers off her shoulders and worked on the sweater. In no time we were free of our clothes and tangled in each other on the lumpy mattress. Sex can be estranging; it can drive two otherwise compatible people apart. I'd had that experience a few times over the intervening years, but with Madeleine I had the sense that sex could actually hold us together. I couldn't go wrong, she was always with me. We kept at it quite a while, rolling off the bed to the floor at one point. At another the bed frame gave a shriek and a loud crack. "Oh no," Madeleine cried and we clutched each other, expecting the mattress to collapse beneath us, but it didn't. I made a lot of noise right at the end. She was nicely twisted with her hips turned one way and her shoulders the other, laughing and gasping for breath. My heart announced its ecstatic condition with a roar and I collapsed on top of her. After a few moments she eased her head out from beneath my shoulder and we had one more distressingly tender kiss. When that was over I rolled off of her and we lay side by side, washed up. The expression "flotsam and jetsam" came to mind, and then, like flotsam and jetsam, drifted away. "I thought that rehearsal would never end," I said.

"Me too."

"Every time you read a line I had to cross my legs."

"Does that help?"

"No," I said. "Only one thing really helps."

She snorted. I turned onto my side and smoothed her hair back with my palm. "I like your hair like this."

"I think Elena will pull it all up."

"But with the curls in the front."

"Um," she said. We were quiet then while the world fell back into place.

"So," I said. "How have you been?"

She gave me an incredulous smile. "Pretty good. Up until last Wednesday."

"What happened then?"

"I found out you were playing Astrov."

"And that was bad news?"

"That was shocking news."

"How did Guy take it?"

"Not well."

"That doesn't surprise me."

"No?" She was pressing little kisses down the inside of my forearm.

"Did he tell you he came to see me?"

She closed her eyes, taking in a slow breath. "When?" she said softly.

"When you were here for the audition. He came to my play and he came to the dressing room and he tried to talk me out of doing the audition."

"I think I don't need to know this," she said.

This annoyed me. "I wish I didn't know it," I said. She was silent. "Do you have any idea how he found out I was up for the part?"

"No," she said. We were very still then, while the specter of Guy Margate slid into the bed between us. "He's been having a hard time," she said, turning away from me.

"I know. He told me."

"What did he say?"

"He said he was killing himself."

"I feel sorry for him."

"You've a funny way of showing it."

She looked back over her shoulder. "What do you mean?"

I gestured to the room, the wreck of the bed, our clothes commingled on the floor.

"He must never know about this."

"He thinks you love him."

"Did he say that?"

"Yes. He said, 'Maddie loves me.' "

She turned over to face me, frowning.

"Maddie," I said. A blush started at her throat and swept up to her cheeks.

"I don't know what to tell you," she said.

"You could start by telling me why you married him."

"I was pregnant. You rejected me. He was so kind, he loves me so much."

"I rejected you?"

"You sent that chilly postcard."

"That wasn't rejection, Madeleine. That was a postcard. I never got the chance to reject you."

"But you would have. I knew that."

I rushed past this arguable point. "Another thing I'd like to know is when you started sleeping with him. Was it before I left for Connecticut?"

She pursed her lips and fluttered her eyelashes.

"It was before, right?"

"By sleeping with him, you mean when did I first have sex with him, right?"

"Exactly. When did you start fucking him? That's my question."

She allowed a dramatic pause, concentrating on the ceiling while tears welled up in her eyes. "I've never had sex with Guy," she said.

"Oh please," I said.

"It's unbelievable, isn't it?" she said.

"Completely."

"Nevertheless, it's true."

I suppose my mouth dropped open and some version of amazement sat upon my brow. It was as if she'd handed me one of those sudoku puzzles everyone is so mad for these days; I was conscious of a pattern I'd never noticed before and certain numbers were falling neatly into place. "So, he's gay," I said.

She gave a sad smile to the ceiling. "I wish it was that simple," she said.

"Madeleine," I said. "What are you telling me?"

She glanced fleetingly at my face then resolutely back at the ceiling. "Guy is impotent," she said. Immediately upon this revelation the tears overflowed and a strangled sob burst from her throat. I rolled upon my back, staring blankly at her crumpled profile and the tears streaming down her cheeks into her ears.

"You mean—" I said.

"Completely," she whimpered.

I rubbed my forehead with the heel of my hand. "So you've been married six years and there's no sex?"

She squeezed her eyes closed, nodding her head.

"He gets in bed with you and he can't get it up?"

A moan, sniffing, and gasping. "I swore to myself I'd never tell you," she said. "I've betrayed him."

"So you haven't had sex in six years?"

"Mumble, director, mumble, mumble Yale."

"What?"

Big sigh. "I had an affair with the director of the Yale play last fall. It was awful. That's the only time, until now."

"There was that time in the bookstore."

"You're right. I should never have done that."

"So you feel guilty for wanting to have sex every few years."

"You don't understand."

"It's crazy," I said. "You know that, don't you?"

She nodded again.

"It's just not normal. Has he been to a doctor?"

"It's psychological. He had a brutal childhood, his father left, his mother did sick things to him."

"You've got to leave him."

She put her hands over her face, wiping the tears away. "I can't. It would kill him."

"It won't kill him," I said. "You're just being dramatic. He has no right to ask you to live like this."

"He took care of me when I needed him."

"That was his choice," I said.

"And he saved your life."

"As he never fails to remind me."

"We owe him so much."

"That doesn't mean we have to like him."

She considered this. "We don't have to like him. But we can't try to destroy him. You must feel that, Edward."

I sat up and swung my legs over the bedside. "I don't feel it," I protested. "I know I should, I know I'm obligated to him. He saved my life and I'm obligated to him, but I don't feel it. I just don't feel it."

Madeleine said nothing. She'd stopped crying and when I looked back she was arranging a pillow under her head. "He told me he wished he'd let me drown," I concluded.

"Perhaps he does."

"So why do I have to care what happens to him when he wishes I was dead?"

"Because he would never do anything to hurt you."

"You think not?"

She pondered this. "He has his own demons."

"Great," I said. "The demon has demons." I got up and went to the bathroom, where I drank a glass of water and looked at myself in the mirror. I had an incipient mustache; I was growing it for Astrov, who talks about his mustache in the first act. It made me look older, sinister. I didn't like it. I raised my eyebrows and made my eyes bug out like Guy's. "What time is he coming?" I called back to Madeleine.

"Late," she said. "His train gets in at ten thirty."

I stood in the doorway looking down at her. She was stretched out with her head propped up, her hair waving out in all directions over the pillow. I felt enormously sad. The cruel irony of her fate wasn't lost on me. She'd been dealt a very poor hand and had tried to make the best of it, but she'd lost the game.

"Are you living with anyone?" she asked.

"No," I said. "There's a woman I see. She's a lighting tech."

"Are you in love with her?"

"No. It's not serious."

"Oh," she said, idly scratching the inside of her thigh. This caused the breast resting against her arm to jiggle lightly. She lifted one knee, the better to get at the thigh, her eyes all the while resting on me. I felt a pleasant tingling in the groin, which resulted in a visible indicator of my emotions. Cause and effect—where would we be without it?

"Oh, look," Madeleine said, pointing at me with girlish surprise.

"What can I say," I said, looking down at my steadily lifting member.

"As I understand it," she said, "only one thing works." She patted the sheet and I crossed the narrow space, clambering in beside her.

Madeleine was as flexible as a reed. She had a remarkably strong back and open hips; she could do a backbend from a standing position and sit in the demanding full lotus for hours on end. She liked being pulled about, folded and unfolded like an accordion. Her ankles were over my shoulders and her knees pressed into the mattress when we heard three sharp raps at the door. We froze, our eyes locked in alarm. "Who is it?" Madeleine called sweetly. There was no answer. "Wrong room!" I exclaimed. Madeleine was sweating; her upper lip gleamed in the dim light. We heard the key slide into the lock—one click. The door, scraping against the cheap carpet, said "Shhh" as Guy, lugging a suitcase, stepped into the room.

Let's play this as a comic scene. The only sound is the obscene pop of my cock coming free of Madeleine as I lurch backward and she dives for the floor. Guy stands speechless in the open doorway with what I take at first to be a grin on his face. Madeleine is scrambling, pulling in articles of her clothing. I arrange myself cross-legged on the edge of the mattress facing him, but he does not move. "For God's sake," I say to him. "Close the door."

His face is a mask, the grin not glee but terror. His eyes take in the room, his panicked wife on the floor, his own reflection in the mirror over the dresser, the disheveled bed, and the unabashedly naked me, facing him, waiting upon his next

move. What's odd is how calm I feel, how guiltless. As our eyes
meet he apprehends this; it does something to him. In that moment it's out in the open between us: we are enemies.

Quietly, still clutching the suitcase, he steps back into the
hall, pulling the door closed behind him. Madeleine is sobbing
on the floor. "Oh God," she repeats, though I know she is not
a believer. No sound from the hall; he's just standing on the
other side of the door. Will he change his mind and reappear,
charged for confrontation? "Calm down," I advise Madeleine,
who sits up dazedly, pulling her blouse over her head. "He's
going."

Another moment. She's holding her breath. Then we hear
the creak of the floorboards as Guy, yielding the stage, treads
stolidly off into the wings.


After Guy left, Madeleine and I argued about what we should
do. I wanted her to leave with me at once; she wanted to wait
for Guy's return. She was certain he would come back. In the
end I left and she waited. Near eleven, the time when he had
been originally expected, Guy appeared at the hotel-room
door, shaken but resolved. He described himself as disap-
pointed in Madeleine, though not surprised that I would take
advantage of her weakness.

"Your weakness," I said. "What century is he living in?"

"He cried all night," she said. "He's had such a hard time.
You and I have been working; we can't understand what he's
going through. It's as if he's been shut out of the theater and

now we have these great parts and the minute we're together we betray him. He trusted us, and we betrayed him."

"He cried?"

"I didn't sleep ten minutes."

"So what is he going to do?" I asked. We were speaking softly in the hall outside the rehearsal stage.

"He's quitting his job," she said. "He's moving to the hotel until we can find an apartment. He's delivering me to rehearsals in the morning and picking me up at night."

"But that's absurd," I said. "You're not his prisoner."

She smiled, misty eyed. "I'm a prisoner of this play. So is Elena."

"What is this, method acting?"

She rested a trembling hand on my forearm. "I can only see you here and only kiss you as Elena."

"I can't stand this," I said. "I'm going to follow you when you leave and punch his nose in."

"Don't," she said. A trio of our fellow actors, exiting the elevator, filed past us to the door. "Don't try to hurt him."

"You've got to leave him, Madeleine."

"Not yet. Not now. I can't be that cruel."

Peter Smythe, peeking gnomically from the open door, announced, "Here they are in the hall. Aren't you coming in, lovebirds?"


In general the actor's memoir is divided into two parts: stirring tales of my youthful artistic suffering followed by charming profiles of all the famous people who admire me. I'm not sure why this genre is popular, as nothing could be more boring than an actor's life and actors are such a self-absorbed and narcissistic lot, they're unlikely to make good narrators. Katharine Hepburn got it right when she titled her tiresome paean to herself simply *Me*.

Fortunately for my readers, this memoir is different. In this memoir something memorable actually happened. If you are over forty you may have read about it in the papers, though it was far from front-page news. It was a curious item quickly buried in the back pages.

Now, as I approach the big event, it occurs to me that there may be those among you who, through some fault in your stars or your education, are unfamiliar with Anton Chekhov's *Uncle Vanya*. In this case you must fail to appreciate how bizarrely the events Madeleine and I acted out upon the stage echoed the anxious lives we put on hold to take our parts. For this reason I pause at what I hope is a suspenseful moment to tell you a little about the play.

There's no summarizing the plot of a Chekhov play. One might say they all have the same plot. A group of unhappy characters come together at a provincial estate and complain about the emptiness of their lives, the hopelessness of trying to do any good in the world or to find satisfaction in work or love. Invariably they imagine real life is elsewhere, most likely in Moscow. The "action" of the play takes place offstage, thereby circumventing melodrama. Dispossession, either of property, of virtue, or of hope for the future, is the process the characters unwittingly facilitate. The world outside the estate is changing. It is coarsening; it is being deforested, developed, and exploited. Through indolence, ignorance, or indifference, in the course of the play each of the privileged characters will lose what he or she most values.

*Uncle Vanya* concerns a family in possession of a country estate that brings in less and less money each year, despite the efforts of the eponymous Uncle Vanya and his niece, Sonya, who labor incessantly to keep it solvent. Of the older generation, only the mother, Maria, a tract-reading feminist in thrall to her son-in-law, survives. The son-in-law, Serebryakov, is a professor of literature at a distant university. His wife, Vanya's sister, Petrovna, has died. It is the visit of this revered professor, in reality an aging windbag in declining health, with his young and beautiful second wife Elena that springs the action of the play. Mikhail Astrov, the family doctor and friend to Vanya, is called in to care for the hypochondriac Serebryakov. In spite of himself Astrov is struck by Elena's beauty and drawn to her. Vanya too is madly, hopelessly, openly in love with her and makes a comic show of his feelings, following her about, teasing her about her laziness and uselessness, complaining to Astrov about what a crime it is that she is faithful to the professor. *To deceive an old husband you can't endure—that's immoral; but to try to stifle your pitiful youth and vital feelings—is not immoral,* he tells Astrov.

Of course, as this is Chekhov, there's a gun and eventually it goes off, though, in this case, ineffectually.

So, in summary, my character, Astrov, is bewitched by the beautiful, useless Elena, who out of sheer perversity has married an old and impotent husband, and now wanders about the run-down estate tantalizing all who see her.

From the first day of our rehearsals, our director expressed his astonishment at the naturalness and sensitivity of Madeleine's interpretation of Elena. He thought she was acting. I wasn't so sure.

Now, one last scene before we proceed to the drama.

It is my habit to arrive early at the theater for rehearsals. I get up, shower, dress quickly, and hit the streets, still in the daze of sleep. At the hall I drink two cups of coffee and eat whatever sugary roll or doughnut is on the table, putting my nerves on the alert for the work to come. I enjoy watching my fellow actors make their entrances, one by one, greeting one another and milling about the ample space. There are always a few who are habitually late, flustered and apologetic, with wild excuses that vary from day to day until their creative faculties are exhausted and they resort to blaming the subway.

It wasn't the subway—the theater was an easy walk from my apartment—but my alarm clock that failed me on the third day of our rehearsals for *Vanya*. I woke half an hour late, curtailed the shower, dressed frantically, and rushed into the street with my hair still wet, hoping my fellow actors would not have eaten all the cheese Danish by the time I arrived. It was a blustery, chilly, gray morning, threatening the dreaded wintry mix, and I bustled along with my cold damp head bowed against the wind. As I ducked under the theater awning, the glass door flew open and a man, his face drawn in under the hood of a heavy parka, burst out, nearly colliding with me. We drew apart and our eyes met. As he ducked past me, an expression of revulsion and outrage which struck me as completely disproportionate to the provocation narrowed his eyes, inflated his nostrils, and doubled his chin. In that moment I recognized him—it was Guy.

This was a confrontation I would have preferred to avoid, but I was still too close to the numbing embrace of sleep to feel anything beyond a mild vexation and surprise. I didn't greet him; how could I? Our coats brushed as he pushed past me, leaping awkwardly upon a wedge of packed and blackened snow at the curb. His boot soles were slick and could find no purchase. Briefly his feet performed a pas de deux on the ice, but he had lost his balance and in the next moment his legs buckled, his arms flew up, he emitted a low cry of alarm, and down he went, flat on his back in the street. His head was protected by the hood, but it was dangerously close to the passing traffic and as I watched in fascinated horror, a car whooshing past threw up a spray of half-frozen muck that caught him square across the face. I released the door handle, and, careful of the ice, hastened to assist him. By the time I got to him he had risen on one elbow, occupied in wiping the slush from his eyes. I bent over, offering my hand. "Are you OK?" I said.

"Get away from me!" he shouted. "Don't come near me!" I stepped back, meeting the apprehensive gaze of a passing pedestrian who veered toward the building to avoid the two crazies at the curb. Dripping gutter water, Guy got to his feet and staggered into the traffic.

"Be careful," I warned. A car swerving to avoid hitting him sent a wave of slush over my shoes. "Christ," I exclaimed.

"Stay away from me," Guy shouted. I watched as he dodged another car and gained the opposite sidewalk, where he stopped, turning to scowl back at me. His face was streaked with dirt, his eyes fierce, and his cheeks flushed with rage. This interested me. Guy had always seemed so studied to me, conniving and artificial, but this was raw emotion.

"Fine," I replied, "that's fine with me," and I stalked back to the theater. I opened the door upon the warm, inviting lobby, puzzling over the whole complicated history of my connection to Guy Margate, the man who saved my life. The cliché "no good deed ever goes unpunished" came to mind. What was that from? I looked back through the glass door and saw, to my surprise, that Guy was still on the opposite sidewalk. He was smoking a cigarette, his back pressed to the building, glaring across the traffic at the door. I doubted that he could see me, but without thinking, as I mounted the marble steps, I raised my hand and waved goodbye.

The rehearsal period for our *Vanya* was intense; we had four weeks to put up a long and complex show. We started in the morning at nine, broke for lunch, which was sandwiches sent in from the deli down the street, and then went on until eight. In the first week we got the blocking down and worked on various separate scenes, but after that we had the whole cast in all the time. It's an eight-character play and the scenes require from two to six at all times, the family passing in and out of the set, just as they would in an ordinary home. At one point Sere-bryakov remarks that the house contains "twenty-six enormous rooms, people wander off in all directions and you never can find anyone," so there's a sense of brooding and empty space outside the circle of warmth where the characters confront one another with their suffering.

Peter Smythe had clear ideas about what he wanted and the ability to express these ideas coherently, which is about as rare in the theater as the ivory-billed woodpecker is in the forest. He was interested in his actors and gave us leeway, even adjusted his own view in the light of an interpretation that he hadn't considered. Soon, with his guidance, we began to cohere into something very like a small orchestra, each instrument in tune with every other and clear about the score. I never worked more confidently and I think the other actors felt as I did. At night I was generally too exhausted to do much but have dinner with a few of the cast. Madeleine was never with us, having been disappeared by her husband for who knows what sort of dinner, a jolly evening of browbeating and guilt-tripping and kvetching. In the second week she told me Guy had found an apartment in the East Village and that Sunday they had driven to Philly with a truck, packed their meager possessions, and moved in. "Is he going to get a job?" I asked.

"Not yet," she said.

We had five days to rehearse on the theater stage itself. The first two were devoted to the ordeal known as tech rehearsal, in which the actors are required to sit or stand for hours on end while the lighting director and the sound director make minute adjustments to their equipment, and the stagehands figure out how they're going to get the furniture moved between scenes, and the set designer instructs the actors about the dangers of the set, which parts move and which are permanent, which doors open in, which out. The union allows two eleven-hour days and we filled every minute of that time, breaking for dinner and then back in the theater until midnight. During the waiting around we familiarized ourselves with the stage, the backstage, and the dressing rooms.

At last we did a full dress rehearsal and I finally got to kiss Madeleine as passionately as I wanted with no interference from our director. She struggled, as Elena must, but I held her tightly until Vanya appeared with his roses and ruined everything.

Peter's notes were brief: an adjustment to the blocking here ("How did everyone get balled up in the corner?"), a suggestion about timing there ("Sonya, start leaving before she says 'Go on'"). In conclusion, he said, "Astrov and Elena, about that kiss."

Madeleine stepped forward, eager for the critique, but I hung back and said coldly, "What about it?"

"Well," Peter said, "actually." He left a nice pause for effect. "Actually, it's perfect."


*Uncle Vanya* opened at the Public in March to notices so overheated you could warm your hands by them. Rory Behenny in the title role was "brilliant, as always," and brought to the outraged Vanya "a wry intensity." Edward Day's performance was "astonishing," also "complex, nuanced, ironic," possessing—I liked this one—"a range Chekhov would have applauded." In Astrov, Day "showed us reason and desire in mortal combat." Madeleine Delavergne was "born to play Elena," her beauty "delicate, ravishing, haunted," her Elena "longing to live but unwilling to sully herself in ordinary life, mesmerizing." "When Astrov and Elena steal their brief kiss, the audience holds its collective breath."

Our director, Peter Smythe, was praised for his "apprehension of the tragic strain in the comic situation of these trivial characters who can't bear the tedium of their existence."

Et cetera. Tickets were hot; cast and crew settled in for a nice long run.

I've never much liked the whole setup of Christianity, with its emphasis on being saved, thereby acknowledging a debt that can only be paid by a lifetime of sacrifice and devotion. Must God's love have strings attached? People who crave salvation should think about how they're going to feel if it turns out that this God who saved them is, upon closer acquaintance, completely alien. He, possibly she (or, more likely, it), is not now and never has been one of us. Jesus clearly was not one of us, with his crypto-stories about the prodigal who is more beloved by the father than the dutiful son and the sliding pay scale for field hands, with his magic powers that run the gamut from improving the wedding beverage to blasting trees to raising the dead. These days we have born-agains everywhere, even in the White House, carping about how clear and meaningful everything is now that they've seen the light and accepted Christ as their Savior. There they were, just sinning along aimlessly, drinking and fornicating down that slippery slope lined with good intentions and ending you know where, when suddenly Jesus reached out or down or across and saved them. And now they feel grateful all the time, every day. If things go wrong, that's God's way of testing their faith, and if they are successful and make lots of money, that proves they have been chosen by God.

It's supposed to be all about free will, but there's not much freedom in it. And if God is really so eager to save the desperate from themselves, where was he when my mother was knocking back the Seconal with her lunatic girlfriend from hell.

These musings are by way of preparation for the climactic scene of our drama, which takes place, appropriately (though perhaps you'll disagree), in a dressing room at the Public Theater between acts 2 and 3 of Chekhov's *Uncle Vanya*.


Mikhail Astrov isn't onstage for the last part of act 2 and he doesn't appear again until several minutes into act 3, so it was my habit to retreat to my dressing room and stay there through the intermission until I appeared in act 3 toting my geographical surveys. Rory Behenny and our Russian, Anton Schoitek, shared the room with me but they had a serious long-running card game going in the greenroom, so I generally had the space to myself.

In the third week of our run I was backstage, exchanging witticisms with the Russian, when Madeleine arrived looking harried and made a beeline for her dressing room. "You're late, my angel," I said, following her. At the door she turned to me. "We've been fighting all day," she said. "Even in the subway. He wouldn't let up."

"Where is he now?" I asked.

"He's here somewhere." She laid her hand on my forearm, her eyes searching mine. "If I leave him, can I stay with you?"

Did I hesitate? Not more than a breath, I swear. "Yes," I said. She squeezed my arm and her eyes softened. Then she disappeared into the room.

The audience that night was a live one; we could feel their attention. Sweet ripples of soft laughter ran up and down the aisles at various points and we fed on them, pumping up the irony, which in this play is sometimes too subtle for lazy auditors. I delivered my last line to Sonya in act 2 and exited stage right. My dressing room was around a corner and down a few steps. I paused on the landing, noticing that the door, which I knew I'd closed, was open.

So no entrance: this time he was waiting for me. The room was long and narrow, the usual bare bulbs and faux-leather chairs lined up before a dressing shelf, a full-length mirror at the far end and two sinks tucked behind the door. He was slumped in one of the chairs, rummaging through an open backpack in his lap. He had on a light jacket, similar to the one I wore as Astrov, and he had a mustache trimmed in the same absurd nineteenth-century style I'd chosen for my part. "Look at this enormous mustache I've grown," Astrov tells the old servant Marina. "A ridiculous mustache. I've become an eccentric." I pushed the door open a few more inches with my foot. Guy looked up from the backpack, raising his hand unconsciously to stroke the bristles over his mouth. "Is it real?" I said, entering the scene.

He frowned. "Is what real?"

"The mustache."

He dropped his hand. "Of course it is," he said.

"How did you get in here?"

"It wasn't difficult."

I crossed to the mirror where Astrov's reflection greeted me. "I'll have to ask you to come back after the play," I said. "I don't like to break character in the middle of a performance."

"Don't then," he said. "That Astrov character is as big a heel as you are. And I've got the same problem with him."

I plant trees, I told myself, because I want future generations to be happy because of me. "And what problem is that?" I asked.

"He's trying to steal my wife."

"Why not come back later and we can talk this over like gentlemen."

He shook his head wearily. "I asked you not to take this part. I knew it would be too much for her. I know you have no sense of obligation to me, you've made that perfectly clear, but you owe it to her to let her get on with her life."

I breathed deep into my diaphragm, lifted my shoulders and rolled them back, shrugging off Mikhail Astrov. "You're always so preoccupied with who owes who what," I said. "It's a real failing of yours."

"How do you sleep at night," he said. It wasn't a question.

"Well," I said. "I sleep well. You're the one who doesn't sleep."

"I don't sleep because I care about other people. If I see someone struggling, someone in trouble, I try to help. I don't just let them drown."

Oh, here we go, I thought. "Look," I said, "I know I've been a big disappointment to you but I just can't keep my mind focused every second of the day on how grateful I am to you."

The sound of applause, like a thousand ping-pong balls simultaneously dropped into play, pattered in over the intercom. The intermission had begun. Guy lurched to his feet, clutching the backpack to his stomach, and with a crabbed sideways step brought his shoulder to the door and eased it closed. Panic turned a screw in my chest and tightened the cords in my throat. The murmuring of my fellow actors as they drifted to their dressing rooms, a cough, a laugh I recognized as Rory's, a ribald exchange as he and Anton sat down to their card game, the creak of shoe soles against linoleum, the glug of water running in the pipes, all these familiar sounds of our daily routine were improbably dear to me. Why was I trapped with this crazed loser and his backpack? I could have pushed past him, pulled the door open, and ordered him out, but I didn't. If I made him leave he would run straight to Madeleine's dressing room and start in on her. She'd gotten through the first act well enough, tearing up prettily during her brief and marvelous response to Vanya's teasing. *Everyone looks at me with pity, poor thing, she has an old husband! This sympathy for me, how I understand it.* Her voice quavered on the last line in a way I hadn't heard before. Our big scene was coming up and I didn't want her distracted, so I decided to have it out, whatever "it" was, with her husband. He had resumed his seat, hunching over the bag like some beggar going through the day's collection of rags and bottles. "What is it you want from me, Guy?" I asked.

He glanced up sharply over the bag. "Don't ask me that," he snapped. "If you had any interest in what I want, we wouldn't be here."

I could think of no response to this assertion, which was, I recognized, indisputable. I twisted the waxed tip of my mustache, gazing upon my unwelcome guest. I knew too much about him, I thought, and though some of what I knew should have made me pity him, what I felt was a steadily mounting irritation, such as a buzzing fly produces of a Sunday morning when one is trying to read the papers. Just as, while rolling up the book review for use as a weapon, one may succumb to a grudging admiration for the doomed insect, I admitted that there was in Guy's persistence, as well as his supremely confident appropriation of the moral higher ground, something impressive. He seemed incapable of seeing himself as anything but wronged. So be it, I thought. "You're right," I said. "I don't care what you want."

He returned his attention to the bag. "That's better. At least you're being honest."

"Has it ever occurred to you to ask yourself what *I* want?"

"I know what you want."

"Do you?" I said. "And what is that?"

I assumed he would say *my wife,* and I was prepared with my response, which was that his wife could make her own decisions. But instead he lifted his head and considered me thoughtfully, his eyes fixed vacantly on my forehead as if he were reading a scroll on a video screen. "You want to be rid of me."

A hoot of laughter followed by a shout of "In your

dreams!" echoed from the card game outside. Then came the rapping knuckles and the repeated warning, "Five minutes, five minutes," from the stage manager making his rounds. I turned to the dressing shelf and opened a stick of liner. "I don't have time for this," I said.

Guy made a sound somewhere between a gargle and a laugh. I could see him in the mirror, pressing his palm into his forehead, smoothing back the hair from his temples. "I think you do," he replied.

"Has she told you that she's leaving you?" I said. "Is that what this is all about?"

"She's not leaving me. What makes you say that?"

"Jesus, Guy," I said. "Why should she stay with you? You keep her like a jailer. She's young, beautiful, talented, she's a successful actress. Once she's free of you, the world's at her feet. Do you think she doesn't know that?"

"Did she tell you that?"

"She doesn't have to tell me. Take a look in the mirror." I stepped aside and his eyes shifted to the mirror in which we were both reflected, but he didn't look at himself. He glared at my reflection. For an eerie moment our eyes met on the surface of the glass.

"Three minutes," the call came from the hall. "Three minutes."

Doors snapped and creaked and the atmosphere between us thickened as the bustle of actors heated up in the hall. Madeleine was out there. When the lights came up in three minutes, she would be onstage, complaining to Vanya about how bored she was. I tried to distinguish her voice, her tread, but it was impossible. Guy wasn't listening. He was back at the bag, which had evidently an endless potential for engaging his interest. He reminded me of Beckett's character Winnie, in *Happy Days,* buried to her waist in sand, reaching for her purse whenever her ruminations veer too close to the abyss. "There is, of course, the bag," she says.

"Look," I said to Guy, "you can wait in here until I get back."

"But you're not going anywhere," he said. He had extracted something new from the bag, something I couldn't make out at first because his head was down and he was turning it over in his hands, fiddling with it. Then he parted his legs, the bag slipped to the floor with a thud, and I saw that he was holding an extremely nasty-looking revolver and pointing it directly at me.

The apprehension of a tight spot always commences with a flush of incredulity. There's a mistake here. This isn't really happening. So it was, without any sense of the ironic potential which strikes me now as charmingly piquant, that I asked, "Is it real?"

"Oh yes," Guy said, narrowing his eyes at me in a way that struck me as absurd. Was he taking aim? Why bother, the pistol was huge and we weren't five feet apart. "It's real, it's loaded, and I've just removed the safety."

I wasn't afraid, though I should have been. The gun affected me as a provocation rather than a threat. I felt elated, light on my feet, and ready to match wits. "I hope you've considered the consequences of your actions," I cautioned.

He rearranged his mouth into a sneer and tilted his head as

if listening to an inner dictate. A sour, metallic smell wafted off of him and I noted a line of perspiration gathering over his brow. "I have, actually," he said.

"Because even though I know you're unhappy and disgruntled, and rightly so, I don't deny that you have a legitimate complaint, I don't see how what you're doing can help matters. Not for Madeleine, and not for you, and certainly not for me."

"You will be the biggest loser," he agreed.

The intercom crackled overhead. Act 3 had begun. *The Herr Professor has graciously expressed the desire that we should all assemble in this room at one o'clock today*, Vanya said.

"That may be," I said, "but you'll lose Madeleine either way."

He blinked, pushing the pistol out over his knees. Madeleine's voice, falsely amplified, said, *It's probably business.*

"This isn't about Madeleine," Guy said. "It never was."

I pressed on. "You tell yourself you care for her, but think about the impossibility of her situation. She can't have children; she's stuck in a sexless marriage. It's unbearable."

Wrong card. We both watched his index finger stretch over the trigger. "What are you talking about?" he said.

"What do you think I'm talking about?"

*I'm dying of boredom*, Elena lamented above our heads. *I don't know what to do.* With a flourish of my hand I indicated the intercom speaker.

Guy followed my gesture, his eyebrows knit, his upper lip lifted over his teeth, completely mystified. "That's good," I said. "You're good in this part."

He returned his puzzled attention to me. "She's not stuck in a sexless marriage," he said. "That's ridiculous. We have sex all the time."

*You must be a witch*, Sonya chided Elena.

I nodded sympathetically. "It's nothing to be ashamed of," I said. "It can happen to any man."

He laughed. "This is rich," he said. "There's nothing she won't say when she wants to get laid. And she's insatiable, but you know that. We had great makeup sex that night after I found you in the hotel room, she was really hot. We called you the warm-up act."

"Guy," I said, "give it up."

Now Sonya confessed her love for Astrov to Elena. *I love him more than my own mother. Every minute I seem to hear him, feel the pressure of his hand.*

It was my cue to head for the stage. I moved closer to the door, oblivious to the armed threat in the chair. The theater chestnut called "Chekhov's rule" popped into my brain: a pistol on the wall in the first act must go off in the third. Guy was still chuckling over the joke he and Madeleine had enjoyed at my expense. "No, really," he said. "She told you we didn't have sex and you believed her?" So great was his amusement that his hand relaxed and the barrel of the gun tilted toward the floor.

I took the chance to push past him, throwing open the door. His head came up and he jerked around in the chair, leveling the gun at me. Who knows what came over me, a near fatal curiosity, an irresistible impulse to risk my life, but I paused at the door and looked back at him. He was hunched forward awkwardly over the gun, as if it was alive and he had to struggle to keep it from pulling him out of the chair. His chin was down, and his eyes, rolled up and fixed on me, brimmed with hatred such as I have never seen before or since. It shocked me, that look, it frightened me, and I dodged away. He's going to hurt someone, I thought as I rounded the corner and darted up the steps to the wings where a stagehand waited to hand me the roll of maps I would display to the indifferent Elena. "Listen closely," I said to him. "There's a man with a gun in my dressing room. Don't go down there. Tell Peter to call the police." His eyes grew wide and solemn and he nodded his head, glancing anxiously past me at the stairs. "Just don't go down there," I said. He nodded, wandering away into the wings.

Sonya came offstage and stood quietly to one side. We both watched Elena, who was alone before the audience, debating with herself the pros and cons of yielding to Astrov's charms. *But I'm a coward. My conscience would torment me. He comes here every day, I can guess why, and even now I feel guilty.*

Gripping my charts, I moved to the dark at the edge of the stage. Elena paced during her monologue, not in agitation, but aimlessly, tormented by her thoughts, too lazy to act, to put herself out of her own misery. *I am ready to fall on my knees before Sonya, and ask her to forgive me, to weep.*

I stepped into the lights, advancing strongly upon this beautiful intruder who was destroying my orderly life. *Good Day!* I said, and we shook hands.

In this scene Astrov has come to show Elena his passion, the geographical charts he has made which detail the gradual degradation of the flora and fauna in the neighborhood. Elena has expressed an interest in seeing them, but this is a ruse; what she wants is to tell him that Sonya is in love with him and, thereby, to draw him out on the subject of his heart, which she believes herself to have captured. I spread out my charts across the table before Elena, fixing them with clips, and began my lecture on ecology. *Now look at this. This is a map of our district as it was fifty years ago. The dark and light green represent forests.*

I loved this speech. Even the most indifferent members of the audience were stirred by the prophetic vision of our nineteenth-century playwright. It's a mighty plea for environmental stewardship but it's also an argument for the vital necessity of art. *On this lake there were swans, geese, ducks, and, as the old people say, a powerful lot of birds of all sorts, no end of them; they flew in clouds.* I raised my hand, indicating an imaginary flock darkening the sky and inviting Elena with an eager, schoolboy earnestness to humor me, to stretch her limited imagination to a sense of natural wonder. Of course, she couldn't do it. She gave me a look of frustrated sadness. She was bound by law and by social stricture to a sick, tyrannical old man who kept her awake all night moaning about his gout. Why should she care if there had once been geese honking across the horizon, wild goats and elk startling the weary traveler in the woods at night?

I returned to my chart. I was dead center at the heart of Doctor Mikhail Astrov, a moody, lonely, cynical man, yet passionate about life and driven to do something worth doing in this world, longing at this moment to share his despair of the present and dim hope for the future with a beautiful, desirable, sexually frustrated woman who is bored by what interests him.

Edward Day was gone; Guy Margate a nonentity, a disturbing dream from which Astrov has awakened. *Besides villages and hamlets,* I continued, *you can see scattered here and there, various settlements, small farms, hermitages of the Old Believers.* I lowered my chin and raised my eyes, letting her in on my skepticism about the "Old Believers."

She isn't listening, I thought. Her mind is wandering. But I won't stop yet. I want her to understand how much is at stake in this world, because men are indifferent to beauty. *This is how it was twenty-five years ago.* I rolled up the top sheet exposing a second chart. *Already one-third of the area is woodland. There are no longer any goats.* I went on, but she resisted me. I made the case that it wasn't a matter of progress, the old giving way to the new, but rather of *a degeneration due to stagnation, ignorance, complete lack of understanding.* When I lifted my finger from my meticulously drawn map, I saw that her eyes were glazed with boredom. I drew away, closing my heart to her. *But I can see by your face that this doesn't interest you.*

*I understand so little of all this,* she said.

In frustration I rolled up my charts. *There's nothing to understand; it's simply uninteresting.*

She gave me her coy smile; really, she was enough to try a saint. *To be quite frank, my thoughts were elsewhere.*

Then we had the whole fraudulent business of her sounding me out about my feelings for Sonya.

Emotionally this is an intensely complicated scene; it's a showstopper. Elena and Astrov are attracted to each other and have been repressing this attraction for reasons that are both personal and social. The attraction is purely sexual; it has been growing on a daily basis for a month in which they have been constantly together but never alone. Now, at last, they are alone. They are as concentrated as two people can be. A tiger could leap through the window and they won't notice. He declares himself: *I submit. Here I am, devour me!* And she puts up a flimsy show of resistance: *Oh, I am not so low—I am not so bad as you think!* But it's a sham. He takes her in his arms, she struggles, but weakly. *Where shall we meet?* he begs her. *Someone may come in, tell me quickly . . . what a wonderful, glorious . . . one kiss.*

And at last, they kiss. We kissed.

Because of the arrangement of the entrances near the stage, the gunshot sounded as if it came from the audience in the right orchestra seats. It startled a few cries out of those closest to the door, but no one bolted. Madeleine jerked in my arms. Had he shot her? I held her fast, running my hands along her spine, releasing her lips and lifting her face so that I could look into her eyes. Her gaze was clouded by desire and she brought her hand to the back of my neck, stretching up to meet my lips with hers. As there was no reaction from anyone resembling an authority, and no further disturbance of the airwaves, the moment passed. Some innocents may have thought the shot was part of the play. I held Madeleine fast, stroking her hair and pulling her in close at the waist, so overcome by desire that I wanted to force her down onto the floor and have at it right there in front of the audience. Who cares? I thought, my brain sparking like a power line cut loose by a lightning bolt. I've got her now. She eased her mouth from mine and I pressed her cheek against my chest, allowing my other hand to stray over her hips. Behind me, Vanya entered stage right, carrying the bouquet of roses he'd gathered for her. Neither of us could see him yet.

Somewhere in my consciousness the gunshot was being judiciously minimized and filed away. There would be some harmless explanation for it; it could have been the blank gun Vanya would fire in the next act, or perhaps it wasn't a gun at all, but some amp blowing out—there was a lot of voltage out there. Elena was strangely limp in my arms. I felt a hiccup against my collarbone—was she weeping? I lifted her chin and looked into her wet eyes. As the tears overflowed she said something that startled me almost as much as the gunshot. *I am not so bad as you think.*

It wasn't her line. The prompter whispered the correction. I held her by the wrist and shoulder, turning her to face Vanya, but she didn't see him. She was sobbing now, but she caught her breath and said, *I am not so bad as you think.* She was supposed to break away from me and run to the window. Again the prompter gave her the line: *This is awful.*

*Never mind, never mind*, Vanya said. He and I exchanged a look freighted with worry. I launched into my little speech about the weather, after which I was to make a hasty, embarrassed exit stage right, while Elena must remain onstage through the long scene in which Serebryakov threatens to sell the house, and Vanya, in a fury, tries to shoot him with the pistol.

*I'm not so bad as you think*, Elena said again.

Vanya dropped the flowers. *I saw everything, Helene.*

*I'm not so bad as you think*, she repeated.

I paused at the entrance to the wings, opening my hands to

Vanya who understood my gesture. We had to get Madeleine offstage. Serebryakov, Sonya, Telyegin, and Marina were beginning their entrance stage left. Madeleine didn't move. She stood there like Lucia di Lammermoor, a pale and fading rose, her eyes clouded, her lips parted, gazing hopelessly beyond the audience, as lost as a soul in hell. I glanced at the prompter, his eyes aghast over his bifocals, giving her, for the third time, her line—*I must leave here*—but she was indifferent to him. Vanya approached her. *You must leave here,* he said. He took her arm and to the relief of the entire cast and crew, now frozen in apprehension, she didn't struggle. *You must leave here this very day,* Vanya said. Cautiously he guided her to me as the others entered the stage in the midst of an idle conversation about the vicissitudes of age. Serebryakov, whose line was *Where are the others?*, cleverly adjusted it to *Where is Maria Vasilyevna?* I didn't get to hear how they improvised for the now absent Elena because Peter Smythe appeared, sweating but competent, motioning me into the wings. Together we led Madeleine through the dark backstage to the lighted landing above the dressing rooms. "I'll send in the understudy for the last act," he said. "It'll be a mess, but we don't have a choice. They'll have to fake it through the rest of this scene."

"She doesn't have many lines," I said. Madeleine stiffened between us, staring in wide-eyed panic at my open dressing-room door. Three policemen were gathered there, two engaged in conversation, the third speaking loudly into a bulky cell-phone precursor. "No," she said, pulling away from us. Peter stepped in front of her, blocking her view. We steered her toward the dimly lit kitchen off the greenroom. "It's all right,"

Peter said calmly. "Let's go in here and I'll fix you a nice cup of tea." Madeleine craned her neck, looking past me. "Is someone in there?" she asked.

"It's OK, sweetheart," I said. "It's nothing for you to worry about."

She gave me an uncomprehending look. Her face was tear-streaked, her nose red and damp. She sniffed, bringing the back of her hand to her nostrils. I pulled my handkerchief from my pocket. "Here," I said, "use this."

"Thank you," she said. She blew her nose discreetly, folded the cloth, and handed it back to me, a faint, diffident smile on her lips. "I don't believe we've met," she said.


To this day I don't know how we managed to get through the fourth act. Of course the audience noticed that Madeleine had been replaced by her understudy, and as they trundled out into the street, they doubtless speculated about what might have happened. Was she taken ill or had some emergency required her to leave the stage? If they read the Metro section the next day in the *Times* they might have noticed a brief article about the suicide of an unemployed actor in a dressing room at the Public Theater. Otherwise, Guy's exit went unnoticed by the wide, searching eye of the press.

Because I was the last to see Guy alive, I was subjected to an interview with Detective DiBanco, a short, hirsute investigator with a Napoleonic gleam in his eye. He was waiting for me in the wings at the end of the show, and he escorted me to the door of my dressing room. The other actors were encouraged by the attending officers to gather their belongings and leave the theater. Guy's body had been removed and Madeleine spirited away by Peter Smythe. Orange tape was stretched across the open door to the dressing room. I tried to avoid looking at the pool of brownish blood congealing on the floor.

It was unusual, Detective DiBanco informed me, for a suicide to shoot himself in the chest. "It's hard to be accurate," he said. "Most choose the temple, or they just put the barrel in their mouths."

"Well," I said, "he was an actor."

"Why does that make a difference?"

I gaped at his innocence. "An actor doesn't want to mess up his face."

"Was he a friend of yours?"

I wasn't sure how to answer this. The scene had a dreamy artificiality about it, and my emotions had simply shut down. I couldn't feel a thing. DiBanco was a professional; he hung on my answer with actor-worthy concentration. What should I tell him? Should I begin on the Jersey shore? At last I punted. "I hadn't seen him in a long time," I said.

"So he just dropped by your dressing room to kill himself?"

I searched for a shorthand version. "His wife is in the play," I said. "We were lovers, he was jealous. I think he planned to shoot me, but he didn't have the courage."

Detective DiBanco pulled down the corners of his mouth, nodding his head ponderously, for all the world like a cop in a TV drama. "Did he threaten you?" he asked.

"In a way. Yes. I'd say he did."

He gazed up at me; he had to lift his chin to do this, and I noticed a red notch on the jawbone where he'd nicked himself shaving the thick stubble that surged over his chin. "He left a kind of note," he said. "But it doesn't make any sense. Maybe it will make sense to you."

"A kind of note?"

"I'll show you," he said, pulling the tape aside. Reluctantly I followed him, keeping as much distance between my feet and the blood as I could. Guy's blood, I thought, and a reflex of nausea fired an acrid shot of vomit into my throat which I swallowed back manfully.

"It's on the mirror," DiBanco said, unnecessarily, for as he spoke my eyes discovered Guy's final condemnation. He'd used a brown liner crayon to draw a picture frame with a small rectangle at the base, like a title plate, in which he'd carefully inscribed my name. Above the frame, scrawled in startling red lipstick, was a single word: INGRATE.

I took my place as he'd known I would, so that I filled the frame. It made me smile, this last joke of Guy's; it was so sophomoric, so ridiculous, so totally Guy.

"I see it makes sense to you," Detective DiBanco observed.

"A long time ago," I confessed, "Guy Margate saved my life."


At my apartment, to my relief, there was a phone message from Peter Smythe, which I returned at once. "How is she?" I asked.

"She's asleep," he said.

"Does she know what happened?"

"It's very strange," he said. "She's calm, but she doesn't

know anything, who I am, where she is. I don't think she rec-
ognizes her own name, but she's decided to believe I know it."

"This is terrible," I said.

"I called a shrink I know. He said she may snap out of it.
She said she was tired, so Mary gave her a gown and a toothbrush, showed her the guest room, and she went to bed. The
door is open; we'll hear her if she gets up in the night. Are
you OK?"

"I have no idea," I said.

"Can you do the matinee tomorrow?"

"Yes," I said. "I can do it."

"Call me in the morning," he said. "We'll figure out what
to do. Do you know Madeleine's family?"

"No," I said. "Guy knew her mother. I never did."

"Jesus, what a thing to do. What was wrong with that
guy?"

"Guy?" I said. "I guess he snapped. He couldn't get a job."

"Yeah, yeah, it's a hell of a profession," Peter said. "We're
all crazy from it."

"That's true," I agreed.

After I hung up the phone I switched off the lamp and sat
in the dark for a few minutes. I could hear Guy laughing at me.
"We called you the warm-up act." Was that the last thing he
said to me? Was there any possibility that it was true, that he
and Madeleine were in some sort of complicity against me, that
there was another cruel story I didn't know anything about? Or
was it just another of Guy's ploys, right there at the end, to
shake my confidence, to get even with me because I had suc-
ceeded and he had failed?

Naturally I preferred the latter proposition, but I also admitted that I would probably never be sure, as Guy was gone and Madeleine, if she could even remember her story, would have a strong personal interest in sticking to it.

Guy is gone, I said to the empty darkness pressing against me. But I hadn't seen his body. They'd taken him and the backpack and the pistol away sometime during the last act. A sinister doubt crept in from the dime-store-mystery plotting lobe of the brain: What if Guy wasn't really dead? Then the police would have to be in on it, also Peter, who had identified Guy. Impossible, right? But no sooner had the thought crossed my mind than a creak and crunch issued from the bedroom, as of someone rising from the bed. My trembling fingers shot out for the lamp switch, but it wasn't where it had always been. "Christ," I muttered, feeling around until I found it exactly where it had always been.

The light blasted my eyes. The bedroom door was ajar. I could see the empty bed and the dresser, just as I had left them, but I had to get up, cross the room, and look behind the door. That was when I decided to go out. It was midnight and it was chilly; people with sense were all in bed. I didn't want to talk to strangers; I didn't want to be alone. I called Teddy.

He was awake; he had, he said, just come in, and how was I.

"Not great," I said. "Guy Margate shot himself in my dressing room during the show tonight."

"My God," Teddy said. "Are you serious?"

"Yes. He's dead; and Madeleine doesn't know who she is."

"Ed," Teddy said. "Where are you?"

"I'm in my apartment, but I can't stay here. I'm too creeped out. I need a drink. Can you come out and meet me somewhere?"

"Hold on," he said. He talked to someone, Wayne no doubt, but I couldn't make out what he was saying. "I'll meet you at Phebe's," he said. "I'll leave right now."

"Thanks," I said. "I'll be there."

Teddy was waiting on the porch but as soon as he saw me he came out and steered me into the small room behind the bar. He had evidently spoken to the bartender, for a bottle of whiskey and two glasses with ice cubes melting in them were set up on a table. This dark room wasn't ordinarily open unless the crowd overflowed, so we had it to ourselves. "I would have told you to come to the apartment," Teddy said, "but Wayne invited some people from the opening in for drinks. Do you want something to eat?"

"Wayne had an opening?" I said.

"No. It wasn't his. A friend. Awful pictures." He poured the whiskey over the ice, his eyes moving from his hand to me and back again, animated by solicitude. He slid the glass to me. After I swilled a good draught, I thumped the glass down on the table with a sigh. "Thanks," I said. "That helps."

Teddy sipped his drink thoughtfully. "So Guy is dead," he said.

"Yes."

"I can hardly believe it."

"Me neither."

"And what did you mean; Madeleine doesn't know who she is?"

"She just lost it all," I said. "Right in the middle of the third act. We heard the shot and she was sobbing in my arms and she kept repeating her line over and over. We had to get her offstage and then I gave her my handkerchief and she asked me if we'd ever met."

"What was the line?"

"What?"

"What was the line she was repeating?"

"What?" I took another drink, washing back the impatience I felt at this question. "I'm not as bad as you think."

"That was the line?"

"Yes," I said. "That was the line. I'm not as bad as you think. Why is that important?"

"Where is she now?"

"Peter took her home."

"Peter?"

"Smythe. The director. He said she doesn't know who she is. He called a psychiatrist who said she might snap out of it. She went to sleep."

"This is awful," Teddy said.

"I don't know what I'm going to do," I agreed.

"No," Teddy said. "I'm sure you don't."

"For one thing, the understudy has a completely different interpretation of Elena. It's all vanity and irritation. I'm not saying it's wrong, but it's just completely different. I'll have to start from scratch."

Teddy was quiet, rotating his glass on the coaster, drying the moisture from the bottom before he lifted it for another cautious sip. His eyes rested upon me with a distant, friendly curiosity, such as one might show for a child who has charmingly botched a recitation.

"I know that sounds incredibly callous," I admitted.

"Well," Teddy said, "it is *one* of the things you'll have to worry about."

I slept poorly and arrived at Peter's apartment fifteen minutes early. He came to the door in his robe and slippers, his eyes bleary, his mop of hair sticking out in all directions. "Come in, come in," he said. "What a night. I didn't get back from the hospital until four."

"What hospital?" I said, looking about the gloomy living room. Why was it so dark?

"Bellevue," Peter said. He shuffled to the window and pulled the curtain cord, vaporizing the gloom. "God it's bright out there."

Bellevue. My legs went rubbery and I sank onto a handy hassock. "Oh no," I said.

"We didn't have any choice. She woke up screaming and we couldn't calm her down. She wanted to get out of the apartment, didn't know who we were, said someone had stolen a baby, at least I think that's what she said. Mary called Dr. Hershey and he said to call 911 and meet him at Bellevue. So that's what we did."

"Did she calm down?"

"They gave her a shot. Then she was just moaning."

I stood up, making for the door. "I've got to see her."

"They won't let you see her," Peter said. "Sit down, have a cup of coffee."

"What will they do to her?"

"It's a hospital. They'll take care of her. You can call Hershey later. She's his patient now. She needs help, psychiatric help. Hershey said she was in a fugue state."

I sat back down again. So Guy was right, I thought. Madeleine was fragile. I hadn't believed it because she was so ambitious and talented and beautiful and sexy, but he knew it, probably from the start, which is why his suicide is so completely inexcusable. He knew what it would do to her; he even made sure she would bear a crippling weight of guilt. He'd kept her up all night, berating her, threatening to kill himself if she left him, and then he sat in the dressing room listening to the play on the intercom, waiting for that moment when her lips met mine, and then he pulled the trigger. When she heard the shot she knew exactly what it was. In the annals of suicide has there ever been a more ignoble performance? If there was any justice and if there was a hell, I thought, Guy was surely in it. I would not waste a moment's pity on him.

Peter brought me a mug of coffee. "Do you want milk?" he asked.

"No," I said. "Black is good."

"Are you sure you can do the matinee? We can get the understudy if we call him now."

"No," I said. "I can do it."

The matinee was a shambles. We were running on nerves, parroting our lines like politicians, all save the understudy, who was in the unenviable position of benefiting from another actor's misfortune. She'd decided to throw herself at the role with a passion that was at odds with the character she was playing. She shivered and fidgeted, had starts and fits. The audience, composed of blockheads with hearing aids, thought she was terrific.

After the show I headed uptown to the offices of Dr. Seymour Hershey, a dour, bespectacled individual with heavy dark lips like two prunes folded under his big nose. He greeted me indifferently, even disappearing behind the desk to pick up a pencil while I inquired about Madeleine's prognosis.

Amnesia, he explained, is a rare condition, usually brought on by an injury, such as a blow to the head. In such cases the effects were sometimes reversible, though not, as so often happens in fiction and film, as the result of a second blow. In Madeleine's case the loss of memory was the result of a psychic trauma. "Typically," he said, "these patients were sexually abused as children. Do you know anything about her childhood?"

"Not much," I admitted. "She didn't like her mother."

"Well," he said, psychiatrically, "she would have buried that too."

"She's an actress," I said. "There's nothing buried in there. She has complete access to her emotions. That's what actors do."

"Pretending to have emotions you don't feel doesn't open the portals of the unconscious," he said.

"We're not pretending. That's the point," I countered.

He probed his chin with his thumb, scanning his desk for something of interest. "Actually in my experience, actors are extremely unstable personalities," he said.

"Will she get her memory back?" I asked.

"If she wants to," he said. "But her memory loss is the least of her problems."

"Will she get well?"

"If she wants to," he repeated maddeningly.

"So your deep professional wisdom is that Madeleine wants to be extremely unstable."

He ran his eyes over me critically, like an antique dealer inspecting a table, checking for cracks in the veneer. "Not consciously, of course," he said.

"Can she come home?"

"Oh no. Not now. She needs to be clinically evaluated. There are medications that may help. I can recommend a mental health facility that should be able to take her."

"An asylum?"

"We don't actually call them that anymore."

"Where is it?"

"In Westchester. It has an excellent reputation. It's called Benthaven."

I sputtered. "Benthaven?"

He removed his glasses and rubbed the lenses with a square of red cloth he kept on the desk for just that purpose. Absolutely humorless, I thought. My poor Madeleine. "Once we get her stabilized I can have her transferred there," he said.

"Can I see her before she goes?"

"Oh, yes. You can see her. It might be helpful; I don't think it can hurt. You should bring her some food. She's refusing to eat anything they offer her at the hospital."

"Why does she do that?"

He gave me another long, magnified look, opening and closing his prune lips a few times like a fish trying to catch a wafer of food in an aquarium. "Why do you think she would do that?"

"I have no idea."

"Then what makes you think I would know?"

"You're her doctor."

"And you're her what? Her friend? More than that?"

I had to think this over. Whatever I was, I knew I was committed to getting Madeleine out from under the thumb of Dr. Seymour Hershey.

"I'm the one who knows what she likes to eat," I said.


In the days that followed, Teddy and I began the process of freeing Madeleine from the mental health authorities. Hershey was having a picnic because Madeleine wasn't capable of making decisions and we couldn't find anyone related to her who was. I knew her father had died when she was in high school and Teddy's investigations revealed that her mother too had died of cancer the previous year. Madeleine was a widow and an orphan.

By the time I got to see her, she was "stabilized," but she hadn't, as hoped, snapped out of it. She wasn't hysterical or frightened, she was unfailingly polite, but she didn't recognize either Teddy or me, nor did she understand why she was in a hospital. Mostly she was hungry, but, as Hershey had told me, she wouldn't touch anything that didn't come from outside. Teddy and I took turns bringing meals from nearby restaurants. One night, as I was opening another white carton of her favorite Chinese takeout, she confided, "If you eat the food they make here, you can never leave."

"So it's not that you don't like it," I said, handing her the box.

She stabbed a water chestnut with the plastic fork. "I'm sure it's perfectly nice," she said in her new affectless voice.

"They make it nice," I suggested, "to tempt you to eat it."

She sent me a conspiratorial glance over the carton. There was just the flicker of a smile at the corners of her mouth as she lifted a long noodle above the edge. "Exactly," she said.

She's still in there, I thought. I just have to find a way to get her back.


Teddy helped me with the other problem that (I can't resist the pun) gravely needed clearing up, which was the earthly remains of Guy Margate. He too was without traceable relations. "We can't just leave him to the city to dispose of," Teddy said. "Should we buy a plot somewhere?"

"I want him cremated," I said.

"Should we scatter his ashes?"

"No," I said. "I want him cremated and in an urn and buried. I want him put to rest."

Teddy, puzzled by my vehemence, acquiesced. "I can arrange that," he said.

Getting Guy out of the morgue and into a grave proved a complicated and expensive process. Teddy took on the funerary arrangements and, with the help of Detective DiBanco, I navigated the murky legal channels. In the process I had to sign a document that made me responsible for Guy's interment, an obligation that gave me a full moment's pause.

"Do you want to see him?" the detective inquired.

"No," I said, scribbling my name on the dotted line.

"We'll release his stuff to you. The backpack has keys in it; must be to his apartment. We'll keep the gun."

"Yes, do. Please," I said.

"We checked him out from his license. He didn't have a record."

"That's comforting."

"You know where he lives, right?"

"Lower East Side," I said. "But I don't know where exactly."

He took up a pen and jotted down the address on a yellow pad. "You actors are an odd bunch," he said. He ripped off the sheet and held it out to me.

"In what way?" I asked. I had the sense that he was about to make some deep and revelatory observation, so I gave him my full attention.

"You know, like a bunch of children. Always in the fantasyland, always waiting for a break, playing make-believe. Your friend was wearing a fake mustache. You'd think if you was going to kill yourself you'd take off the costume."

So the mustache wasn't real.

"It's a calling," I said to DiBanco.

"Yeah, right. Like I was called to be a detective."

"Weren't you?"

"No, I wanted to play baseball. But I had to be realistic. That's the difference."

I took Guy's bag back to my apartment, dropped it on my kitchen table, and made myself a cup of coffee, postponing this final encounter with all things Guy. It had seemed bulky when he had it on his lap, but in fact there wasn't much in it. A shabby wallet with his license, a bookstore ID, one credit card, and thirty dollars in cash, one of those collapsible leather coin purses containing sixty-seven cents in change, a leather key ring with five keys. A travel toothbrush and a travel-size tube of Colgate toothpaste. A comb. A wool muffler. A pair of wool socks and an unopened box of white Jockey briefs. A blank notebook and a pen. A copy of the *Playbill* for *Uncle Vanya*. A paperback sci-fi novel, *God Emperor of Dune*. I flipped through the *Playbill*. My name on the cast list had been scratched out with a red marker; my listing in the Who's Who box was entirely blotted out in red.

The sun streamed through my kitchen window as I drank my coffee, considering the last hours of Guy's unhappy, unlucky life. According to Madeleine they had been fighting all night, even on the subway. At some point, either before or during that argument, he'd packed this backpack. What was he planning? The underwear and toothbrush suggested he intended to be away, at least overnight. The gun must have been in the bag already. Did Madeleine know he had it? Was that why, when she heard the shot, she knew what it was? The mustache, I thought, why the mustache? Did he plan to murder me and then take my place onstage after the intermission? What a bizarre idea, but not impracticable.

I put everything but the keys back in the bag and stowed it in my closet. Someone had to clear out the apartment and let the landlord know his tenants wouldn't be returning. I dug the address Detective DiBanco had written for me from my coat pocket, took up the keys, and went out into the street. Maybe there would be some clue—a diary, perhaps—that would clear up the mystery of Guy's intentions toward me.

The East Village is still a gritty territory where the opportunities to enjoy a tattoo session are limitless, but it was worse then. An evening stroll required making a choice between dodging the rats on the street or the dope peddlers on the sidewalk. These denizens weren't much in evidence in daylight, but the occasional syringe or strung-out, babbling addict lolling curbside provided helpful reminders for those who might be duped by the run-down gentility of the buildings. One had to circumvent the black steel doors flung open like bat's wings over steps descending vertiginously into the gloom of various basements, a vast underworld of violence and criminality.

The Margates' apartment was in a brick-fronted building with a fire escape laced across the front. Steel steps rose over the used-clothing store at street level to a bright-red, triple-locked steel door that had been installed during a recent, hopeful makeover. I mounted the steps and plied the keys until I found the ones that fit, hauled the heavy door open, and stepped into the foyer. It wasn't bad. Black-and-white tile floor, red walls, a line of steel mailboxes, and a dusty but solid concrete staircase leading to the upper regions. Apartment E was on the third floor, behind a wooden door with only two locks. I tried the keys again; the door glided open before me.

I'd been expecting penury and grubbiness, but this was bourgeois respectability. Guy and Madeleine had been playing house. Very small house, there were only two rooms and a bath, but house all the same. Dishes stacked in the kitchen cupboard, geraniums on the windowsill off the fire escape, a flowered cloth on the two-seater table tucked into the corner between the fridge and the sink. They'd only been in the place for a month, but it was seriously furnished. Well, I told myself, they'd been together for six years and they'd acquired stuff. A painted bookcase containing the books I would later pack up and move to Connecticut, a wicker couch with paisley cushions, a lady's desk with a few envelopes on top, a swiveling desk chair on wheels. A curtain of the same paisley cloth as the cushions hung from brass rings, pulled partially aside to separate the space. Behind it was the bed, an iron bed frame painted shiny black. The patterned sheets and quilt were thrown halfway back over the mattress, as if the sleepers had leapt up and rushed away. Perhaps they had, I thought. Homely items, fuzzy slippers, hers, and leather slippers, his, a half-full glass of water on the night table, a dresser with one of her blouses folded neatly on top. Oddest of all was the double frame with two photos propped on a ledge that must once have been a fireplace mantel. The frame was hinged and had an antique look to it, black glass mat and pewter filigree edging. The photos were professional head shots, his and hers. They appeared to be looking at each other, his expression cool, masculine, serious; hers demure, but with a frank sexuality about the mouth. I laid the frame flat and stood looking down at them. His wasn't recent; he had more hair. "This is too sad," I said to the empty room. They slept in this bed every night as innocently as children, with these artificial selves framed and elevated like devotional images of saints gazing at each other in the upper atmosphere.

Or perhaps they didn't sleep like children. Perhaps they had screaming fights all night, as Madeleine claimed, or perhaps they had, as Guy insisted, sex all the time.

I left the bedroom feeling oddly chastened, and approached the desk. The papers were just bills and lists. I opened the drawer: a box of paper clips, an open package of loose-leaf paper, a checkbook. It was a joint account, Guy Margate and Madeleine Delavergne. I found the name of the realty company to which they were paying the enormous sum of four hundred dollars a month. Guy had written a check for twelve hundred the month before, first month, last month, and damage deposit. The second payment was overdue by a few days; the balance in the account was three hundred and seventy-five dollars.

This was sad, too, so sad that I sat down on the desk chair, completely enervated by the turmoil of my emotions. Noise from the street assaulted the building, shouts, cars, sirens, trucks with the reverberating backup beeps, a revving roar that sounded like a leaf blower, though there were no dead leaves in the world just yet, a dog barking and barking, and beneath all this the persistent thrumming hum that was the city itself, the living, breathing, pulsing, all-consuming heart of it, the never-ending beat that elated some and pursued others to oblivion.

That was when I decided that once I got Madeleine out of the hospital I would take her out of the city.

I put the checkbook in my pocket—I would contact the Realtor and arrange to pack up the apartment—and let myself out the door. I had only an hour before I had to be at the theater. The understudy wasn't bad, but I couldn't warm up to her. When Madeleine's Elena complained that she was bored it was a shameful confession. In the understudy's interpretation it was an accusation. My Astrov was becoming something of a clown, frantically trying to amuse her.

The next morning Teddy called to consult with me about the urn for Guy's ashes.

"I don't care," I said. "Just make sure the lid is tight."

"Should it be metal or ceramic? Wayne thinks it should be bronze."

"Do they have lead?"

There was a moment of silence. "Here's one that's copper lined in lead. Not bad-looking."

"Get that one."

We had a simple ceremony at a funeral home in Queens that Wayne recommended because two of his uncles were interred in the adjoining mausoleum. Teddy put an announcement in the papers, and to our surprise a few people showed up—two clerks from the store in Philadelphia, the manager of the Columbus Circle store, and a few actors Guy had worked with in the Italian play and the Broadway disaster. His agent, Bev Arbuckle, didn't show, though I'd left her a message on her answering machine.

I got Guy's birth date from his driver's license and Teddy

had his name and dates carved on a marble panel, behind which the urn was safely sealed away. Teddy had paid for something called "perpetual care," which meant, once Guy was stowed in his slot, we didn't have to come back.

Guy was thirty-nine years old. He shot himself in the heart a week before his fortieth birthday.

Now for a final leap across a canyon of twenty years to the present. Madeleine and I are married and live in a small Connecticut town near the regional playhouse where I spent that mystical summer with Marlene Webern and where I now serve on the board. As it turns out, I have a knack for fund-raising and am much valued both by the playhouse and by the local prep school where I chair the theater program. We do a lot of dining out with the well-heeled.

In that first year Madeleine was in and out of Benthaven having her mood swings adjusted and calibrated and gradually recovering most of her memory. There are still gaps, the night Guy died being most notable. She knows it happened because she's been told, but she has no memory of it. She generally dislikes talking about the past and I sometimes suspect that considerable swatches are still largely blank. Every morning she takes an antidepressant pill; she never forgets that. It alters something fundamental in her; it narrows her range. For obvious reasons, but also, I think, because of this medication, she has no interest in acting. She doesn't like going to plays; she says the theater makes her anxious. She prefers movies.

Yet she often quotes lines from plays. She still has a lot of

Shakespeare, which crops up in her ordinary conversation. If I read her a bit from the newspaper about political skulduggery, she nods quietly and observes "Some rise by sin, and some by virtue fall" or "Knavery's plain face is never seen till used," that sort of thing. These lines drop from her lips without intonation, like a bag of chips falling into the tray of a vending machine when the correct code has been punched.

She's Madeleine but not Madeleine, though she doesn't know it. She laughs more easily, seldom weeps, has no ambition, is affectionate and loving and warm, but she's not passionate about anything, including me. She's a serious gardener, but she's still a miserable cook.

I don't act much anymore myself, though occasionally I take a small role in a school production or fill in for a bit at the playhouse. I keep track of what's on in the city and go in whenever Teddy has a role, which, these days, is more and more often.

In the '80s, as everyone knows, AIDS wiped out a sizable percentage of the arts community in New York; Wayne Lee was a casualty. Teddy spent two desperate years trying to find some way to save his partner, but there was almost nothing available in the way of treatment, and Wayne's last months were gruesome. To make matters worse, some secrets about Wayne's financial dealings and, of course, sexual meanderings surfaced, and Teddy was forced to see his beloved in an unflattering light even as he was giving every ounce of his energy and patience and affection to the dying man. Was Wayne grateful? I went so far as to ask this once, and Teddy replied without hesitation, "I couldn't care less. I'm losing him."

By the time Wayne died, Teddy was mentally and physically worn out. He couldn't bear being in the city, where
everything reminded him of his lost happiness. Around that
time I bought the small house I still live in, with a big yard
which Madeleine straightway turned into an Eden complete
with apple tree. There was a guest cottage at the back which I
fitted out. Teddy became a regular visitor; especially welcome
for his cooking skills. Often we stayed up late, after Madeleine
had retired for the night, drinking and talking. At first all
we talked about was Wayne, but gradually the subject turned to
old times and to acting. I encouraged him to go upon the
boards again and he admitted that he missed the theater, though
he never wanted to attend an acting class again in his life. I
pulled a string or two and he got a slot in the company at the
playhouse. He spent the summer living in the boardinghouse,
working hard and sleeping well, absorbed in an energetic group
of actors, mostly younger than he was. He played Malvolio in a
production of *Twelfth Night* to great acclaim—he was riotously
funny, with such perfect comic timing that the audience began
tittering the moment he stepped onto the stage. His fellow actors admired him, he made a few connections, and in the fall,
when he returned to the city, he acquired an agent and threw
himself, with a good will, into the grinding business of auditions. He began to get parts, mostly comic, and to live the life of
a working actor. Young men were drawn to him because he was
kindhearted and he fell in and out of love, but he has never lived
with anyone again. He's working too hard.

So happy ending all round, more or less. I know you're relieved. But much as we might imagine we can leave the past

behind, it has a nasty way of pressing its hoary old face against the window just as we are sitting down to the feast.

About a month ago I was taking the train down to the city to meet with a select group of theatrical high rollers who might throw some money Connecticut-ward, and to see a new play in which Teddy had a role. It was a chilly January day. Madeleine dislikes going to the city in the winter, so she opted to stay at home. I was staying over in a hotel because the rollers did business at breakfast, so I packed an overnight bag. I was closing the lid of my faithful but battered sidekick of many years when the zipper jammed. Pulling it back didn't work; it locked up like a safe and wouldn't budge in either direction. Bracing against the bed with knee, gripping of the tiny metal tab, furious yanking accompanied by imprecations followed by the sudden disheartening thweeeet as the placket parted company with the suitcase, ensued. Renewed curses brought my lovely wife to the bedroom door. "Is something wrong, darling?" she said mildly.

"My suitcase is completely fucked!" I exclaimed.

She joined me in examining the damage and agreed with my diagnosis. "Take mine," she offered.

"I don't like yours. It's too big."

"I used to have a smaller one," she said. "Where is it? Is it in the attic? I think it's in the attic."

Together we ambled down the hall to the attic door. As I climbed the narrow steps ahead of her, it occurred to me that a trip to the attic is an excursion into history, and that all over the world the present unravels beneath the stored detritus of the past; that's what attics are for. At the top I pulled the light cord and turned to watch Madeleine trudging up behind me. The harsh light from the bare bulb illuminated the fine creases around her eyes, the deeper lines around her mouth. She is still a beautiful woman; age only serves to accentuate her aura of refinement and sexuality. Her face was lifted to mine and she was smiling in a distant, distracted way. "Don't look back," she said.

"Why not?" I asked.

"You might lose me," she said, arriving at my side. "I think it's inside a bigger case. It's part of a set."

We proceeded to examine the area I call Mount Luggage, a museum of the improvements in the design of the wheeled suitcase over the years, including the steel-trap-on-wheels that pinched so many fingers around the world and the equally hazardous four-wheeled hard-side. "It's here," Madeleine said, pulling out a gray two-wheeler.

"Why did you say I might lose you?" I asked.

She bent over the case and unzipped the top, revealing the promised smaller bag within. "I was following you in the dark and then you turned on the light and I thought I might be coming up from the underworld."

"Like Eurydice," I said.

"And then you looked back." She pulled the smaller case out and set it between us. "Will this do?"

I put my arms around her, resting my cheek against her hair. "It's fine," I said, but I was thinking, as I often do, *What is in my wife's head?* My hand strayed to her breast.

"You'll make yourself late," she cautioned.

She was right. I snatched the bag, carried it back to the bedroom, transferred my travel togs, kissed my helpmeet, and headed for the door.

"You have time," Madeleine cautioned as I picked my way around the ice on the walk. "Don't rush. Drive carefully."

A few hours later in the hotel room I unpacked Madeleine's bag, carefully hanging my cashmere turtleneck and Armani jacket in the closet, so as to appear fresh, stylish, and wrinkle-free for the millionaires on the morn. I removed my underwear and socks and slid my fingers inside the back pocket where, in my rush to change bags, I had stuffed my oral hygiene products. In this process a card, stuck against the side of the case, was dislodged. As I extracted my toothpaste, the card edge peeped mischievously out at me. I pulled it loose. It was a note card with a faded Japanese block print on the front: a waterfall, pedestrians with umbrellas crossing a bridge. The edges had been pressed together so long they were joined and I had to pry the top loose with a fingernail.

Inside I recognized Madeleine's handwriting.

*My Darling,*

*Your beautiful flowers were in the dressing room when I arrived. How heartening to read your sweet note with the fragrance of roses filling the air. I got right over my jitters and the performance went amazingly well. I died beautifully, everyone agreed.*

*I can hardly wait to see you and you to see the play and tell me all your thoughts. Dearest, I miss you awfully. "The*

*heavens forbid but that our loves and comforts should in-*
*crease, even as our days do grow!"*

*And grow. Come as soon as you can and rescue me from*
*this villainous Moor. He's killing me.*

*Love, kisses, M.*

I sat on the bed and read this billet-doux a few times over. The quote I dimly recognized, Desdemona to Othello. It took about three minutes to commit the whole message to memory. Then I put it in my jacket pocket, changed my shoes, and went out to the street. Teddy's play was a longish walk from the hotel, but I had only one thought, which my brain repeated every step of the way: So she loved him.

The play was at the Laura Pels, a fairly new theater, small and well-appointed. It was a comedy about a dysfunctional family, not great but not bad, not very funny, though Teddy was ripping in the role of the father who can't say consonants, a little quote from an old Feydeau farce brought nicely up-to-date. All the acting was top-notch and the audience liked it well enough. One feels relieved these days when a play is not like television.

I concentrated on the stage doings with difficulty, distracted by a voice from the past, one I'd never heard before. "Dearest, I miss you awfully." Guy too was piping up from the memory vault. "She did Desdemona last year. Rave reviews." And of course the immortal line "We called you the warm-up act" smacked around the walls of my brain like a racquetball. It was sickening.

After the show I met Teddy at the dressing-room door and

we walked a few blocks to the West Side Café, a place I like because there are usually a few actors hanging around and the food is good. I praised Teddy's performance and we discussed the merits of the play and the reviewers' comments, which had been largely positive. "It's a great group," Teddy said. "We all get along. No one is crazy. It's good fun."

"It's always better when no one is crazy," I agreed. When we were seated, with drinks in hand and had ordered our dinners, I pulled the card from my pocket and passed it to Teddy. "I want you to look at this," I said. "I'll tell you what it is after I ask you a question about it."

"It looks old," he said. "Is it something mysterious?"

"Just read it," I said. I sipped my wine while he gave the writing close attention.

"All right," he said. "Who is it?"

"I'll tell you in a minute. I want your opinion."

"It's very sweet. She's playing Desdemona. That's the quote, right?"

"Yes," I said. "It is."

"So what's the question?"

"In your opinion, is the person who wrote that note having sex with the person she's writing to?"

"Well, it's very affectionate. She misses him. Or her. I suppose it could be between two women. But yes, I'd say they were lovers."

"I thought so too."

"So, who's it from?"

"It's from Madeleine. To Guy."

"And?"

"I found it in her old suitcase, tonight, just before the play, at the hotel."

"In *her* suitcase?"

"I borrowed it. I broke mine."

"So maybe she never mailed it."

"Possibly. I figured he used the suitcase later and left it in there."

"That could be. They were married a long time."

"That's what I thought."

Our meals arrived and we had a moment's banter with the waiter. Teddy broke a piece of bread, frowning in puzzlement. "I don't get it," he said.

"What?"

"Your question. About the sex."

I laid down the fork I had picked up. "Madeleine told me she and Guy never had sex."

Teddy sawed at the small roasted bird on his plate. "Wow," he said. "She told you that?"

"A long time ago."

"Why would she tell you that?"

"Exactly. Why would she make something like that up?"

"So he was gay. Wayne thought he was."

"Really?"

"He thought Guy was in love with you."

"He did?"

"He just said it to be catty; he hardly knew either of you. Wayne thought everyone was gay, actually, just half the world represses it, hence the human race."

"So he thought I was gay."

"He thought you and Guy were in love but you were both in denial and used Madeleine to get at each other." He slathered butter onto his bread. "You're not eating."

I picked up my fork again and speared a green bean. "I'm dumbfounded," I said, chewing the bean. "That's so ugly."

"It is. I never believed it."

"Anyway, Madeleine said Guy wasn't gay. She said he was just completely impotent."

"Wayne would love that."

"Can we just leave Wayne out of this?"

Teddy pulled his chin in and made his eyes round. "Touchy," he said.

"I'm just trying to figure out what the truth is."

"Guy's been gone a long time. He was a terribly unhappy man."

"He denied it."

"That he was unhappy?"

"That he was impotent."

Teddy took a swallow of his wine. "You asked him?"

"I didn't ask him. I told him I knew and that it was too bad and could happen to any man."

"When was this?"

"That night. In the dressing room."

"Oh, my lord," Teddy said slowly, addressing his quail.

"He said Madeleine made fun of me. He said they had sex all the time and they made fun of me."

Teddy pulled a tiny bone clean between his front teeth. "This is sick," he said.

"I assumed he was lying. I always have. Then I found this note."

Teddy picked up the card and read it over again. "There's nothing in here that proves anything either way," he said. "She doesn't say, 'I miss your erect penis,' or anything; it's just affectionate. So maybe she was telling you the truth."

"But it's very affectionate. You can't deny that."

"Why don't you just ask her, Ed?" he said softly.

This irritated me. "You can't ask her anything about Guy. She just says she doesn't remember. Her memory is full of holes. She doesn't want to talk about anything that happened before we were married."

"Well, then, why don't you forget about it too?"

"It's just that I've always believed she didn't love him. I thought he trapped her, and then he made her feel sorry for him, but that really she disliked him as much as I did."

"No one disliked Guy as much as you did."

This surprised me. "Did you like him?" I asked.

"Guy was OK. He was funny sometimes, and he was so awkward and he had such bad luck, I felt sorry for him. I didn't agree with Wayne. I think he was madly in love with Madeleine. And she was fond of him. Sex or no sex, they had a close relationship. Whatever it was that held them together, it lasted several years."

As Teddy advanced this reasonable view, I tried to eat another bean, but it stuck in my throat. I started to cough. I was thinking of the photo in their apartment, Guy and Madeleine on the mantel over a scene of domestic harmony. The cough turned into a frightening wheeze. I couldn't catch my breath. I clutched my throat and tears filled my eyes. The attention of our fellow diners began to coalesce upon our table. Teddy got up and, with remarkable ease and speed, whacked me twice high on my back. This helped. A brief series of coughs, through which I was able to suck in a few swallows of water, opened my windpipe. Teddy sat down again as I pressed my napkin against my lips, holding it there while I breathed in slowly through my nose.

"Are you OK?" Teddy asked.

I nodded behind the napkin.

"I think you should throw this note away and forget you ever saw it. Send Madeleine some roses and tell her you love her."

I nodded again. He was right, of course. But not roses; she didn't approve of out-of-season flowers. Chocolates. I knew her favorite shop, Upper West Side. I pictured her, brightening up at the sight of the cunning brown box. I lowered the napkin and drank a swallow of wine.

*But that our loves and comforts should increase, even as our days do grow!*

Guy, opening the card, moving his lips over that line.

Maybe I was just tired. I hadn't slept well the night before. Or the night before that. In fact, I hadn't slept well in years. I didn't like thinking about the past, it was pointless, it was over, but as I sat there it all came stamping up around the table legs, hauling me down like a pack of demons into a dark and fiery furnace, where Guy Margate rolled over on a spit and fixed me with the burning coals that were his eyes.

"Are you OK?" Teddy asked again.

A shudder ran up my back, gripped my neck, and rustled my jowls. My throat felt tight. My eyes were stinging and I squeezed them shut.

"Ed?" Teddy said.

My head was filling up with fluid. I sniffed as it slid down my nose and I opened my eyes, releasing a mini-flood of tears. "I don't know what it is," I blubbered. "All of a sudden I feel . . ." A sob strangled whatever it was I felt, so moist and respiratorially calamitous a sob that, once again, our fellow diners turned our way. What was I thinking about? I hardly knew.

Death? My mother's and Guy's, a frame of suicides, one pushing me into the theater, the other driving me out, and my own mortality, and the thought that Madeleine might die, and Teddy, my dear friend, he might die. I opened the napkin and swabbed my eyes and nose, but it just kept coming, this viscous flood, and I wondered how a head, which looks relatively dry from the outside, could dump, without warning, so much liquid. "I'm sorry," I gasped, covering my face with the cool linen and boohooing like a diva. I heard Teddy fending off the tentative approach of a concerned waiter. "We're breaking up," he said in a voice so arch and fey that I laughed through my tears. I lowered the napkin; all eyes were on us. Teddy was holding his hands out, his mouth set in an insipid pout, turning from one group of alarmed diners to another, repeating vapidly, "We're breaking up. What can I sa-ay, we're breaking up."

"You're killing me," I moaned, hiding behind the napkin

again. The fit was easing off, but, in spite of how Teddy amused me, at bottom I was still sad. I dried my eyes and dabbed my nose, while he returned to crunching up his quail. "I hope you don't mind," he said, between bites. "I'm really hungry."

"Go right ahead," I said.

"So what was that all about?"

"I'm not sure," I said, tearing up again. "It's that stupid note. It brought the whole thing with Guy back. I never could figure out what was going on there. I couldn't get to the bottom of it. And now I guess I never will."

"So you were moved by your own touching saga."

I drank some water, dried the last tears, took out my handkerchief, and gave the nose a serious blow. "Yes," I agreed. "I was."

"Well, it is a good story. You ought to write it down."

"No one would believe it." I straightened my spine and slid my eyes along the tables nearest us. The chatter level had returned to normal, clinking cutlery provided a reassuring white noise. At the bar a woman with a loud laugh laughed loudly and, as I glanced toward her, a tall, dark-haired man, dressed in an impeccable three-piece suit, came into view. Our eyes crossed, his intent on contact, mine on escape. He approached us, gliding stealthily among the tables.

"Do you know this guy?" I asked Teddy, tilting my head to indicate the potential interloper.

"Never seen him before," Teddy said. "Great suit."

Then he was upon us, his handsome face emanating goodwill. "Excuse me," he said. He nodded first to me, then to Teddy, and back again to me, feigning hesitancy. "I'm sorry to disturb you, but, I hope you won't mind, I just had to ask, are you, by any chance, Edward Day?"

I set down my fork and gave him my attention. He had the manner of a supplicant. He was blushing, his eyelids flickered nervously, but his voice gave him away. It was an actor's voice, perfectly controlled and pitched for this complex public space. "I am," I said.

"You are," he agreed. "I thought you must be." A self-conscious, oh-silly-me laugh escaped him and he shifted his weight from one foot to the other.

"Do I know you?" I asked.

"No. That is, we've never met. I saw you on the stage, years ago, it was at a theater downtown, very small. You played the valet in a Strindberg play."

"*Miss Julie,*" I said.

"Yes. It was an incredible performance."

Teddy leaned over the table, grinning from ear to ear. "This is great," he said.

"It's kind of you to say so," I said, frowning at Teddy.

"That play changed my life."

Teddy was chortling. "But you must have been, what, twelve years old?" he said.

"I was eighteen," my fan replied. "It was in my first year at NYU. I wasn't certain what I wanted to do. I'd always loved the theater, but I'd never seen anything like that play. Your performance, well, this may sound odd, but I'd never understood what the expression 'truth' in acting meant until I saw . . ." He paused, opening his palm to acknowledge the master, "Edward Day in *Miss Julie*. When I left that theater I knew I wanted to be an actor."

"Really," I said.

"You changed my life," he said.

## Acknowledgments

I want to thank, in roughly chronological order, the following actors, playwrights, and theater enthusiasts who helped me along the way to this novel: Christine Farrell, Robin Day, Laura Shaine Cunningham, Anthony Giardina, Patrick Pacheco, Peter Schneider, Sarah Harden, Nicole Quinn, Jack Kroll, Janet Nurre, Mikhail Horowitz, Christine Crawfis, Ean Kessler, Walter Bobbie, Mary Willis, and Geri Loughery. Thanks also to playwright Nina Shengold, who responded to my query about the possibility of talking to actors with the message, "You want actors, I'll give you actors." The next thing I knew I was at a rehearsal of a Broadway play. I am grateful to Adam LeFevre, Robyn Henry, and Christopher Durang, for graciously agreeing to let me watch.

Thanks are also due to Erin Quinn, who unknowingly suggested the plot; Nicole Drespel, who gave me a backstage tour of the Public Theater; Peter Skolnik, who answered my questions promptly and told great stories in the process; Ronit Feldman, who gave the manuscript an early and actor-oriented reading, and my energetic and hardworking agent, Molly Friedrich.

I owe a special debt to John Pleshette, who was there then. His memory for detail is truly astonishing, and his descriptions of the daily grind of the actor were harrowing. There may be actors who remember what they got paid in 1973, but I suspect not many recall what the set cost as well. John also read the manuscript and offered invaluable suggestions.

I am and will continue to be indebted to Nikki Smith, my most trenchant reader and valued friend.

For the unwavering support and enthusiasm of my nearest and dearest, John Cullen, Adrienne Martin, and Christopher Hayes, I am continually grateful.